Butterflies in Production

Five Short Stories

J.L. Caban

Rare Jewels Literary Works

Dedication

In loving memory of my father, the greatest man in my life

Joe Caban

In memory of my cousin

Carlos

For my mother

Lisa

For my brother

Ivan

For my wife

Cecilia

For my children

Ashley, Jesiah, Joey, Julian

For all my brothers of Kappa Alpha Psi Fraternity Incorporated, especially my Line Brothers

Kurt

Chris

Thomas

Clyde

Gene

Malik

To the one whose music moves my soul

Elif Tanverdi

To the men and women of the United States Armed Forces & Police Departments across the country. Thank you for your service.

Contents

Note from the Author

Before I begin, I would like to take a brief moment to share with you a very personal loss in which I suffered while writing this book. With Covid-19 running rampant all around the world, the disease hit home, literally, and took my father, Joe Caban, from me. He was seventy-one years old at the time of his passing, far too young to be called; but, that is not for any of us to question – only God knows when we will leave this Earth, which is why I implore all of you to live life to its fullest. Go for that walk, start that project, call that loved one… because you just never, ever, know what is around the corner for us. I had the fortune of having my father in my life, raising me from a pesky little kid until the day I flew the proverbial coop, something that I will always treasure and hold dear to my heart. His accomplishments served as a template for my drive and passion towards whatever thing in which I set my mind. For him, his achievements were many. Growing up in the South Bronx, on Caldwell Avenue, he rose to success, enjoying a lucrative career as a Latin nightclub owner in the nineteen seventies, *Caramba* and *La Mariposa (Lady Butterfly)* serving as two of the leading venues of the Salsa sound, with *'A List'* artists, as it were, such as Tito Puente, Willie Colon, Hector Lavoe, and a slew of others gracing his stage. His passion and love for the musical arts continued into the nineteen eighties with the creation of In Production, which served as a platform for anyone with musical talent having a desire to be discovered. Artists such as Judy Torres, Cynthia, Johnny O, The Cover Girls, and many more went on from his stage to the recording studios, performing their sizzling hot *Freestyle Music* at night clubs around New York City, Miami, Los Angeles, and the like. Some even *crossed over* to the more profitable Latin industry, becoming staples of that genre for many years, all in large part to the opportunity given to them by my dad, Mr. Joe Caban. More importantly than all of that, to me at least, was the time in which he and I spent together; and, for that, I thank God for every moment that I was given. He will always be with me in mind, heart, and spirit; so – as the axiom goes – he is not *truly* gone. All of that being said, without further adieu, I will begin this book – because I know he is looking down upon me from above, patiently awaiting its completion. *Quia nunc vale,* my father…

The Christianson family, who are the focal point of the first four stories of this book, make their inaugural appearance at various moments within my first publication, *Moving On,* in the form of the protagonist's father and mother (Louie and Laura), his cousins (Felix and Juliana), along with a brief mentioning of three other cousins of Justin's (Rachel, Anthony, and Barbara), as well as his Uncle and Aunt (Felix Senior and Gloria, respectively). I chose to tell of their anecdotes in the form of four separate stories in one publication, incorporating different time periods within their lives in which I felt most significant and relevant to the larger purpose of this work, which was to create awareness to certain occupations that, in this author's humble opinion, warrant the attention and respect of all that call the United States of America their home; additionally, I wish to bring consciousness to the impecuniousness that plagues our nation, often causing otherwise decent human beings to subject and reduce themselves to shamefully dishonest deeds, not because they are innately bad human beings, but rather because they have never been educated, or perhaps have no alternative due to their social and economic conditions… moreover, if given a legitimate opportunity to excel, some of these individuals could very well lead productive and rewarding lives, as you will soon discover while reading their chronicles. Other essential and pertinent topics covered in the novella include biracial prejudices that many members of our society must endure, abuse in the household, as well as the difficulties faced by women in the workforce. I will briefly provide – that is, I will make the greatest attempt at brevity – to you, my dear reader, a synopsis of the work in which you are about to immerse yourself upon.

I wanted very much to become a brother of the United States Marine Corps when I was a young man of eighteen years old; however, this did not come to fruition due to circumstances of my doing; which, I shan't share with you just this very minute, my friends. Perhaps one day, we could sit down to a quiet cocktail and cigar (of the flavored variety – because I do detest the taste and smell of the harsher kind), at which time I will share the *hows* and *whys* of the thing. Just know, for now, it was a decision in which I will always foster regret, simply because it was a goal left unaccomplished. Many of my friends and family – including those that have the honor and distinction to call themselves brothers and sisters of the United States military – tell me that it was for the best, often citing the somewhat hackneyed maxim, *'everything happens for a reason;'* although, I often find myself – still to this day – wondering exactly what that *reason* is. There are, however, several members of my family who *have* served their country (my brother, Ivan; one of my sons, Joey; my Uncles, Eddie and Hector; and, my cousins, Carlos and Jose 'Papo' Rosa). It was for this *reason* that I chose to scribe the rite of passage diegesis in Story One, *'Felix Junior,'* in which the protagonist, whose name is one and the same with the title of that particular chapter, endures the hardships not only of basic training in the U.S. Marine Corps, but the effects it possesses on the family dynamic as it relates to this particular young man going away overseas during wartime. Felix Christianson makes his initial appearance in 'Moving On,' where the protagonist in that novella, Justin Christianson (Felix's cousin), shares with the reader two different moments in which Justin and Felix have occasion to spend with one another; during one of these moments, Justin mentions Felix's intention to join the Marines during the height of the Gulf War. Now, in this current tale which you are about to embark, in Story One, Felix's experiences are brought to light; the grueling weeks of basic training, or boot camp, as it happens, are explored, as well as the challenges in which he is faced before deployment, with a particular focus on his family and the love of his life, Ronnie, whom he adores and wishes to marry, all of whom must deal with the ramifications of Felix's decision to join the military.

In Story Two, 'Louie and Laura,' the reader will go back in time to the late nineteen sixties and early nineteen seventies to meet the parents of Justin Christianson (once again, the protagonist of the original book, 'Moving On'). This story will first explore the plight of a young Louie who grows up in poverty, having chosen the less than stellar life of a dealer in narcotics within the inner city area of Manhattan; however, being given the opportunity of a second chance – albeit subsequent to an arrest - through a lifesaving social program far up north, which attempts to teach the young men, all of whom find themselves in a similarly hapless situation, basic skills, working together as a team to accomplish their goals. Through this program, he very well may be able to turn his life around for the better. The second half of Story Two will concentrate on the life of an adolescent Laura (Justin's mother) who deals with growing up in a household riddled with verbal and physical abuse. In spite of being subjected to daily domestic mistreatment, Laura will attempt to rise above it all and escape her world of torment, something which has plagued most of her life. As a member of the New York City Police Department, I have had the great misfortune of seeing many types of these cases, each one breaking my heart more than the last, owing to the fact that many victims are never quite able to free themselves from their utterly morbid realities. I thought it important to sort of focus the proverbial microscope, as it were, onto this particular topic by allowing the reader into Laura's emotionally and spiritually agonizing world.

In Story Three, entitled '*Juliana & Robert,*' the reader will make their acquaintance with Juliana Christianson, Justin's elder cousin by just a few years, and her boyfriend, Robert. She was first introduced via correspondence in '*Moving On,*' wherein a post written by her is shared at the conclusion of the book. One might, from the way in which the letter was written, come to believe that Juliana may be content in her life – her advice to her cousin appearing so judicious, filled with the confidence of a person that possesses a soundness of heart and spirit; however, what the reader does not know – or has not had the opportunity to discover – is that she is dealing with a most challenging situation of her own. In the message to Justin, Juliana makes mention of 'her dear Robert' who has recently graduated from NYU and is not adjusting well to life after his collegiate career; however, the reader, at that point in time, is not yet informed that Juliana and Robert are a biracial couple, experiencing all of the social injustices and hardships that accompany such relationships. This story will explore the intricacies of this *affaire de coeur*; and, hopefully, bring awareness to the difficulties endured as a result.

Story Four, '*Selena,*' who is not a member of the Christianson family per se, will focus on Selena Martin, the childhood friend of Justin in '*Moving On*,' who was an integral part of his finding himself. She is described by him as someone who had "… this militaristic, commanding, tone that made you wake up if you were in the deepest of sleep;" and, who "… could have been a damn drill sergeant doing reveille…" Yet, in spite of this apparently negative implication, she was clearly someone of great comfort to him because, as he further states, "… she always sounded like she was in high spirits and that sort of thing can be contagious; it winds up putting me in a good mood." Justin also makes clear to the reader that Selena would, in fact, be the type of person in which he could love, but is not yet prepared to engage in such intimacies due to his inability to – at that time - achieve self-love. In her story, we will find her in the present time (which would be about twenty-three years subsequent to her appearance in '*Moving On'*). Now, at forty-one years old, and at the twilight of her career as a member of the Police Department, she will reminisce upon some of the many trying events of her twenty years on *the job* and, in addition to this, will reflect on the disadvantageous circumstances in which many females must endure in a predominantly male occupation.

The novella will conclude with Story Five, '*Memoir of a Broken Hearted Gentleman; Introducing Jasper Loring*,' a short story having no connection with any of the other stories in the Christianson universe. In this brief excerpt of Jasper's escapades, which – unlike the preceding four stories - is written in the first person, we will find an unhappy twenty-nine year old man who shares with the reader his displeasures – and there are many – of the human race. He has been plagued with negative experiences most of his life, the majority of these experiences including, but by no means limited to, his romantic relationships, and he now finds it almost impossible to establish healthy and meaningful liaisons with nearly everyone in his world... at least, in his mind he does; thereby, spending most of his time in mental purgatory, unsure of who he is and in what direction he is destined to go.

Now that the précis, if you will, is out of the way – I truly and humbly do thank you ever so much for patiently enduring it; for, I know that many a reader wants nothing more than for the author to get on with it, dispensing with the ghastly forewards, prologues, author's notes and such – make yourselves comfortable and please enjoy reading my evocative vignettes, as I have most certainly enjoyed writing them for you.

Jose 'Joe' Luis Caban, III… A Hero in the Universe

(Pictured above from left to right, Tito Puente & my dad, Joe
Caban, at La Mariposa)

Story One

Felix Junior

From the Halls of Montezuma
to the shores of Tripoli
we fight our country's battles
in the air, on land, and sea.
First to fight for right and freedom
and to keep our honor clean; we are proud to claim the title
of United States Marines.
Our flag's unfurled to every breeze
from dawn to setting sun; we have fought in every clime and place
where we could take a gun.
In the snow of far-off Northern lands
and in sunny tropic scenes; you will find us always
on the job - the United States Marines.
Here's health to you and to our Corps
which we are proud to serve; in many a strife we've fought for life
and never lost our nerve.
If the Army and the Navy
ever look on Heaven's scenes, they will find the
streets are guarded
by United States Marines.

Marines' Hymn, Unknown Author

The television in the hospital room was turned on, but silent. Someone had muted the volume in a sort of valetudinarian effort because it was too loud, and it might have disturbed him; although, if anyone had bothered to ask Felix what he would have liked, he would just as soon raise the volume to the maximum, most ear piercing decibel level available. Anything was better than the mind numbing and, quite honestly, morbid, beyond humanly tolerable conversation – or incessant bickering, to be more accurate - that was going on around him. As if sitting in the droll, sterile, hospital room – void of any warmth, both literally as well as figuratively – was not bad enough, he had to endure the interminable squabbling that engulfed him in this God forsaken place; a place that had become an unwelcome second home, as it were. It was the typical hospital room, complete with beeping and blipping vital monitors; medicine bags hooked to the access point in his arm that hung from the poles beside his bed; frigid temperatures comparable to that of the Antarctic; and walls void of any color. The white walls, riddled with scuff marks all about from the crashing and scraping of the portable machines brought in at all hours of the day and night, used to poke and prod, were all that surrounded him. The paintings that hung from these walls were thoughtless; and, much to Felix's displeasure, each wall possessed one, as it happens. One illustration was of a steel-grey vase filled with the most hideous purple, green, and pink flowers that, quite honestly, made him uneasy. The color scheme was revolting, making him angry and confused for reasons he could not comprehend; therefore, he avoided eye contact with it as much as he possibly could. Another painting was of two little children – a boy and a girl of about twelve and ten respectively - standing in some sort of marsh or river (he couldn't tell which) at low tide; they were depicted painting on canvasses of their own, the subject of which could not be seen. From the angle of the work, it appeared as though the children may have been standing ankle or knee deep in the water, their countenance one of absolute abhorrence… the youngster's frowning faces giving the impression that they were dragged there against their will, kicking and screaming the whole car ride over. One could imagine, as one continued to gaze at their downcast faces, that the juveniles, in all likelihood, received numerous bribes, perhaps in the form of either delectable confectionaries or some little trinket from the local toy store, in order for the artist to complete his painting of them.

Felix was dying. Literally. The cancer - lung cancer, which was most likely caused by the years of smoking like a chimney - had eaten through him with the rapidity of a locomotive at its maximum speed, and the doctor's prognosis was grim. He was originally given up to six months to live, but – in truth - could *expire*, as it was so very eloquently phrased to his mother and father (Gloria and Felix Senior) at any time. He, Felix the younger, had been battling the disease for a little under a year now. He was diagnosed in early 2012, just before his fortieth birthday, which was in March... it was now August. In addition to tearing apart his constitution, his physiognomy was currently decaying with similar perilousness. What was once a fine, chiseled, facial structure, complete with a perfect set of dimples whenever flashing his room-brightening smile, was now languid, sunken, and wan. His gorgeous locks of light brown hair, always classically styled, resembling a *young* Marlon Brando – not the old version that appeared in *The Godfather*, but more like the debonair version, having a closer likeness to Brando's character, *Johnny Strabler*, in *The Wild One* - was now reduced to mere sporadic strands here and there about his head. In short, he was what one might call *a shell of himself.*

He, Felix, most desperately tried not to focus on the unremittingly galling dialogue that presently encircling him, similar to the way in which a shark swims around a scuba diver who has somehow slashed his epidermis and is actively spewing blood into the ocean water, enticing and inviting the predators to draw ever so close; but, it was impossible. The room assigned to him was about the size of a broom closet; therefore, with four people – besides himself - packing into it like a can of sardines, he had no choice but to painstakingly listen to the obstreperous visitants clamoring on as he stoically lay in his bed, staring at Jeopardy – a show he had no interest in – made a thousand times worse by the muted volume.

"I don't understand why it takes so long to have the nurse come in. Honestly, it's been… *over thirty minutes*! since we asked for her." Said Gloria, Felix's mother, to her husband while frantically peering out of the room, looking for the nurse; although, at that point, she would have settled for an orderly, a maintenance worker, or any other warm blooded individual employed by the hospital that would give her the attention she required. Gloria was the epitome of an overprotective mother… the Queen of such people. She would strike at anyone, like a mama grizzly defending her cubs against the slightest indication of a threat, large or small. At sixty years old, she appeared more like seventy; her face fatigued, bordering on haggard, with bags and crows feet under and around her brown eyes, accompanied by strands of gray hair running amok amongst her once beautifully flowing light brown hair. She wore no make-up of any kind, which made her countenance particularly more lamentable; however, nothing was more disagreeable than her unpredictable temperament, which made most everyone avoid her like the worst plague in the history of plagues. One never knew what version of Gloria they would encounter… that is, if one had the nerve or courage to engage her in any conversation. A mere 'good

16

morning' could land one in a world of hurt if it were not literally a *good* morning for *her*. In addition to her violent, roller coaster-like ebullitions, she had a propensity to embellish the truth, especially when it pertained to a cause or subject matter in which she felt wholeheartedly about. Such was the present case at hand when she strongly exaggerated the time which had elapsed since calling for the nurse.

"Ma, it has not been over thirty minutes. It's been like -" Anthony, Felix's younger brother by three years – and the second of her three children – paused when he realized the wall clock was no longer functioning, to glance at his oversized, faux gold, Rolex watch (spelled *Rulex* across the white face), which he purchased at the corner variety store a few blocks from where he bought his last bag of marijuana, a drug of which he was an avid user, causing the whites of his eyes to retain a permanent cotton candy-like pinkish tint. " – it's only been like fifteen minutes."

"First of all, young man, it has *not* been fifteen minutes." Gloria rebutted, with a hint of vexation. "I know for a fact it hasn't been fifteen minutes because Jeopardy is at the half-way part. I distinctly remember the show was just starting when I asked for the nurse. *Distinctly.* And secondly, this conversation is between your father and I. What would possess you to involve yourself in an adult conversation?"

"Ma, I'm thirty-seven, not seven. I think that qualifies me -"

"Don't argue with me!" She interrupted. "I'm still your mother, no matter how old you are. Do you hear me, *young man*? You're never too old for a closed fisted knock across that fresh mouth of yours! I brought you into this world, I have no problem, whatsoever, taking you out!" Gloria bawled, as she wildly gesticulated her fist in the air to accentuate her point.

Anthony, who was quite accustomed to these idle threats of misdemeanor assault, merely rolled his eyes, sucked his teeth, and looked away in the opposing direction of where his mother stood.

"Gloria, what do you want the nurse for, anyway? I don't understand what you think she's gonna do for you. They got other patients, you know. Felix ain't the only one, you know." Said Felix Senior, much to the chagrin of his ex-wife, and with instantaneous regret for having committed what was once considered a cardinal sin of epic proportions in the Christianson household, as it pertained to what one should and should not utter to the family matriarch. He knew what cork he had popped; although, in part, he no longer cared, since their marriage had come to a much welcomed – at least on his part - end nearly two decades ago. They had been divorced for about twenty years now. Irreconcilable differences was the declaration which had been forged on the legal documentation, which brought an official end to their matrimony; a convenient little legal catch-all that was used by couples who simply had no idea – or no desire to know - how to repair their marriage. At least that's how Felix Junior always phrased it to anyone who asked.

"Oh, I see. So, I suppose I should let my baby just rot away here without any food or anything, right? *That's* a good idea. I'll just let him *starve* to *death*. That's such a *good* idea, what a *great* father you are!" Exclaimed Gloria in her infamous melodramatic fashion. She often spoke in italics when passion ignited her, this being one of those instances.

"Nobody is saying for him to starve, Gloria. Nobody ever said that. You need to calm down. You ain't gonna get nobody to come in here if you act like a mental patient, except maybe the hospital police to drag you outta here in a white straight jacket. That's what they're gonna do if you don't take it down a few notches." Felix Senior replied in monotone. He always mistakenly rationalized that keeping absolutely calm – more like completely void of emotion – would defuse any volatile situation. This never worked in his marriage and it was successful a million times *less* now. This, incidentally, was the default personality in which the Christianson men were blessed… Felix Senior; his older brother, Louie; and many years later their youngest sibling, Julian, all who grew up on the mean streets, as it were, of Spanish Harlem in New York City, had a propensity to make a powder keg scenario *nth* times worse with their nonchalant method of engaging in disagreements. In defense of these gentlemen, for utilizing such flippant techniques during intense conversations, one could easily place blame on their upbringing. Having to essentially raise themselves due to the fact that their parents were far from omnipresent (with the exception of Julian who was the product of a second marriage on their father's side), some elements of common courtesy, etiquette, and compassion were wanting in the two elder brothers.

"So, I'm *crazy* now, huh? Is that it? I'm *crazy*? *Very* nice. A *very* nice thing to say in front of *my* children." She was now raising her voice at an alarming level, as she continued to rant. "You *hear* that, kids? You *hear* how your father speaks to me? *Now* do you see what I'm always saying? *Do* you?"

The '*children*,' altogether possessing a median age of thirty-two years old, responded by offering absolutely *no* response.

Felix Senior, at this point, threw his hands up to the air, letting out a breath of frustration and subjugation. He knew, from years of experience, that there was no way of defeating the mother of his children, whether the strategy be a battle of locution or placating her with kindness. There was no solution to her enigma. "That is not what I said or what I meant. That's your problem, you know that? That's always been your problem. You are a drama queen, Gloria. That's exactly what you are." His hazel grey eyes sunk into despair, as he frustratingly ran his calloused hands through his hair in utter exasperation. He was too old for this, he thought… too old to get into such *tit for tat* with his former ball and chain.

Thus far, the youngest of the Christianson lot present in the hospital room had been silent, quite aimlessly glancing over the scores of social media pages on her cell phone; however, the ruckus of her parents' wrangling had awoken her from the somnambulant trance caused by endless postings of food, cats doing carnival tricks, and gratuitous selfie snapshots of people who were - for the most part, and in all honesty - unknown to her and vice versa. "Oh my God, you guys are so loud right now. Can you not? So embarrassing." Exclaimed Barbara, never breaking eye contact with her phone, continuing to peruse through the infinitely brain numbing postings. At twenty one years old, she was the typical self-absorbed young woman of the 'millennial' zeitgeist, who had no time to waste with trivial and ignominious matters such as her parents' squabbling; which, incidentally, could potentially taint the very delicate reputation that she spent her entire adolescence – up into young womanhood – fashioning… a reputation that not only came complete with a singularly horrific attitude, but also with the dyed silver-pink hair that roosted atop her head, matching her finger and toe nails. She had every social media outlet known to the human race, along with thousands of *'friends'* she never once actually met in person, and every moment of every day was spent tending to them. Still very much entranced with her task, she managed to blow a bubble, pop it, and - just as quickly as she cameoed into the world of the living – she transported vacuously back into her cyber existence.

"Are you satisfied with yourself? now you have my children turning against me." Gloria exclaimed, her voice now commenced to tremble whilst the waterworks began welling.

"No one is turning anyone against -"

"It's what you do." She interjected. "It's what you've always done. I'm so sick and tired -"

"Hello, family, did you guys call for me?" Interrupted the nurse who, at some point during the spat, entered the room, cutting into Gloria's award winning conniption. "I apologize for the wait, I've been with other -"

"What kind of a facility *is* this?" Gloria broke in. "My son has been laying there for *hours* practically dehydrating and starving. We called for you almost *an hour* ago -"

"It has not been almost an hour, Gloria." Felix Senior chimed in, subsequently turning towards the nurse and apologizing, "I'm sorry, nurse, please excuse my wife -"

"*Ex-wife.*" Gloria corrected.

Turning his head again, shooting a quick glance towards

Gloria, Felix Senior corrected himself, "Please excuse my… *ex-wife.*" Then returning his attention to the nurse, he continued, "We were just wondering, if at all possible - and if it doesn't inconvenience you in any way - could we please get some water and food for my son? I know it's not meal time, but maybe just a little turkey sandwich and some apple juice… or something like that? I mean, whenever you can." He said this in, what he believed to be, his most seductive voice; however, in all actuality, it sounded more like a predator in the wild attempting to lure its unsuspecting prey into its talons. He was sixty-five years old; but, in the depths of his imagination, he was decades younger (and on a really good day, when he wore his best polyester butterfly collared shirt, pressed bell-bottomed slacks, and ultra-pointed, magnificently shined Florsheim shoes, *he* would easily pass himself off as a young bachelor just turning thirty). His gray hair, which was full of life, was always combed to perfection, topped with grease (even on days wherein he was home with no intentions of going out), and he always kept in good repair by frequenting his local community center gym, attending at least three times a week. Mr. Christianson, the elder, was of the axiom, 'you're not as young as you used to be, but you're not as old as you're going to be,' words that he wholeheartedly lived by.

"By all means, make *me* look like the deranged lunatic." Rambled Gloria.

Leering for a brief moment at Gloria, with a look of displeasure and slight disgust, the nurse swiveled her face in Felix Senior's direction, rearranging her countenance to one of ebullience, complete with a flirtatious smile. She then replied, "Of course, I'll get it right away. Again, I'm so sorry for the wait. You wouldn't believe how swamped we all are here. We're so understaffed and

I've been running around like a chicken without a -"

"Ok, thank you so much." Gloria cut in. "The water and food, please."

With an expression of discontent, screwing her face and scrunching her brows, the way in which one would when one has been rudely interrupted, the nurse turned around and walked out of the room. Gloria traipsed past her ex-husband and, without looking in his direction, muffled under her breath, "Could you *be* more disgusting? She's half your age… *Pig.*"

Felix Senior, disregarding the insult – far too accustomed to the slight to be affected, but more importantly, for him, to gander at the sight in which, at the present moment, was seizing his attention - watched, the way a mountain lion would espy a scrumptious deer that it wished to devour, as the nurse glided out the room, swaying her rear end back and forth, similar to that of a pendulum in a grandfather clock, glancing back at him with a coquettish smirk, and he returning the gesture.

Felix, the younger, who had all the while been helplessly and haplessly laying in the bed, staring lugubriously at the ceiling, unable to bear one more single, solitary, minute of the conversation and happenings swirling around him like a tornado blasting through a village, destroying all in its path, closed his weary and darkened eyes, putting himself into a somnambulant state, where none of them could reach. As he closed his lids, he slowly began drifting off into his own thoughts… drifting off to a time far away from the aching, insufferable, pain of the cancer, as well as the unpleasantness of the bickering and bantering of his *loved ones.*

***

When his eyes reopened, he was no longer in the sterile, bleak, and utterly dispiriting hospital room, but on the rickety transport bus, which reeked of underarm, uncleaned ass, and whatever other un-Godly odor that is caused by forty-four perspiring young men trapped in a conveyance, with no air conditioning, in the middle of the summer, smells like. They were all headed to the intake area of Parris Island to begin the thirteen grueling weeks of boot camp in the Marine Corps; subsequently, to be shipped off to the burning sands of Baghdad, Iraq, to fight in the war – the Gulf War; or, as it was dubbed by the powers that be, as well as the entirety of the media outlets in the year 1991… *Desert Storm.* Felix, then, was a young and quite virile man of twenty; ironically, old enough to die for his country, but too much of a *babe in the woods*, as it were, to waltz into a watering hole to order his favorite libation of rum and Coke, a thought that frequently ran through his mind since signing the military contract which, as it happens, would commit him to four years of service.

The thirty year old ramshackle bus rocked back and forth like a small vessel caught in the turbulent waters of the Atlantic Ocean during a tempestuous storm, causing various men on the bus to dry heave; Private Howard McGovern, being one of the aforementioned men, actually regurgitating his Irish breakfast of black pudding, eggs (over easy), sausage, bacon, baked beans, tomato, and mushroom. To make matters worse, it was raining torrentially; therefore, it prevented anyone from opening the windows of the bus, which made the temperature inside about fifty degrees hotter than the ninety-five degrees of sweltering, inferno-like, heat outside. Felix – the recipient of Private McGovern's aforementioned regurgitation - was still very much in a state of incredulity due to the fact that this was, in fact, really happening… He was really on this bus, really headed to boot camp, really going to the Middle East, really going to fight in a war; therefore, it was for this reason that he did not initially realize he had been the victim of McGovern's purge.

It was all very surreal, these thoughts in Felix's mind; but, not nearly as palpable as the chunks of McGovern's extremely potent cud, which reeked of addled eggs, now splattered all over Felix's trousers, having had the great misfortune of sharing a seat with the man of weak constitution. "Jesus, man!" Said Felix, snapping out of his state of stupefaction, looking down at the remnants of what was – at the original time of consumption – a singularly savory meal for McGovern.

"Oh man, sorry man. I'm so sick. Fuck. Sorry, man." McGovern said, attempting to wipe the lap of his victim with a handkerchief… a handkerchief that his mother insisted he place in his pocket for calamitous and unforeseen circumstances such as this.

"Dude, no, stop that. Hey, stop!" Felix insisted, mortified at McGovern's irresponsibly gross negligence of the unwritten rule in the man-code manual, which clearly states - paraphrasing, of course – *'thou shalt not swab another man's crotch region (which includes any area three feet above, below, and/or all other adjacent portions of a man's body) for any reason whatsoever, so help you God.'*

This grandiose and quite catastrophic error in judgment by McGovern led to an undulation of snickering, whistling, and cat-calling from all throughout the bus (various puerile exclamations, such as *'get a room,' 'me next,' 'do you ménage a trois?'* and so forth were amongst the few), as Felix – now utterly humiliated - seized the handkerchief and completed the task of purification. "Dude, what in the fuck did you eat? It looks like goddamn Alpo dog food!"

"Lock that shit up right now, or you *will* be road kill!" Thundered the Sergeant, launching up and out of his seat from the front of the bus, with a God-like voice analogous to something right out of the worst parts of the Old Testament. He scanned the entire bus – much the way in which a silverback gorilla would when leering at a group of on-lookers at a local zoo - which was now deathly silent, before returning to his seat.

"I'm so sorry, bro." Whispered McGovern to Felix. "My mom made me a big breakfast. It's made of a bunch of stuff, dude. I don't even wanna think about it. Hey, man, you sure you don't want me to get that for you? I feel real bad, man." McGovern made an attempt to retake control of the handkerchief.

"Bro, no. I definitely do not want you to get it for me!" Felix implored, while contorting himself to avoid McGovern's grasp. "What's wrong with you, dude? You don't go around scrubbing a guy's junk area. That's just a huge violation, brother." Felix lamented.

"Sorry man, I don't know what's wrong with me. Damn it, sorry."

"Alright, alright. Stop apologizing. Just stop apologizing all over the place." Felix implored, as the heckling voices (taunting echos of *I'm so sorry, my love,' 'Please forgive me, my sweet'*) now circulated all around the two interlocutors in undertones, so as not to alert the Sergeant to their shenanigans.

As the bus approached the compound, the silence grew deafening in anticipation of the hell that was expected to be unleashed. All that could be heard – if one had the ability to hear such a thing – were the pounding of forty-four heartbeats awaiting the worst level of Dante's vision of hell. Those that dared to gander out their windows, which, incidentally, were all tinted black - having little cracks and tears here and there for limited voyeuristic viewing - did so only by bringing their eyeballs to the most extreme point in which an eyeball can be brought without turning their heads one single iota. What they would have seen on the other side of the window, between those cracks, however, was nothing but more darkness, as it was nighttime when they finally arrived. The Sergeant stood up from his seat, ducking to prevent his head – which was attached to his six foot five frame – from hitting the roof of the bus. He turned and addressed them with the look of death in his steel gray eyes; a look that pierced their very souls. He neither yelled nor whispered, but his authoritatively sonorous voice made all of their rectums tighten with a vice-like grip just the same. "Now listen up, when this goddamn thing comes to a stop, you will get the fuck off of my bus. You will gather your shit and you will get the mother-fuck off of my bus." With that simple declaration, the Sergeant's stoic countenance returned, and the Privates, whose throats all filled with un-swallowable thick saliva, tried – however they could – to mentally, physically, and spiritually prepare themselves for the unknown terror that loomed ahead.

The bus pulled up to the barracks, coming to a halt; the dusty brakes of the conveyance creating a nails-on-a-chalkboard sound, sending a chill throughout all of their spines. The door flew open and what occurred next was somewhat of an eerie revelation for the forty-four souls who were in anticipation of bedlam. Instead of pandemonium, they were, quietly and very calmly, directed to exit the vehicle and, subsequently, told to place their feet upon the yellow-painted footprints embedded onto the ground in which they stood. "These iconic footprints," began one of the multitude of Sergeants now beginning to take their places around the newly arrived Privates, "represent the men that have stood in your place long before your miserable selves had the bright idea of joining my Corps. Not everyone standing next to you today will be here in thirteen weeks, but that's just fine by us! We only want the absolute best, only the strongest of mind, body, and soul. From this point forward, you will answer as such, 'Aye, Sir!' Do you understand?" He roared.

"Aye, Sir."

"I said, do you understand?!" He shouted, louder than the first time.

"Aye, Sir!"

What occurred subsequent to this speech is best described as sheer chaos, coupled with a complete breakdown of what the human mind has so carefully placed into wonderful little categories for its human hosts. "Get the fuck inside! Get the fuck inside! Grab your shit! Grab it! Go!" The same command flew out many different mouths, as all of the Sergeants present were now in full 'Drill Instructor mode,' *directing* them; although, ironically, in a manner that gave them the least bit of orchestration.

Privates flew to and fro in every possible direction due to an endless array of conflicting orders from the now thirty other Drill

Sergeants swarming around like attacking wasps – or, as it is referred to in the proper vernacular, and entirely more apropos due to the fact that it was still raining, a *shark attack*. As Felix frantically grabbed his gear and headed towards the muster area, as instructed, his bag was ripped from his hands by one of the Sergeants, who took off like a bat out of hell, as it were, in the complete opposite direction from that of the muster point. Unsure of what to do, Felix continued on to his original destination, forsaking his belongings, leaving it in – as he rationalized – the capable hands of his superior. Seeing this, yet another Sergeant intercepted Felix and tore into him. "You're gonna let him take your shit?! Is that it, Private?! You're just gonna let him take your shit, huh?!" The Sergeant ejaculated, apparently in opposition to Felix's decision to abandon his things.

"Yes, sir. No, sir. They told me to go to the -" Felix stammered before being interrupted.

"It's '*Aye, sir.*' This is the Marines, not the Army. Shut the fuck up and go get your shit, Private!" The Sergeant exclaimed.

"Aye-Aye sir!" Shouted Felix.

"Damn you, Private! it's '*Aye*', not '*Aye-Aye*'… we're Marines, not pirates! goddamn it!"

"Aye, sir!"

Felix then pursued, as fast as he possibly could, the thief who hadn't gone far - expecting very well, at some point, for the young Private to retrieve his belongings - as this was something that had been performed years upon years before this day, and will very likely continue to be an integral part of basic training for years to come. As Felix approached the bandit in question, the bag was given to him freely with a lesson, "Don't ever let nobody take your shit, Private."

"Yes, sir. I mean, Aye-Aye, sir. I mean, Aye, sir… Thank you, sir!"

"Well, what in the fuck are you standing around here for?! Get the fuck outta here! Go, go, go!"

With that, Felix resumed his flight to the muster tent where almost all of the other Privates had already made their way. Attempting to enter, he was abruptly halted, told to drop his *shit* outside of the tent and to get into formation which, at first – after his recent debacle moments before – was met with apprehension; but, realizing that all the other bags were, indeed, piled alongside each other outside of the tent, the young Recruit was somewhat convinced he was not the recipient of another dupe, therefore did what he was told. After leaving his bag outside with the others, he reentered the tent with the intentions of following his orders; but, the formation to which the Sergeant referred was as good of a guess as anyone else's. Felix watched in dubiety as all of the other Recruits bumped into and off of one another like old fashioned wind up dolls, not knowing in which direction they were supposed to be going. He had positively no clue what, on God's green Earth, would have been the appropriate formation to assume. At this point, he was just overjoyed to be out of the rain. His jubilation was short lived, however, when the Drill Instructors made their way into the tent and unleashed all hell; within seconds, the chaos resumed and Felix found himself under the shark attack once more. Seven mouths wailed at him from every direction, shouting seven different commands, each and every one of the convoluted orders contradicting the other.

"What's your name Private?!"

"Shut your mouth, shut your fucking mouth right now, Private!"

"Give me twenty push-ups right now, you scum of the Earth!"

"I asked you what your name is, Private! Are you fucking ignoring me?!"

"What are you doing push-ups for?! Get the fuck up off the floor right now, Private!"

"Didn't I tell you to give me twenty push-ups, Private?! Are you trying to cheat me outta my twenty push-ups?! Is that it? Now give me thirty, you worthless piece of shit!"

"If I ask you one more time for your goddamn name, I *will* put my foot so far up your ass you'll know what the bottom of my boot tastes like! You hear me, Private?!"

Felix could feel himself passing out; his knees began to buckle under his body, followed by a tingling sensation all about his face. The tent was filled with forty-three other Recruits, all undergoing similar hazing rituals, which produced an oven-like atmosphere inside of the tent; oxygen levels depleted by the microsecond. His face was flushed; the sweat from his back plunged deep down into the crack of his rear end, cascading down his legs, and into his boots. The irony of wishing he were back out in the rain was comical, almost making him laugh out loud; that, along with the delirium felt in his brain, causing a meltdown of epic proportions within his psyche.

As a matter of fact, unbeknownst to Felix, he just so happened to let out a snicker, drawing the attention – yet again – of the *sharks*, which caused him to end up in what was called the *front leaning rest* position, wherein one holds themselves in the upper push-up pose until one's humerus, radius, and ulna bones feel as though they would – if they were animate beings having the ability to make their own choices - prefer to disintegrate post haste rather than endure one fraction of a second more of this torment. The Sergeants around him were all a blur now. The only thing he could see – barely - were the other hopeless lot scattered around the tent; and, from what little he was able to make out, no one else was better off.

Not far off from where Felix was being smoked like a well rolled cigar, McGovern, the Private who ejaculated his victuals onto Felix's lap in the transport bus, was apparently fairing just as well, or, more accurately, just as poorly. "Goddamn it, Private, what in the hell does your mommy feed you?" One of the Drill Sergeants shouted to McGovern. "Is there ever any food left over for the rest of your family? It sure as hell doesn't look like it! I'll bet your mama is saving a shit ton of money on groceries now that your fat ass is gone! Give me a hundred jumping jacks… hell, never mind the hundred; just keep going. You'll need at least a million to get that sack of shit you call a body into shape!"

To Felix's right, another poor sap was getting his end of the business handed to him. "You look like a liberal, boy." An Instructor addressed a young man who possessed the appearance of a typical *gamer* (the kind that sits in his basement all day long with *mission control* type headphones wrapped around his head, playing video games whilst screaming, "Hey Ma! where's my sandwich?!"), complete with long hair down to his shoulders, John Lennon style spectacles, and acne all about his bloodlessly etiolated face. "Are you a bleedin' heart liberal, boy? Don't they got barbers in the hippie city that you live in? I bet you're a member of every tree huggin', animal lovin,' foundation there is. We're gonna make a man outta you, don't you worry, little boy!"

Felix wasn't the religious sort, but he – like many thousands upon thousands of other poor souls who find themselves in the most precarious, agonizing, and unfortunate state of affairs – developed a one on one internal dialogue with his Creator, right then and there in that *front leaning rest* position… a conversation which mostly incorporated pleas of mercy in addition to beseeching requests of forgiveness for what he had ever done (and, incidentally, for what he would ever do in the future), in exchange for an expeditious liberation from the madness at hand.

Just then - just when he was convinced that not a moment of physical endurance, nor mental capacity, remained - the Drill Sergeants ordered all of the poor, defeated, creatures out of the tent. God only knew, thought the neophytes, what was in store for them next; however, the mere thought of the blessed cessation to the hostilities at hand gave them the will to move forward as they all, including Felix - albeit begrudgingly - headed out of the tent and back into the tempestuous storm, still raging and awaiting them outside.

As the rain pounded down upon their heads, they immediately desired to return back to the sanctuary of the tent. The juxtaposition of these two feelings was, undoubtedly, brought upon by their befuddled minds, no longer functioning at full capacity. At this juncture, in the middle of the storm, they were ordered to retrieve their *shit* and form up in front of the tent. This was no small task, as the bags that the future soldiers placed neatly outside the tent before they entered, were now scattered all about in the muddied waters in no discernible order. The Drill Sergeants were not at all sympathetic to this quandary, having been the perpetrators of the imbroglio. "What in the fuck are you waiting for, Private?! a goddamn invitation?!" One of the *sharks* cried, directing his attention to Felix who was in a state of the utmost perplexity as to what exactly to do with himself.

"Sir, I don't know where my bag is. I left it right here, right here in this spot." Felix pointed and cried, almost instantaneously wishing he hadn't done so.

"Oh, that's terrible. You can't find your bag, buddy?" The Sergeant replied superciliously, using an eerily tranquil, condescending tone of voice that made Felix regret his decision to utter even one syllable to this evil creature from the deepest bowels of hell. "Get the fuck out of my face right now, Private!" The Sergeant resumed, now with the chilling and petrifying fury of Mephistopheles. "Get out of my face and find your fucking shit right fucking now, you worthless piece of pig shit! Go! Go! Go!"

With that, Felix was off to find his bag, along with the other forty-three compatriots, who were all now bathing in wet, brown, slosh. As Felix sifted through the bags, he found himself haphazardly tossing the belongings of the other Privates to the side. This, he would soon learn, was a grave mistake. "Goddamn you, Private!" Roared one of the Sergeants. "Why on sweet Christ's blessed Goddamn Earth did you just chuck that mother fucking bag to the side?!"

Felix, shooting straight up, now completely erect, splattered with mud all about his face and clothes, his hair completely saturated from the rain storm still being jettisoned from the heavens above, shouted in reply, "Sir, it wasn't mine. It wasn't my bag!"

"Really?! Is that right?! It wasn't your bag, huh? Did I get that right, you selfish son of a bitch? So this is all about you, huh?! You are less than zero! You are lower than dirt! You disgust me! For the love of God, why are you here?! Why on Earth are you trying to become part of my beloved Corps?! Goddamn you, Private, these are your fellow earthworms! These pieces of absolute dog shit are your fellow Privates! Go back and get that piece of shit bag, find out who it belongs to, and give it to that low life piece of monkey manure! Help him out, you low life loser piece of shit! Do it now!"

Felix obeyed the command; he retrieved the bag he had hoisted off to the side, scurried back to the Sergeant with a look of incertitude, and meekly, with a voice shakier than a California earthquake, said, "Sir, I don't know who it belongs to."

"Hail Mary, full of grace. You dumb shit, what does it say on the damn bag, Private?!"

"It says Forester, sir, but I don't know who Forester is."

"Here's a real smart idea. Hows about yelling out the name and see what fly you attract with the shit you're holding? How does that sound, maggot?!"

"Oh, good idea, sir!"

The Sergeant, who could've *smoked* Felix with some push-ups or sit-ups for that last reply, could no longer stomach his ignorance, gaping at him in complete disbelief instead, as the Private yelled and searched for Forester.

"Forester?! Forester?!" Felix yelled, to no avail. Forester was on the other side of the bedlam in progress, searching, apparently in vain, for his bag.

"Man, forget Forester, let's help each other find our bags." Said another recruit who was also covered in mud from head to toe, resembling what looked like thick chocolate syrup.

"The Sergeant told me to find Forester. He'll kill me if I don't." Answered Felix.

"Dude, that Sergeant's already gone to the other side of the tent. Help me find mine and I'll help you find yours!"

"Alright… what's your name, by the way? I sorta need it in case I see your bag!"

"Serrano, man, what's yours?"

"Christianson."

"Hey, you guys helpin' each other? I'm in. What's your names?" Said a voice that was familiar to Felix.

"Serrano and Christianson, man. You?" Inquired Serrano.

"McGovern." The infamous, notorious, McGovern who unleashed the inner workings of his digestive system on Felix earlier inside of the bus now stood beside them both.

Between the three of them, they managed to find not only each other's bags, but a few others that were in the vicinity. Once this mission was complete, the fifty pound bags, now soaked and muddied, were ordered to be heaved up above their heads and kept there while various calisthenics – such as squats, shoulder raises, and other corporal torment - were performed until most all of the men dropped from utter and complete enervation. The monsoon continued to pour down upon them in huge waves; Felix could hardly see a thing because of the blade-like shards of rain, seemingly coming at him sideways, piercing his eyelids. With an unseen force of sheer will, he trudged forward, following command after command. "Keep breathing." He thought to himself. "Just keep breathing. That's it. Deep breaths. Breathe in – hold – breathe out. Nice and slow. I can do this. I can make it. I'm going to make it."

Finally, after what seemed like an eternity, the Drill Instructors ordered the men into the barracks, where the Recruits would be housed for the next three months. Felix entered the structure, which was made mostly of oak wood, giving off a pleasantly nostalgic smell that reminded him of a much simpler time in his life; evocations of the days in which he would spend countless hours up in his treehouse traversed through his mind as he walked through the threshold of his new dwelling place. He also detected the pungent odor of bleach and mustiness which filled the air as well; but, welcomed it because he was no longer outdoors in the middle of the vicious torrent that ensued on the other side of the walls. There was no time to get the lay of the land now, though; the forty-three other recruits were, at present, picking – in a first come, first serve manner – their bunks, which was like placing a succulent steak in the middle of a pack of starving wolves. It was every man for themselves; the Corps' mantra, *the goal is to become an integral component of the team*, did not exist in this space and time. "Sorry, big guy, this one's mine" or, "Oops, I got this one, fella" or, "I don't think so, squirt, dibs on this one" were some of the utterances spewed. After three failed attempts, most accurately characterized as a perfect display of Darwin's *survival of the fittest,* with the men asserting their dominance over one another to acquire the bunks of their choice, Felix finally secured a resting place. With no time to lose, he unpacked his gear as best and as rapidly as he humanly could. The recruits had but minutes – which felt like seconds - to unpack their gear and get all of their belongings into their footlockers.

As the men scrambled to complete their mission, the Senior Drill Instructor – the man who would be responsible for disassembling the souls and spirits of these men, subsequently reconstructing them to form the soldiers that would fight for the very freedom of the country – stormed into the room. He was a larger than life figure; from head to toe, he exemplified professionalism – the personification of a true soldier. He wore the classic *smokey* campaign hat, which – tilted downward – revealed only a portion of his sinister eyeballs… eyeballs that would penetrate the immeasurable depth of any human soul – or inhuman soul for that matter - that dared to peer into them for a protracted period of time. As he ploddingly traversed the isle which separated the two sides of the room, with rows of bunks on either side of him, the Sergeant slowly moved his head methodically from left to right, left to right, left to right, barking orders in monotone to no one in particular. "Hurry up. Faster. Move it. Hurry up. Faster. Move it. Hurry up." Arriving at the equidistant portion of the room, he now brought to the attention of the men that their time was running out, in somewhat indiscernible *'D.I. talk' (Drill Instructor talk)*, which, much like pig-Latin, were, essentially, cut up words, forming sentences that were hardly lucid to any of the consortium. "You ha' twen' secon' ta ge' yo shi' in yo foot locks'. Afta twen' secon's, you will freeze in frona' yo bunks. Twen', ninetin', etn', se'ntn', sixt'n," The men were in a frenzy at this point. With sixteen seconds left, there was no hope of placing all of their effects into those footlockers. The Drill Instructor, in spite of knowing this fact very well, decided to skip the chronological order of the countdown. "Elev'n, non, sev'n,"

"Goddamn it, he's skipping numbers, mother fucker!" Said an unknown soul, out of the Senior Drill Instructors earshot, of course.

"Fi', 'ree, 'woo, one!" The Instructor concluded, unleashing all hell on the first Private with whom he locked eyes; which, as luck would have it, just happened to be our protagonist. "What in the name of all that's holy and pure are you doing, Private? Goddamn it, Private, I told you to freeze at the count of twenty!"

Felix, not realizing that the countdown had reached its climax, was still attempting to put his things away; however, at the untimely tongue thrashing from the Sergeant, he snapped to attention, still holding tight to his underpants, which were dangling from the clutches of his fist. "Sorry, I was -"

"Damn it, when I say something, you say 'sir' before you say something! Do you understand me?"

"Sir, Aye, sir!"

"Do you understand me?!" The Sergeant, not satisfied with the volume in which Felix offered his response, repeated.

"Sir, Aye, sir!" Felix shouted, apparently not appeasing the headman.

"Get your ass down and lock into front leaning rest, Private!"

Now addressing the entire room, with Felix in *front leaning rest* - the upper push-up position, as previously mentioned - the Sergeant bellowed, "I thought it was clear, you miserable maggots, that the first and last words out of your mouths will be 'sir.' When I say something, you say, 'sir!' Do you understand me?"

"Sir, Aye, sir!" Cried the room.

"Do you understand me?!" He repeated, unsatisfied at the decibel level he received from the platoon.

"Sir, Aye, sir!" The room ejaculated louder than the first time.

For the next five minutes – what felt like five hours to Felix, who was still in *position* on the floor and, incidentally, somehow still maintaining a vice-like grip on his under-briefs – the Sergeant proceeded to read the proverbial *riot act*. He went over the expectations as well as the daily schedule in which the men were to adhere and, in between the very lengthy instructional lecture, somehow found time to sling around deleterious insults about everyone's significant other; things like, "While you wastes of human existence are here on the Island, *Jodi* is back home banging your girl!" This was, incidentally, received with much vexation by some of the weak minded young men who actually bought into the Sergeant's propaganda, thinking of some guy named Jodi actually fornicating with the love of their lives; thus, thoroughly marring the profundity of the psyche, pushing it off of the precipice, sending it into a steep nosedive towards the depths of despair.

Meanwhile, during the harangue, our poor Felix's arms felt as though they were ablaze, trembling and buckling like a bridge on the verge of collapse; his lower back finally beginning to give way bit by bit, sinking towards the floor. In an attempt to combat this blunder, he compensated by lifting his rear end straight up to the sky, forming the Greek letter 'lambda,' an entirely improper position to hold when performing the task at hand; a point, however, rendered moot due to the fact that he was only able to maintain this position for but seconds before sagging downward again. The sweat from his face, neck, and arms began to dribble onto the floor, forming a considerably sized puddle below him. The unknown, he pondered to himself, was the killer. Not knowing when he would be able to remove himself from this wretched position, Felix began to panic and concede defeat. His mind had given up; therefore, his body stood no chance. Involuntary moans of agony hurled from his mouth, but its point of origin generated from within the depths of his soul; the lamentations, oddly enough, supplied him just an ounce more resistance from caving in and laying prostrate upon the floor. As his body commenced to launch into spasms – nearing the brink of utter muscular failure - the Senior Instructor ordered Felix to get to his feet; and, as he did so, the uncontrollable shockwaves could be felt from his hair follicles to the hangnails on his toes, which involuntarily caused his nerves to jerk incessantly. He was, to put it in layman's terms, mush.

The Drill Instructor, unsympathetic to the Private's agonizing state of affairs, instructed the men to report to Room B137 for orientation. Then, as swiftly as the Sergeant entered, he made his exit; at which point the men all continued to unpack their belongings. At this juncture in time, still clinging onto his skivvies, Felix wondered how he could possibly endure this punishment any longer. He was not built for this kind of mental and physical anguish. He was a pampered city boy, born and bred in Staten Island, New York, in a modest home somewhere between the Goethals and Verrazano Bridges. Growing up, before the divorce, his parents demanded very little, aside from the typical chores given a teenager, such as throwing out the garbage, which he frequently neglected… and perhaps keeping his bathroom clean (his parents possessed an en-suite bathroom, so the second floor hall lavatory belonged to Felix and his little brother, Anthony); however, this task was also, for the most part, forsaken. Never a finger was lifted to conduct any extremely difficult manual labor; therefore, this present physical exertion was too much to bear. He began to fantasize a million and one ways about cutting and running from this crisis of epic proportions, but knew it was a pointlessly futile pipe dream. There was no going home. He was here to stay.

At about five in the morning, in the middle of their fourth and fifth dreams, the men were awakened by the clanging of what sounded like a thousand metal objects being thrown in every direction; the Senior Drill Instructor, along with a few other Sergeants, were conducting reveille, and doing it ever so gracefully by striking their batons against large, metal garbage cans. Felix wondered if these men ever slept. There they stood, in all of their splendor, wide awake and attired in their green smokey hats, donned with a black Eagle,

Globe, and Anchor emblem; beige, short sleeve, military button-down shirts that wrapped themselves tightly over a white Fruit of the Loom crew neck style undershirt, which peeked out between the upper button and the collar; green trousers, neatly pressed to perfection, held up by a darker shaded green belt containing a buckle, which proudly displayed another Eagle, Globe, and Anchor (this one gilt in color); and, shiny patent leather shoes to complete the ensemble, emitting the essence of sheer flawlessness. "Wakey wakey, hands off snakey, you worthless pieces of pig shit! Get your pretty little asses up and get your bunks wrapped up!" Every order that was barked was followed by a countdown (a countdown that somehow never included the proper numeric order). The men scrambled to put on their clothes, which included the standard mucus green socks; slightly darker colored boxer underwear and tee shirt; overlaid with camouflage trousers and a button down shirt of the same pattern; and, of course, black combat boots. The Senior Drill Instructor walked up and down the aisle as the men garbed their uniform, verbally *smoking* those that were either going about the charge in a dawdling manner or not accomplishing it with the level of excellence that was expected of them as Privates of the United States Marine Corps.

Once this daunting task of getting properly dressed was completed, the men began wrapping up their bunks, which was no easy task for many of them… and Felix was amongst the many. The beds were expected to be impeccable, as if out of an IKEA showroom, which, needless to say, was an especially impossible mission for Felix, due to his aforesaid lack of domesticated training. After approximately three legitimate attempts at dressing his rack, McGovern and Serrano – the two recruits that aided Felix with the *bag fiasco* the day before – came to the rescue. Like worker bees in a hive, they banded together to execute the quest for the perfectly made bunk.

"I appreciate this, bros. I don't know how to thank you guys. I would've been here for a year trying to figure this shit out. My mom always makes my bed, so I don't know what in the hell I'm doing." Felix admitted, with the utmost humility and sincerity. This was no jest. Gloria Christianson, in all actuality, was the maidservant of the entire household; moreover, in consequence of this woeful fact, Felix had not made a bed in his entire life… and, in all probability, would have continued this trend, had it not been for the opportunity given to him courtesy of basic training.

"Dude, that is definitely *not* something you should be sharing!" Serrano declared with a modest chortle. Serrano was the confident sort. Most of his life, he got by on his strikingly prepossessing facial features; that, and a body toned to perfection, resembling, somewhat, the hallmark features of the statue of David – which is to say, he was small in frame; however, every muscle that was part of the human body was prominently accentuated. Having crystalline blue eyes that resembled that of a cloudless spring day did nothing to contradict his self-proclaimed declaration of world's hottest guy, incidentally… not to mention his flawless, jet black hair that never seemed to concern itself with the harsh conditions of torrential rain or gale-force winds.

"Is that bad?" McGovern, the antithesis of Serrano in every way, shape, and form chimed in. "My mom makes my bed every day; and, she makes me whatever I want to eat. All I gotta do is ask. Once, my mom made me a whole lobster dinner, just 'cause I said it looked good on this Red Lobster commercial that I saw on TV. It was so good, too. She made it with butter and garlic and - "

Serrano interrupted, not willing to listen to McGovern's fatuous babbling for even a second longer. "That's real nice, McGovern; but, if you don't wanna have your head ripped clean off, followed by a loogie spit down your neck, you need to hurry up and lock down your corner of this bed."

"Right!" McGovern agreed.

Felix chuckled. He felt content. No longer was the sense of isolation and forlornness running rampant in his mind. He was now part of something… something bigger than himself. At this moment in time, three individuals became a single unit, working at a common goal, operating together as one entity – albeit simply making a bed; but, in life, sometimes something as simplistic as dressing a rack can produce such grander things that create bonds, solidify even greater friendships, and eventually give birth to the quintessential ethos, Semper Fidelis.

Learning how to walk and turn in unison occupied the time of the men for the next week or so. At the onset, it was – as one might expect – a cumbersome undertaking. What made it worse was that Felix had issues, to put it mildly, differentiating his left from his right; when the troop went this way, he went that; while the troop completed a one hundred and eighty degree about-face, Felix barely achieved ninety degrees. One might think that this inability to distinguish ones left from right would be far too satirical to be true – something that, perhaps, this historian conjured up with the intentions of providing a sort of comic relief to his readers; but, there it was nonetheless. He was quickly identified as the *weak link,* becoming the frequent recipient of what was officially referred to as *incentive training;* or, as it was better known, and in the vernacular of the victims, being *smoked.* "Take a real good look at this complete waste of life, he is the one that's gonna shoot all of you, instead of the enemy, because he doesn't know his left from his right!" Howled the Instructor. "Now, everyone get down into front leaning rest and give me fifty!" Then, focusing in on Felix, who began to descend to the ground with the rest of his platoon, the Sergeant addressed him solely. "Not you, waste of life… you get to stand at attention and watch all these lovely ladies getting smoked."

Felix's heart leapt into his throat as he stood up tall whilst closing his eyes, knowing full well that this would not go over well between he and his troop.

The Instructor had given everyone a severe consequence for Felix's shortcomings, which changed the game entirely. The fact of the matter was, Felix frequently became the recipient of a smoke, which meant that the group had to suffer the sequela; therefore, after about a week of paying for *his* mistakes, the other men were now beginning to turn against him. The menacing looks at chow were a forewarning of what was to come, and it would most likely be in the form of a vigilante-style strike in the middle of night, when no one would be the wiser. Felix, McGovern, and Serrano sat together in the Mess Hall, taking advantage of the Drill Instructors' inattentiveness to dialogue with one another about the crisis at hand.

"Man, these guys are ready to eat you alive." Serrano leaned in and whispered to Felix.

"What am I supposed to do, I have a legitimate handicap. It's a real problem, you know; it's no goddamn joke." Snapped Felix.

"That's true, it *is* a real thing. My third cousin, on my father's side, kinda has the same problem, 'cept he can't see colors too good. He can only see like gray and green and stuff." McGovern babbled.

"Now what in the holy hell does that have to do with left from right?" Scolded Serrano.

"Well it's kinda the same thing." Rebutted McGovern, displaying a countenance of extreme earnest, not understanding Serrano's inability to connect the two ideas.

"You explain to me how in the hell that's the same goddamn thing. Explain that right now." Serrano began to lose his cool, his voice elevating to inappropriate octaves, to which a couple of the Sergeant's responded with a look askance in the general vicinity of the trio; however, unsure from where exactly the disturbance originated, the gendarmes resumed their tête-à-tête. The triumvirate, satisfied that they had not been detected, and in a more subdued tone, continued their dialogue.

"Guys, guys, settle down. We're gonna have bigger problems if any of these D.I.s catches us talking." Felix warned, causing the three of them to sink their heads into their shoulders, like frightened turtles, and reconnoiter around the room once more to assure that the authorities were not afoot. The proverbial coast was clear, as the D.I.s were deeply engaged in their own conversation about high powered rifles, the ammunition in which it accompanies, the multitude of animals that would be on the receiving end of the spent projectiles, and other such leitmotifs. Felix continued, "I need to figure this right-from-left thing out real quick before I get myself a blanket party."

"That sounds like fun. I didn't know we were allowed to have parties. Can we really have parties here? If so, my birthday is coming up and I want a big -"

McGovern's blundering was impeded once again. "It's not a real party, numb-nuts. It's when a bunch of guys gag you and tie you down to your rack in the middle of the night, then take turns *whack-a-mole-ing* you over and over with a pillowcase full of soap bars." Corrected Serrano.

"Well, I'll tell you what, where I come from, that could very well constitute a party." McGovern informed, with a straight face, showing no signs of his utterance being made in jest.

"Where on *Earth* do you come from?" Serrano replied, shaking his head, supplemented with a look of sheer repugnance.

"Guys, focus! I need help here." Pleaded Felix.

The three of them sat pensively for a brief moment before McGovern's proverbial light bulb went off. "Hey, why don't you guide yourself using that big ol' pimply looking birthmark on your face?" He was referring to a small, flesh colored beauty mark, about the size of a tiny ladybug, which lay on the right side of Felix's face, just below his bottom lip.

"Come on, McGovern, no more clowning around." Said Felix, with agitation.

"I'm not clowning. I'm serious. Your birthmark is on your right side. Just remember when they say *'right face'*… or whatever… just remember and say to yourself, 'I got a pimple -' I mean, birthmark '- *right* on my face;' and then go in the direction of the pimple… I mean, birthmark. And when they say left face, just don't say the pimple thing and go the other way."

"McGovern, you're a regular idiot savant – more *idiot* than *savant*, but that's pure genius." Said an elated Serrano.

"That's actually a damn good idea. Damn good!" Felix approved, giving McGovern a slight, inconspicuous nudge of approval, so as not to alarm the D.I.s.

The men finished the rest of their chow of dry, tasteless, chicken; wet, loose mashed potatoes; and pruned-up green beans, in silence. Felix wore a slight grin on his countenance at the newfound solution to all of his woes at the present. McGovern sported a slightly larger grin for having been the hero for that brief moment in time; that, and - most importantly to him - he could finally concentrate on devouring his chow.

Physical training, after Felix's directional epiphany, thanks to McGovern's timely flash of brilliance, graduated from impossible to excruciating; which was, essentially, an improvement due to the fact that, in effect, it was now on par with all of the other men in the platoon. Felix was now marching alongside his troop with minimal mistakes. He was no longer the source of their extra curricular calisthenics and that made *everyone* happy… as happy as one can be when being subjected to torturous exercises for hours upon hours a day. For weeks, the men endured grueling ten mile hikes and marches, often falling to the ground in all out exhaustion, only to be lifted to their feet again by the Instructors or each other. They trained to endure *weapons of mass destruction* attacks, which included being led like cattle into a small gas chamber, in what resembled a kind of outhouse that one would find in the backwoods of some far off, desolate place, getting doused with the mephitic fumes of chlorobenzylidene malononitrile (or CS gas), which was considered to be a non-lethal substance, normally used as a method of riot control; except, when released into vents while trapped inside that oubliette, it felt – to the Recruits – like the worst verses of Revelations, as written in the New Testament. Some of the men passed out, having to be dragged out of the place, with drool and mucus spewing out of their noses and mouths. They were learning to face their worst nightmares; to grow not only physically stronger, but mentally unbreakable. There were certain days that Felix wished to be back in his bed, watching his favorite programs on television – perhaps some Star Trek, or maybe Battlestar Galactica, episodes – and eating his favorite food, which consisted of, basically, anything breaded and fried with a garlic dipping sauce on the side. He thought about how, just before he left for basic training, he'd had a falling out with his cousin, Justin, who expressed his severe and explicit opposition to Felix joining the Marines. Some days – most days – he wished he had heeded his cousin's stern reservations in the matter.

Today, though, Felix was not as apprehensive. On this particular day, after what seemed like a three thousand mile hike through rugged and craggy terrain, leaving his feet to feel as though someone had poured gasoline upon them and, subsequently, lighted them on fire, the Drill Instructor mercifully brought the troop to a halt somewhere in the middle of the forest, at an area where Felix could see the various pine, red maple, and American beech trees soaring above his head, which, incidentally, screened them all from the searing heat of the sun. There was a slight breeze undulating through the trees that brought with it the scent of lush, green vegetation, a smell that reminded Felix of his childhood, playing in the backyard of his parent's house, not too many years ago. He recalled, once more, sitting for hours on end, inside of his treehouse, wishing he could sit atop his little kingdom in the trees forever. Smells of crisp leaves, bark, and fresh soil danced through the noses of the men as they sat on the ground with legs crossed, welcoming the respite… it made them feel at ease. He, the D.I., had the men form a complete circle as he stood amongst them in the center. It was at this moment that the soon-to-be soldiers had reached the turning point of their basic training. It was here the Instructor gave them – for the final time as his neophytes – the allocution that all those that proceeded them, as well as all those to follow, would receive right before the most infamous, notorious, terrorizing, and blood chilling final obstacle course they would encounter during their initiation… the Crucible.

"Today," the Sergeant began his soliloquy, "is a meaningful and memorable day for all of you earthworms. Today is the last day of your civilian lives. Up until now, you were all posers trying to infiltrate my beloved Marine Corps. Just a bunch of weekend warriors thinking you could waltz in and call yourselves Marines. Well, you still are, you miserable maggots." He said, jocularly.

The men laughed.

The Instructor continued. "But after tomorrow, after you've bled, sweat, and wept your eyes out; after your body has been through the worst pain it's ever endured; after you've cried up to sweet Jesus to rescue you from the absolute hell that you will find yourselves engulfed in, you will be United States Marines. Remember that fact when you feel like you can't move one more inch, when the pain is so bad you'll be crying for your mamas, when you want to quit and die, when you wish you'd have joined the Navy, instead."

The men interrupted with jeers of "No! No!" and then laughed once more.

"When you're feeling all of these things, I want you to remember one thing… Adapt and overcome. Take hold of all the doubt, the uncertainty, and convert that useless, negative energy into motivation. You are, even right now, where very few have had the fortitude to be. You soon *will be* what very few have ever been. You will be this thing for the rest of your lives."

The men were filled with pride and motivation. *Felix* was filled with pride and motivation. He felt, at that moment, as though he could hike another twenty miles; the adrenaline flowed through him like an intravenous drug.

"Now on your feet, you piles of horse manure. Fall in and head back to camp." And with that, the men marched back, with a pep in their steps, to the barracks, carrying within them a sense of purpose and honor.

The next morning was the day of the dreaded Crucible. Over fifty back-breaking hours of endless marching and countless exercises, navigating through complex obstacle courses with what seemed like every single piece of accoutrement the Recruit possessed, weighing close to sixty pounds, having only two meals to get them through it all. The sole purpose of this trek through perdition being to work together as a single, solitary, unit to – when it was all said and done - form the unbreakable and indisputable bond of brotherhood that has existed since November 10, 1775, nearly – at that time - two hundred and fifteen years ago. A brotherhood that the men would cherish and defend to their last breath on their dying day.

Felix stood abreast of McGovern and Serrano, his heart pounding against his chest like the bass of a speaker inside of a nightclub; his breathing was labored and his vision tunneled. He tried all he could to clear his mind, which was, at present, inundated with incessant and uncontrollable thoughts of the impending journey, through the abode of the damned, in which he was about to plunge upon. They wore the tactical uniform of the day, which consisted of a green armored helmet; buttoned down camouflage shirt and pants; their beige Danner Reckoning combat boots; along with all of their gear in a duffle-bag, which they lugged on their backs; and, finally, a black M16 rifle strapped alongside their shoulders. Twelve weeks had passed. Twelve weeks of torturous, relentless training of the physical, spiritual, and mental variety all summing up to this moment, time, and place. It was here at the Crucible - on this crisp, early morning in September, about two hours before the sun would expose its torridity above the easterly horizon - that the men would be made or be broken, once and for all.

Felix would have been just fine standing in that very spot, just before the starting point, for eternity and would have done so without hesitation or shame if not for the Drill Instructor's orotund command. "Let's go!"

His feet proceeded to move, left foot… right foot, before his mind could process what was happening. He was on auto-pilot, no thought process was involved. The grueling three and a quarter mile hike en route to the obstacle courses was underway, whether Felix desired it or not. As they marched through the woods, Felix gazed up at the sky, which was still inundated with stars that twinkled brighter than that of a pirate's bountiful booty, containing the most precious of jewels, and he wished, for a moment, that he was up there in the heavens amongst the celestial wonder. The full moon, poised directly above, illuminated the path in which the men traversed; without it, not a one would have been able to see anything around them. It seemed so very serene; the expanse appeared before him as a comforting quilt that would cocoon and protect him from all the evils of the cruel world. This was a fantasy that assuaged many a fear during his childhood and, quite incidentally, his adolescent as well as young adulthood years, if one was being completely forthcoming about it all. It was a defense mechanism of sorts, wherein he would remove himself from the harsh realities of the consequences of his actions; essentially, placing himself in a fantasy world, subsequent to being punished for some infraction or another, and transporting himself to a distant world, light years away, far from anyone's deleterious clutches.

It was about five in the morning at the onset of the hike, and, as mentioned, still very dark; the sun would not rise for about another hour, so the temperature was, yet, very comfortable; not too cold, not too hot. He would have liked very much for the entire event to have taken place in the nighttime, to avoid the unbearable heat that was expected to arrive. In anticipation of the grueling task ahead, his mind burdened him with the delusion that his entire body was already aching beyond belief. Every muscle, every joint, every sinew, ached as though a three ton elephant had been taking a nap atop his entire body; however, in reality, he had only just begun. This hike was only a prelude to the actual obstacle course, and he wondered why they simply could not have just driven them all there; it was – he thought – the least that they could do. Halfway through the march, Felix felt the sensation of lethargy coming on… he especially felt his legs grow extremely weighty, as if two concrete cinderblocks were tied to each of them, and wondered how he would persevere; but, somehow, someway, his body continued to move forward, in spite of his mind's apprehensions, precisely the way in which the weeks of training conditioned him.

After some time, the platoon finally reached the first obstacle course, which was a structure meant not only to climb up and over, but also for the purpose of completing a daunting - and from the looks of it through an enfeebled Recruit's eyes, quite impossible – mission. The object was to deliver a large piece of equipment, made of pure steel, up, over, and finally onto the opposite side of the edifice. The chunk of steel equipment to be hoisted, incidentally, weighed more than the typical Recruit - no one man could complete this objective; therefore, it could only be completed as a team. The platoon of forty-four Recruits were broken into groups that would remain together for the entire quest; but, before the task commenced, each group had to choose someone amongst themselves to lead their particular pack. "Pick your Team Leader, maggot scum! One of you numbskulls – Sweet Jesus help you all - has to be the leader of the group, so choose now!" The Senior Drill Instructor bleated to Felix's group. Someone, anyone, needed to step up and be a figure head. The men surrounding Felix looked around to their left and to their right in the hopes that one or the other would take on this disconcerting responsibility; but, alas, *Bibb Latane's 'Bystander Effect'* was in full force. No one desired to be the guinea pig, and all expected the other to volunteer. No one wanted to fail… not just fail themselves, but be responsible for the failure of all. In certain situations, it is the mere *fear* of failure, rather than any other conceivable factor, that will prevent one from grabbing the proverbial horse by the reigns. This was one of those situations.

"Move" … the Sergeant commenced the order in a yell, "your" … his voice ascended to a scream, "asses!" … he crescendoed to a roar.

Felix's instinct kicked in – an instinct emanating from a quality he had absolutely no idea he possessed. Something within him - some unexplained, quite innate, and involuntary drive that he could not comprehend at that moment - took control of his body; in an almost somnambulistic sort of manner, he assumed the role of Team Leader and shepherded the operation, beginning with instructing the men on where they ought to be positioned to complete the job they were given. "Ok, guys, we'll use the rope right there to get this hunk of junk over to the other side. McGovern, you're the largest of us, so you get up there and get the piece up and over the top. Serrano, you head to the opposite end and guide it down. I'll position myself halfway on the front end of the structure." Felix then directed the other two Recruits in the group to take positions on the opposite end; one to mirror his own position on the alternate side, and the second to make steady and pull the rope in the direction they needed the piece to eventually lay.

The men took their places without question or hesitation.

They were happy to have anyone but themselves take control of what appeared to be a paradoxical situation. At the onset, it was slow going. A portion of the rope was first secured around the steel object and then, afterwards, slowly lifted up. As it passed each man, he would let go of his portion of the rope, transferring the weight onto his back and shoulders, heaving the object up by using his individual body weight, while the others continued pulling upwards. There was moaning. There was groaning. Cuts. Scrapes. Bruises. Tears. Finally, after much trial and error, the *Rock of Gibraltar* was delivered to its final resting place on the other end of the structure. There was no time to celebrate, though, as this was only the beginning; it was only the first of many other obstacles to come. Feeling somewhat invigorated after successfully completing the first hurdle, the men – with somewhat of a spring in their steps – made their way onward.

For the next few hours, it was much of the same; except, of course, for the dreariness that now surged within them, sending their morale into a nosedive. In addition to the litany of climbing and pulling structures, there were the fields of mud in which the men had to crawl through (on their backs, no less), with their rifles held up to prevent them from getting muddied – all the while the booming, deafening sounds of makeshift bombs and loud pops of simulated gunfire, crackling like a Fourth of July fireworks display, reverberated all around them, creating an atmosphere of all out war. If this were not bad enough, there was barbed wire everywhere. As Felix trudged through the brown slop, he came to an area that was inundated with large and extremely sharp circular wire that could, with the utmost ease, slice a phalange, or two, clean off. The men were wearing their black leather gloves, though, which was insulated with Kevlar material, to prevent them from getting nicked about the hands and fingers. As Felix passed half-way underneath the wire, he sagaciously recognized that the men behind him would have an easier time getting through if he could somehow keep the wires lifted up as they passed. Using his rifle, he raised the wire above him high enough that they could all slide underneath, unobstructed and unscathed. As Serrano began to slither passed him, Felix adjured, "If you hold your rifle up like mine, we can create more space and get these guys through easier."

"Good thinking, bro!" Exclaimed Serrano, and with that he now carefully slid to Felix's left, also using his rifle to expand the passing.

The men, seeing this, swiftly glided through on their backs and out onto the opposite end. As McGovern passed, he praised the two with much ardor. "You guys are my fucking heroes."

Subsequently, once the group was safely on the other end, Felix and Serrano, ever so gingerly, still using their rifles to keep the wires at bay – with surprisingly minimal scrapes to their arms and legs – passed through. Once they cleared the wire, they had to then flip over onto their bellies and continue to crawl through the mud, all the while, again, without getting their rifles dirty; which was a nearly implausible thing to do. Felix used his elbows and forearms to advance himself, while his hands gripped the rifle as if he were doing a bicep curl exercise with a small, straight, barbell. The pain endured from holding it in this position soon became too much to handle, and so the gun, from time to time, splashed into the mud, which would, in turn, infuriate the Drill Instructors walking along the side of the embankment. "Get that fucking gun up, recruit!"

"Sir, aye, sir!" was his reflexive response. Felix resented the barks from above, thinking to himself that he would love to see *them* trying to do the damned thing; but, quickly remembering that these prophytes had already passed through and completed this place of condemnation, continued to advance without further thoughts of malice; the rifle was then raised but for a brief moment until his arms gave way once more, causing the gun to plunge, yet again, back down into the mud. It felt like a thousand pounds to Felix. He wondered how the others managed to keep theirs lifted up; but, as he scanned his surroundings, he quickly realized that they were far from better off.

They made their way out of the obstacle now with mud completely covering the tops of their heads, running down the inside of their shirts, and finally spewing to the bottom of their boots, adding what felt like twenty pounds to their already heavy and weary bodies; all of which made the laborious journey ahead of them even more cumbersome. Before they could move any further, the gunk from their rifles that bonded during the mucky peregrination needed to be cleaned out… and it needed to be done before it caked; for, once this occurred, it would be nearly impossible to clean out, not to mention the significantly more important fact that the gun would not fire if it weren't freed from the obstruction. Felix, McGovern, Serrano, and the rest of their group settled in a cool spot, away from the sun's rays, shaded by a collection of large trees that towered above them, to complete this task. They planted themselves next to a few large rocks with flat, smooth, surfaces in which to sit while conducting their gun cleaning and, at the same time, to hydrate the insides of their arid mouths.

"This is insane, bro. I don't think I'm gonna make it. I

really don't." Serrano execrated, while clumsily disassembling his rifle, feeling the effects of intense heat and acute lassitude.

"Don't talk like that. You're gonna make it just fine." Rebuffed Felix, also feeling as though he were barely hanging on, but not revealing it to any of the men.

"Mind over matter. That's what my dad always says." Added McGovern, vigorously scrubbing away at the inner workings of his rifle.

"Your dad ain't never had to do the Crucible. What the hell does he know?" Snapped Serrano, impetuously.

"Hey, my dad knows plenty! He's done a bunch of stuff." McGovern shot back with an expression of indignation.

"Oh yea? Like what? What in the hell has *he* done? please tell me."

"Plenty, Serrano, more than *your* goddamn dad, I'll tell you *that* much!"

"Guys!" interrupted Felix, in the nick of time, just before they pounced on one another like two alley cats fighting over the forsaken victuals of a garbage can. "Cut it out and save your energy! This bickering back and forth isn't helping a damn thing and only gonna wipe you out more than you already are."

"I'm not gonna make it. That's all I'm saying. I know my body. I know what I can do and what I can't, and I'm telling you right now, I ain't making it." Serrano reiterated, standing down from his 'DEFCON one' posturing with McGovern, resuming his cleaning.

"Serrano, you can't say stuff like that, bro. No matter if McGovern's dad knows shit about anything or not, he's right about the mind over matter thing. You gotta make yourself believe you can do it, bro. It's all in here." Felix encouraged, gesticulating his index finger toward his temple to accentuate his point.

"My dad knows plenty." McGovern mumbled, without looking up from his gun.

Serrano did not respond. The three of them sat in silence whilst they swabbed and reassembled the firearms; each drifting into his own thoughts for the few remaining moments in which they had left.

***

Felix thought of his girlfriend, Ronnie, who was less than thrilled at his enlisting in the military. She thought he should have tried to figure out a better way. Originally, he had planned to go to college and maybe get a part time job to make a few extra dollars on the side; but, when he applied for financial aid, he received a grand sum of seven dollars and twenty eight cents. Never informing his parents, nor ever even attempting to ask them for help beforehand, he waltzed into his local recruiting station and signed up to become a Marine… much to the dismay, he was almost certain, of his birth-givers when they would eventually become aware. He wanted to show them that he could make a grown-up decision, without the need of burdening them. They had enough on their plates, dealing with the pending split of their union, without having to wonder how on Earth to pay for his college education. He had known for quite some time that they were thinking of getting a divorce. Felix's father, Felix Senior, sat him down one day and informed him that he and the Mrs. would not be an item forever; they were together primarily for the kids. Felix did not want, in any way, to be a part of that problem; therefore, he gallantly did what needed to be done in order to remove himself from the quandary.

Upon exiting the recruiting station, Felix walked to Ronnie's place with the intentions of telling her the news. The Staten Island recruiting station was not very far from where she lived; it was about a fifteen minute walk, so he possessed some time to figure out how in the world he was going to explain the whole business to her. He knew very well that the news would not go over smoothly; therefore, practiced numerous versions of the disquisition that would provide the rationale for his actions. How to begin was the key; a masterful prolusion was needed to quell the anxiety… an icebreaking circumlocution to pave the way. "Ronnie, I'm a Marine…" no that wouldn't do; "Ronnie, you're looking at the Marines' newest member…" no, not that; "Ronnie, I joined the few, the proud, the Marines..." corny; "Ronnie, where's my salute? Don't you know you're supposed to salute a soldier?" Each catchline sounded more ridiculous than the last. He reached into the inner pocket of his Kenneth Cole, black, leather jacket and took out a pack of Newport menthol cigarettes, a new vice of his, typically flying through an entire pack in one day. He pulled one out, placed it onto his lips, angled it to the side and downward – James Dean style - lit it, and took a prolonged drag. He allowed the smoke to sit deep within his chest for a second or so before slowly allowing it to release from his lungs and out of his mouth, all the while continuing to think of all the different ways in which he would tell the love of his life that he was going off to war.

As Felix approached her house, her parent's house, he took the nearly finished cigarette – his third in a matter of the fifteen minutes it took him to get there – and tossed it onto the sidewalk, crushing the butt with the bottom of his Timberland boot. He rang her doorbell, continuing to practice his speech in vain, aware of the fact that nothing he said to her would serve as a buffer for the hard truth. She opened the door, greeting him with a huge hug and kiss to the lips; a kiss in which he returned with fervent passion encompassing every bit of his feelings for her… feelings unmatched by any other in his world; she was luminance in a gloaming reality. After their embrace, he stared at her, soaking in all of her beauty; she was perfect, he thought to himself. Her light brown hair was tied up into a bun because she had been reluctantly performing the tedious chores of cleaning the bathroom and kitchen, assigned to her by her parents. They, her mother and father, were of the strong opinion that she was at an age where free room and board was no longer a viable or pragmatic option; therefore, she had to earn her keep, as it were. Her light, almost translucent, brown eyes – blended together with just a hint of green - twinkled at the sight of him, forming little crows feet at the corners of the lids, caused by the larger-than-life smile that seemingly extended from ear to ear. She was always so very happy to see him and he was equally happy to see her. They were in love. He even contemplated asking for her hand in marriage; although, such an act of prematurity - they being only eighteen years old and practically jobless - would pose somewhat of a problem for them. There was also the matter of the enmity it would cause certain family members… not to mention the complete and utter pandemonium the prospect of matrimony would spawn from those that knew *'pre-love struck'* Felix, who happened to be somewhat of a Don Juan... a real lady's man, if you will.

"Hi honey bunny, I didn't expect you until later today, I look like a complete mess!" Ronnie said, attempting to stuff the rogue strands of hair that were running amok back into her head wrap, which was, in actuality, a standard blue bandana with designs consisting of white swirls, the type that one could find in a typical discount store.

"You look gorgeous, babe... as always." He cooed, meaning every single word. She could have been in overalls, fresh from feeding pigs on a farm, and it would not have changed what he felt for her; such love transcends the realm of the material and superficial.

"You're insane, I look like an absolute train wreck!" She said, continuing to adjust herself whilst simultaneously sneaking a peak at her reflection in a mirror that hung in a large wooden frame next to the doorway.

"Never to me, my love... Never to me. Listen, I have to talk to you. It's kind of important." His countenance blanched, as his eyes now suddenly avoided hers.

"Oh. Okay, what is it? You look like you've seen a ghost. What's wrong? Is everything okay at home? Did your parents have another huge fight?" Ronnie began to fret. She was well aware of the domestic challenges that faced the Christianson home, serving – many a night – as the sanctuary and escape from the madness that frequently took place in Felix's humble abode.

Felix's countenance suddenly grew cadaverously white.

Beads of glacial sweat now began to trickle down upon his forehead; his legs feeling enervated, barely able to withstand his weight. He had worked himself up while trying to figure out exactly how to break the news to her; and, now that she was standing before him, all of the effort of his practicing rendered itself inert. "No babe. Well, yes they did, but that's not it. Let's sit inside. I need to sit."

Ronnie, now possessing a look of consternation, followed Felix into her living room, where they sat themselves on the large, brown, leather sofa; she, grabbing and clutching close to her chest a throw pillow of Native American design… a pillow in which, since as long ago as her childhood years, was used as a metaphorical shield against any unwanted forces of negativity. Now a young woman of eighteen, she found herself, once again, under its protection, curled up onto the sofa with the pillow against her core, which was now ice cold in anticipation of, what appeared to be, an augury of extremely disagreeable forthcoming news. "Felix, you're scaring me. What is it? What's going on?" A million thoughts – entirely unfavorable – raced through her head; although, none of the postulations were of anything specific… just random visions of every possible unpleasant, worst case scenario, end of the world, situations that she could conjure up in the seconds leading to Felix's explanation.

"So, you know how I applied to a bunch of those colleges and got in, but got gypped with the financial aid?" Felix reluctantly began. Ronnie, now realizing in which direction the conversation was headed, relieved at the fact that it was not within the realm of her worst nightmares, internally exhaled a sigh of relief and continued to listen with a more lightened countenance. "Well," he continued, "I thought… I mean, I figured… I just decided it'd be best – you know, for everyone's sake – that I'd just go ahead

and… you know… join the military or whatever. The Marines."
He stammered and stumbled over his words, his mouth feeling as
though he were noshing an entire package of cotton balls.

A look of absolute nothingness – void of any indication
of emotion - initially shone in her eyes, but was quickly replaced
by utter bewilderment and horror. Unsure of how to process the
information that was being delivered, she perplexingly – while her
mind painstakingly made heads and tails of the words that ejaculated
out of her boyfriend's mouth – and impetuously, inquired, "What are
you talking about? What do you mean?"

"I mean, I went to the recruiting office and signed up to be a
Marine. I have to report to Fort Hamilton, in Brooklyn, in a couple
of days to start the whole process." He tried reading her, but her stoic
disposition left him in the dark. He thought of repeating himself, not
certain if the issue was her inability to understand what was going
on at the present moment or her unwillingness to understand it.

Still very much in a state of shock, her eyes now stared not
at Felix, but *through* him into oblivion… completely disconnected.
Having absolutely no idea how, or what, to respond, she repeated,
almost mechanically, "What are you talking about?"

Now quite annoyed at her inability to focus on the information
that he was attempting to convey, he snapped at her. "Babe, are you
listening to me? I'm trying to tell you that I enlisted in the Marines.
I'm going into the military."

Suddenly, like a sharp smack to the face by a large, calloused,
opened hand, she awoke from her stupor; in an ebullition of
exasperation, she stood up from the sofa - causing her throw pillow

to fall to the floor - and replied, "You did what? You… you joined the military? Felix, you… why? Why would you do that?" She bellowed, her voice now an octave higher.

"Babe, you know that -"

She cut in not allowing him to complete his plea to be understood. "Do you hate me? Did I… Is it *me*? Did I do something to… why would you do something like that?"

"My love, why would you think I hate -"

"Shut up, stop talking. Stop talking. Are you telling me… are you seriously telling me that you joined the *military*? Like, you are going into the *military*?"

He stared at her, obeying her wish for him to be silent, instantly coming the realization that – having known her for nearly two years - it was most likely a poor and unwise gesture.

"Hello?! Answer me!" She yelled.

"You told me to shut up." His impassive demeanor, he was sure, would add fuel to the fire. It was not his wish to infuriate her; however – he not having the wherewithal to successfully douse the flames of her inferno – it was the only viable course of action in which he could think of to resort. He took a deep breath, preparing for the backlash.

"Are you kidding?! You're giving me sarcasm? Are you kidding me right now?"

"I'm not, I don't want to upset you. I -"

"You don't want to *upset* me? Oh, really? You don't want to *upset* me. Are you totally fucking insane? If you didn't want to upset me, Felix, you wouldn't have done such a stupid, stupid, thing."

"Ronnie, I don't want to fight. I just -"

"Oh we're *going* to fight. You better *believe* we're going to fight." She answered, folding her arms together across her chest, implementing the classic defense mechanism posture.

Felix refrained from replying, lowering his head, fixing his eyes onto the floor, allowing his subjugated fizzog to express his unconditional surrender and submission, much like one would see in the animal kingdom, wherein a creature of the wild, who has offended the alpha of the pack, wishes to convey a sentiment of deference and a want to return to good graces. There was no winning this battle. He had only one course of action and that was to weather the proverbial storm. He would have to wait it out like a poor, soaking wet flop waits under a bridge for a passing torrential storm to subside. He retrieved the fallen throw pillow that hit the deck, when Ronnie shot off of the couch like a rocket, attempting to return it to its owner, but it was snatched and launched across the room as she continued her tirade. "I cannot believe you would do something so selfish. You are so fucking selfish, do you know that? Did you think about *me*? Did you think about me for one second while you were doing what you did?" She was crying now. A sense of abandonment rushed through her, feeling, quite psychosomatically, the overwhelming sensations of asthma... the tightness of the chest, the shortness of breath; the thought of her being all alone in the world was too much for her to bear. All she had was Felix. He was more than just a boyfriend and a prospective fiancé; he was her best friend. She had grown to become dependent upon his companionship; in quite the same way he developed a proclivity to her warm and tender presence – that is, when she wasn't flying off the handle at some insanely foolhardy thing that he happened to do or to say, such as the particular moment at hand. She couldn't imagine a day without his being present; and he, if left to his own devices, would not choose to spend a moment away from the love of his world. This wasn't the life – the life of a would-be soldier, off to the trenches – that he freely chose; and, in spite of his forbearing demeanor, he, too, was experiencing every single bit of the dolorousness in which she now endured. Given a choice, if financial obligations were not a factor, he would just as soon get a job in some fast food restaurant or work as a stock-boy in a local clothing store; but, that was not a very pragmatic life-plan, and they both knew this to be an unfortunate fact in which neither of them could dispute.

The two sat in silence, deep in their own rumination, looking, very obstinately, in opposing directions of one another for quite some time before Felix, in a tender and soothing manner, attempting to assuage his heartbroken beau, held onto her hand and said, "You know I wouldn't have done it if I thought there was a better way. You think I *wanna* leave you? You're everything to me."

"So why? Why did you do it? You didn't even *talk* to me about it. That's what I really don't understand. You didn't even tell me you were *thinking* about it." She answered, still avoiding his eyes, her voice slightly subdued. The initial shock was wearing down, but she was still somewhat dismayed, continuing to feel the fire deep inside of her chest.

"I know… you're right. I should've… I'm sorry."

He could hear a slight exhale venting from her mouth, but she did not verbally respond. She was crying again; but, this time, hardly making a sound. The tears quietly trickled down her rose colored cheeks as she unremittingly imagined an existence without Felix by her side. She thought of all the lonely days and nights in which she would now be subjected; all of the conversations she would no longer be able to share; all of the little things that she usually had taken for granted up until now, knowing that he was always there when she needed him.

"Babe, I know it's going to be hard;" Felix continued, "but, it's the best thing. It really is. In the long run, you know? The recruiter says I can get all kinds of training… to learn a skill and stuff, so when I get out I can get a really good job."

"*If* you get out. There just so happens to be a goddamn war going on, if you didn't already know."

Felix didn't want to think about that. He knew it was an indisputable fact that he was going to Iraq to fight; but, it was not a reality right now. It was just an awful, distant, nightmare that he chose to repress, deep down into his cerebellum; therefore, he did not respond to the comment. Instead, he continued to console her. "Love, I'll call and write every single chance I get. I swear I will."

"Oh, yeah because that's just the same as you being here. I'll just go around holding hands with and kissing the goddamn letters you mail me."

"Babe, cut me some slack here." Felix was beginning to lose his patience. The feelings he was so desperately trying to suppress, for his sake as well as hers, were now shooting forward like a slingshot. After all, wasn't *he* the one going off overseas to a foreign country, thousands of miles away from all he had ever known? Wasn't *he* the one that was going to be shot at from every which direction, beginning from the moment he awoke to the moment he closed his eyes? Wasn't *he* the one that could possibly return home minus one or more vital body parts? He could contain these thoughts no longer and ejaculated, "The way I see it, I've got the shitty end of the stick here. I'm really sorry you feel I've offended you in some kind of way; but seriously, I think I'm a little bit worse off."

"Yeah, the thing is, *you're* the one that caused this to happen. *You're* the one that decided to slither into the recruiting station and sign the dotted line, without so much as a single, solitary, word to me about it. *I* didn't do that, *you* did." She quickly shot back.

"I understand that; but, as I already told you – as you already know, very goddamn well, I might add, I didn't have much of a choice. I know I should've told you. I know I should've. I also know that you probably would've tried talking me out of the damned thing; and, quite honestly, it would *not* have taken much to make me change my mind. I don't especially enjoy the thought of going half-way across the world, where people are gonna try to kill me every goddamn single second of the day, so I'm pretty sure you would've had a very easy time changing my mind... and I couldn't chance that because, in all reality, I have no *real* choice… in spite of what you may think. It's not a *real* choice when one of the alternatives is a goddamn substandard way of life."

Ronnie, whipping her head around, glowering at him with

contempt, replied, "And that's such a bad thing? A substandard life is still a life, the way I see it. If you go over there and get yourself killed, then guess what? the *substandard life* – as you so eloquently worded it – would be the winner between the two, let me tell you!"

"Ron, if there was *any* other solution… look, all I want is a good future for us. I want to be able to take care of you. I can't do that while working at some part-time grocery store, packing bags or stocking Twinkies, now can I?" With that, Felix got up from the sofa and walked over to the window. He watched as someone passing outside was walking their dog; or, to put it more accurately, the dog was walking the person. The chocolate lab was about three feet in front of its owner, pulling with all its might, causing the leash to be taut to the brink of obliteration, violently yanking its human counterpart, making it abundantly clear that he, the dog, was the leader of that pack. Felix reached into his jacket pocket to take out his pack of Newports, wanting nothing more than to fill his lungs with the sweet heavenly bliss of nicotine and tar… with a hint of mint, as the Newport variety provided.

As he slid one of the cigarettes out of its packaging and nestled it between his lips, she scolded, "You know you can't smoke that in here, my parents will murder me if they smell it."

"Relax, I wasn't gonna light it up. It just feels good between my lips. It's like a placebo, you know what I mean? The placebo effect?"

"You shouldn't even be smoking at all, you know that? Why on Earth did you even start to begin with? It's disgusting. You're gonna end up smelling like a goddamn ashtray. You know I won't come near you if I even remotely smell it, you know that, don't you? Not even remotely near you."

"Add it to the list of disappointments I've caused." He mumbled out her earshot. Then, turning around to face her, he said aloud, "Listen, I had better go. I gotta figure out how in the hell I'm gonna tell my mom and dad about this. You're not the only one that's gonna give me all hell about this crap."

Ronnie said nothing, but watched as he opened the front door and closed it shut behind him; then, hearing the click of the latch, believing he was gone, unable to hear her, she placed her hands over her face and burst into an uncontrollable, convulsive, fit of tears. He did hear her, though; never feeling more helpless in his entire life, the reverberation of her agonizing pain impaling his heart like a thousand stings from a wasp. He hated that she was suffering, but had no words to console her. How could he make her sorrow go away when he had his own turmoil to deal with? Still, he despised the idea that she was hurting in any way. He remained on the opposite side of the door for a brief moment, contemplating on going back inside; however, he ultimately decided against it. Instead, he took out a lighter from his pocket, lit the cigarette that was still loosely dangling from his lips, took a deep, long, drag, placed it between his pointer and middle finger, exhaled, and began the trek home.

***

Felix was abruptly pulled away from his thoughts by the Drill Sergeant's sonorous voice, which penetrated his ear like the sound of a blaring trumpet. With his rifle now cleared of obstruction, he was ready to push forward onto the next obstacle. The midday sun was high overhead, the air was still, creating a sweltering, oven-like heat that could fry an egg to perfection. Felix had never endured a suffocatingly searing air such as this, with the exception of that one time he was on vacation in Daytona, Florida when he was about ten years old; but, even then, the relief of the Atlantic Ocean waters provided some succor. There was no such relief here, deep in the woods of South Carolina. The humidity was what drove him nearly mad; that, along with the weight of the gear, culminated into what could be best described as a severe case of calenture, causing him to experience bouts of delirium. At certain points during the hike, he believed that he was surrounded by a deep blue ocean, longing to dive into it, so as to refresh and relieve himself of the infernal stewing caused by the rays of the sun; other times he could have sworn, to all that was Holy and pure, that he lay eyes on his beloved, Ronnie, and called out to her, wishing to collapse upon her bosom to be pampered with kisses and strokes of the head, like a child being lovingly cradled by his mater, only to be reminded of the harsh truth whenever the Instructors barked their commands. As the men marched along the dirt path that would lead them to their next task, Felix focused his attention downward at the ground below him and spotted an army of ants, in perfect formation, working as a single unit to accomplish a common goal, which, at present, was delivering a microscopic, grain sized, comestible toward their place of residence … his Drill Instructor would be proud, he thought; they would, most certainly, make commendable soldiers. He almost wished he could be one of those ants, instead of having to deal with this unbearable course; that is, until the men began to crush them by the dozens as they marched by. Still, he wondered what was worse; death by a combat boot or the Crucible.

After about a mile hike, they reached a structure that resembled an 'end of the world,' apocalyptic type, fighting pit; something right out of a Mad Max movie. Felix half expected Mel Gibson to pop out to make a cameo appearance. It was circular in shape, stood approximately fifteen feet high, and was made of stone and metal; its sole purpose was to contain the combatants inside of the small structure to battle one another, the way in which the courageous gladiators of Rome once did in the days of yore within the lionized Coliseum. The men strapped on protective gear that consisted of a football helmet, shoulder pads, and mouthpiece. They were then given either boxing gloves or pugil sticks, which were long, pole-like, objects with padded ends; then, once garbed, they were brought to the center of the arena to beat the living hell out of each other. Felix, McGovern, and Serrano watched in horror as the preceding Recruits viciously thrashed one another about the entire body, some of them the recipients of some extremely violent blows to the cranium. "Guys," McGovern began with much trepidation, "please, no matter what happens... no matter what you do... no blows to the belly. I will seriously vomit all over myself. You *know* I have a weak constitution."

"And no blows to my face... or my nuts." Added Serrano. "Those two things are essential in my life."

"Jesus, these guys are are killing each other. It's like they're possessed." Felix said, growing sick at the sight of the slaughter taking place before his eyes.

They three hoped to get paired with one another; but, their unfortunate reality was that, at the very least, one of them would have to fight another Recruit, one of whom was apart from their clique; and, in this case, there would be no ground rules, *their* ground rules. When the other fighters, the ones currently in the pit, were done beating each other senseless, the Drill Instructor called out for two more assailants. "You two ladies, let's go!" He was referring to McGovern and Serrano. They were relieved beyond measure, shooting to each other a look of solace, a look that signified to one another that the impending, now innocuous, boxing match was *in the bag*, as it were. There was a pact; no belly shots and no strikes to the face or nuts, was the verbal agreement in place. Felix, however, was disheartened. He would have to fight someone who had no such desire to make a similar gentleman's entente; nor would his fellow pugilist have any concern for his preferred *off-limits* clobbering locations. At the command of, "Fight!" Felix watched in bewilderment as McGovern and Serrano went at it like two roosters in a cockfighting ring. There was absolutely no stratagem applied by them whatsoever… the deal that was struck before the match had flown out of the proverbial coop due to sheer and utter lack of skill in the art of hand-to-hand combat. The two possessed zero presence of mind as to what was happening at that moment, as they recklessly wielded the pugil sticks in all directions, with absolutely no regard to the prospective landing sites; the duo inadvertently pummeled one another in every single spot in which it was agreed *not* to violate. In any other circumstance, it would have been comical – something right out of an old Abbott and Costello or Laurel and Hardy skit.

The match mercifully came to a conclusion with no clear victor… both were defeated. Felix wished for it to have been prolonged, not just for the sheer satirical value that it provided to him, as well as all that bore witness; but, also, so that he would not have to participate in this madness. Unfortunately for him, however, the inevitable moment of truth, as it would seem, had arrived. He placed on his gear, initially having trouble with the straps for both the shoulder pads and the football helmet; the assistance of the Instructor was needed, as he struggled to secure the protective equipment. As Felix was being suited up, he glanced over at his opponent, Private Bernard Blaze, who had already garbed himself – with no support from any other – now leering at him with evil intent, whilst simultaneously fleering in such a way as to convey a most unsavory presentment in his favor for the outcome of the skirmish. Felix felt sick to his stomach. He wanted positively nothing to do with this; never having fought anyone in his life, except for his little brother, Anthony, which did not count because it was no real contest – Felix, being the older and larger brother, always ending up the recurring victor of those backyard brawls.

The combatants were ready; they were now face to face, awaiting the signal to begin the fray. Felix struggled to stay awake, as he felt the beginning stages of a faint coming on; his brows engorged with a deluge of perspiration; heart rate elevated above healthful levels; and, a severe case of tunnel vision was setting in… his legs feeling somewhat similar to the consistency of gelatin. The pugil stick felt like a thousand pounds of weight in his hands, barely having the ability to hold it steady, his arms trembling like the brittle branches of a tree against an impending storm. The Drill Sergeant took his position in the center as referee between the two when finally, and much to the displeasure of Felix, the signal to commence the carnage was given. "Let's go! Fight!" Roared the Sergeant.

Private Blaze, whose entire body was already layered in a pool of perspiration in anticipation of the looming clash of titans, attempted to spill first blood, taking a wild, uncontrolled, and miscalculated swing towards Felix's head, so ferocious that, if contact were made, it would have the potential to instantaneously send Felix into a long, deep, slumber; however, the target was missed, as Felix somehow managed to quickly duck under the swing and, as he ascended, jabbed his stick into Blaze's solar plexus, which brought him quickly to his knees. Seeing an opportunity to exploit Blaze's lack of oxygen consumption, Felix swiftly followed up his blow with a lightning quick left and right thrust of the pugil to the head – more specifically, the temples - of his opponent, knocking him flat to the ground, prostrate and unconscious. It was Mike Tyson-*esque*. Felix couldn't believe what he had just done; it was an amalgamation of shock, pride in his accomplishment, and sympathy for Blaze's misfortune, all wrapped into one singular emotion… relief.

One of the Sergeants who had been standing off to the side, unmoved by any of what had just transpired, having neither sympathy nor the slightest bit of empathetic solicitude to the plight of either of them whatsoever, latched onto the pendulous, practically lifeless, body of the defeated Private Blaze, dragging him off to receive medical attention, whilst the other Drill Instructor – the one acting as referee - merely barked, "Next two, lets go!"

Those having concluded their participation in the slugfest gathered their gear and were led to a location about a quarter of a mile from the arena; at which point they were told to chow and rest, albeit (and much to the disappointment of the Recruits) located in the middle of the woods - as opposed to a mess hall with tables, chairs, napkins, and every other humane item one might expect, and desire, when consuming their victuals. What was worse, it was now nighttime, which made it all the more difficult to dine – having to *break bread* amongst the nocturnal creatures that roamed the area, creeping and crawling all about. Other than the absence of the Sun in the sky, which gave them somewhat of an idea where in time they existed, the precise hour of the day was unknown. It was evening, that much is all the men knew. They all made themselves as comfortable as one possibly could under these circumstances; one supposes, one could only wish for smooth ground nowhere in the vicinity of an anthill, filled with flesh piercing fire ants, or anything else that could cause bodily harm, when one finds oneself in such precarious situations at this… this chronicler would have little idea as to the specifics of this kind of plight, having squandered his opportunity to experience this quandary for himself when he had the chance. There was complete silence during this period of repose. No one spoke. No one had the energy to utter a word. Each man pulled out their meal ration, which consisted of a small, pre-packaged jerky-type meat, washing it down with whatever tepid water remained inside of their canteens. This would be the first of only two opportunities to consume any sort of nourishment during the Crucible – as well as the only other time in which they would possess to get some rest.

As Felix ingested his meal, trying desperately to chew without swallowing it whole (as one would expect when one is feeling the sensations of food deprivation), he thought of his contest with Blaze, and was still in awe of it; although imbued with a sense of commiseration for his opponent, genuinely hoping he was well, there was, yet, a sense of fulfillment that flowed within… something that he had never before experienced. He glanced around, but did not see any sign of his fallen comrade, as he quenched his extremely parched throat with the water from his canteen - some spilling out of the sides of his mouth. After placing the top back on the bottle, he lay his head on his bag, now doubling as a pillow, closed his eyes, and began to, once again, think of home and the days before beginning his journey at Parris Island.

***

When Felix arrived at home, he decided not to enter; instead, he traversed along the side of the house - where a string of vibrant, six foot tall boxwood shrubs, serving as a natural fence between properties, made their humble abode - and into the backyard to the treehouse he and his father had built around a large elm tree many years prior. He was about eight years old when it was constructed (Anthony was only five at the time and Barbara was yet to be a member of the human race, as she would not be born for another eleven years at that point); it was a project that Felix and his father worked on exclusively. He considered it all his, not taking pleasure in having to share – even though Anthony made sure to be allowed access any time he so desired. Felix, now eighteen years old, looked up at the treehouse and began to climb the wooden blocks that were hammered into the bark for the purpose of ascending into the structure. Once at the top, he began to look around and reminisce the years that seemed not too distant in the past. Remnants of his childhood could be seen scattered all about the floor in the form of action figures, along with other random toys that, once upon a time, meant the entire world to him. There were drawings on construction paper of all different colors that had long begun to yellow and deteriorate, obstinately holding tight to the walls by an assortment of multi-colored thumb tacks. There were so many good times and, conversely, so many bad times growing up in the Christianson household; but, right then and there, he yearned for it all again; every up and every down. He desired nothing more than to be that little eight year old child, sitting high up above the world atop that tree, with no responsibilities or cares… no *real life* trials and tribulations to burden his mind and make heavy his heart.

He took a seat by one of the framed cut outs on the wall that served as a window, entering into deep rumination about all that was happening to him. Prior to the conversation with Ronnie, it hadn't really set in – his joining the Marines. It was surreal. Now, similar to the way in which shock sets in some time subsequent to the calamity from which it originates, it was all becoming reality and the thought was unsettling. He imagined all of the worst case scenarios. He visualized himself there, in the Middle East, attired in full regalia, engaged in a fierce firefight, surrounded by the enemy. Of course, having never been remotely close to being a part of such a schema, having no true reference point, he had no idea, whatsoever, what he was imagining. The closest postulation he possessed of war were the comic books he read and movies he had seen, which was far from reality; yet, it was all his mind knew… therefore, it wandered freely without boundaries leading him down a morbid path of negativity, doubt, and regret. Perhaps, he pondered, he ought to have thought it through more assiduously; he should have talked it over with Ron before making such an important life altering decision, thereby allowing her to refute his choice to join the military – as he knew very well she would. He could have gotten a job at a local hardware store, or fast food restaurant, or anything other than what he was about to embark upon. He began to weep; just small tears at first, until the corners of his mouth began to slope downward, just before his bottom lip commenced to quiver, culminating, finally, into a steady bawl, crying himself a proverbial river. All of his fears and frustrations poured out of him like a compromised dam, purging all that he had been bottling up since the start of the whole predicament.

"Are you crying?" Inquired a voice from behind. Felix had not realized that Anthony – who spotted his brother from the bedroom window – made his way outside to find out, as Anthony so eloquently pondered to himself, 'why in the hell is he climbing up to the treehouse?' something that neither of them had done in years. Anthony was now halfway though the hatch that opened from the floor, only his lower body being excluded, awaiting the answer to his query.

"What? No! What are you doing up here? Get outta here!" Felix was now frantically wiping his tears. He didn't want his fifteen year old brother descrying him in such a condition, lest Anthony should use it as ammunition for any future indiscretion perpetrated by his elder sibling.

"You *are*! You *are* crying! What happened? Why are you crying?" Anthony exclaimed in ardor, probing his brother's face, not yet believing that his *grand frere* was in tears… crying was not something that Felix did very often, if at all.

"I am *not* crying! Would you get the hell out of here!" Felix stammered while continuing to wipe the evidence from his cheeks.

"Why are you crying? Did you and Ronnie break up? Did you totally catch her *riding dirty?* She cheated on you, didn't she? I knew it! I knew she would! Bro, she's *way* too hot for you, I always told you that! Haven't I always told you she's light years out of your league?!" Scolded Anthony, half doleful for his sibling and half enthralled at the fact that his premonition had come to pass after many an admonition given.

"Nobody… are you stupid? nobody cheated on anybody!

What are you talking about? I told you to get out, why don't you get the hell out of here before I send you flying out this window?!"

"Then what is it?" Anthony continued to delve, ignoring the threat. "What happened? Why are you crying?"

Felix fell silent.

"Hey, I know we fight a lot; and, most of the time, we hate each other's guts; but, we're still brothers and all. You can talk to me, you know." Anthony now said, conveying a much more sincere sentiment.

"There's nothing to talk about." Felix replied, looking out of the window, a million and one thoughts flashing through his mind at once.

"Well, something made you cry, so -"

Felix whipped his head around with the look of the infernal Apollyon. "If you say I was crying one more goddamn time, I swear I'll -"

"Alright, alright, you weren't crying. Something made you… *upset*; so, what gives?" Anthony corrected, now taking a seat next to Felix, placing his hand on his brother's shoulder.

Felix quickly swiveled his head in Anthony's direction, at first leering at the hand that was placed upon his person, then, subsequently affixing his eyes onto his interlocutor's, for but a brief moment, to assess his earnestness; and, having reached a presentiment of satisfaction that the gesture was sincere, returned to looking out the window before responding, "I joined the Marines."

Laughing at what he thought was uttered in jest, Anthony answered, "Very funny. No, seriously."

"I'm serious." Felix responded, with a blank expression on his countenance.

"You? The Marines?"

"Yes, me… who in the hell else?"

"Honestly? Anybody else!"

"Hilarious."

"Sorry, bro, I just can't believe it. Wow. What in the hell made you do that?" Anthony exclaimed in disbelief.

"I have no idea. I'm trying to figure all of that out myself."

"Damn, bro. Can you get out of it? Can you quit?"

"Yeah, I think so, I haven't taken my oath or anything like that, yet… but, no, I can't do that. I mean, I *won't* do that… that's not a realistic option."

"Of course it's an option. You just said you haven't taken an oath; so, just quit. Don't go back. You can live up here in this tree if they come looking for you. I could bring food up to you every day and Ronnie could sneak up here for some conjugal nookie time." Anthony giggled.

"And then what, huh?" Felix began, ignoring Anthony's untimely wisecrack. "Then what am I supposed to do? I can't afford college… you know mom and dad can't afford to send any of us to school. What am I supposed to do? work at some fast food joint for the rest of my life? Is that it? Flipping burgers for the rest of my miserable life?”

"Easy now, Mr. Ambition… I don’t think you start on burgers, bro. You gotta work your way up to that. You’ll most likely be washing lettuce for a hot minute.” Anthony said, chuckling, until he realized that Felix, not appreciating humor in time of crisis, was not joining in on the laughter; then, clearing his throat, he said, “Sorry. Go on.”

You keep joking. Let’s see what happens to *you* in a few years. Let’s see what *you* do when you’re in *my* shoes.”

"No offense, big brother, but I don’t intend on being in your shoes. You know I got my D.J. thing going on. I plan on making it big. International, you know? D.J. Tony Temptation! Spinning his way into the ears and hearts of club-heads around the world! Can you see it? Can you see my name in flashing lights?” He said, gesticulating his hands in a manner that indicated his name appeared on a massive billboard in the sky.

Felix, shaking his head, rolling his eyes, and resuming his gaze out into the yard, replied, “Well, that’s great for you. Good luck with that… sincerely.”

"Look, maybe it won’t be that bad. I mean, plenty of guys go into the military and end up coming back perfectly fine. I’m sure you’ll be just fine.”

"It’s not about being fine when I come back… *if* I come back… it’s about me not wanting to go in the first place. I don’t want to leave home. I don't want to leave Ronnie."

"What, you think she's gonna bang some dude while you're gone or some crazy thing?" He paused before continuing. "Actually, I could see that. I mean, she's nice enough and all; but it happens everyday… that's all I'm saying. They get lonely, you know? She'll probably meet some super hot guy who will act like her best goddamn friend and let her cry on his big burly shoulders, telling her how *he'd* never have left her alone if she were *his* girl. Then, just when she's at her weakest point, he'll dive right in there like a goddamn bird of prey… like a goddamn vulture." He taunted, mimicking the shrilling mating calls of the aforementioned vulture.

"*Not* helping, Anthony. Not helping at all."

"Oh, yeah. Sorry, brother." There was a brief moment of silence before Anthony resumed speaking. "I'm assuming you haven't told mom and dad?"

"No, I haven't."

"When are you gonna?"

"I don't know. Tonight, I guess."

"What time, I don't wanna miss it."

Felix flashed a look of disdain in Anthony's direction. "Can you please give me some time alone? I really need to think things through… please."

"Fine. I have to work on my new mixed tape, anyways. I have a fan club that's waiting very patiently for my next cassette to drop." Said Anthony, now simulating with his mouth a kind of monotonous beat that one would hear at a nightclub.

"Wonderful."

Anthony headed down the makeshift ladder and back into the house, leaving Felix to contemplate on his woeful state of affairs. As he sat there on the warped wooded floor, he took out a cigarette, lit it, and took a long pull; which – on an empty stomach – made him instantly lightheaded and numb… a feeling he welcomed at the moment. He longed for an alternate life; any life other than the one in which he currently lived, wondering why on Earth he was born in the first place, as the plume of smoke exiting his lungs emanated around him, forming a white, foggy, haze. He decided, after some deliberation, that he would not discuss joining the military with his parents today. He would go inside the house, grab a bite to eat, take a long, hot, shower and put the day out of its misery. Tomorrow was a new day and he would be, he hoped, in a better frame of mind to break the news to them. More importantly, it would give him some much needed rest after a mentally trying day.

***

The sounds of gunfire and heart wrenching explosions violently woke the men from their slumber. Only three hours - though it felt like three minutes to the Recruits - had passed since they closed their eyes to lay and recover. Felix forgot where he was for a moment. It wasn't until the Drill Instructors commenced their cries and screams for the men to get on their feet that he finally collected his senses and grabbed his gear. There was sheer chaos around him. An endless barrage of detonations and artillery discharges sounded all around the Recruits as they scrambled with rifles at the *low ready* – a position the rifle is held wherein the muzzle of the firearm is lowered to allow clear observation over its top - as per the Sergeant's instructions. The air around them was filled with a thick, white and grey fog which smelled of freshly dispensed fireworks; the men could not see more than one foot in front of them, moving ahead slowly in a tight pack, with their eyes darting back and forth, not knowing what was to come and fearing the absolute worst.

Felix could feel his heart beating from his throat. His mouth was as dry as the burning sands of the Mohave Desert, but he dared not reach for his canteen for fear of the unknown. After some time, the men found themselves trudging in the mud once more. Now on their bellies, they waded in the thick mud, with their rifles – for the second time – above their heads; but, this time – having already experienced this type of obstacle and learning their lesson as to the consequences of getting the weapons caked with mud - the rifles were held high, with only just a very few splashing down into the brown slush. As they glided forward, the thunderous explosions continued to sound all around them, creating an aura of total mayhem… creating an atmosphere, again, of all out war; something that, in a very short time, would be a grim reality for them all. In the distance, Sergeants were shouting orders here and there; some of the men were hollering at the top of their lungs in what sounded like pure agony, but was, in actuality, a sort of war cry, emanating from the very inner depths of their souls, to keep them moving forward. Felix, making his way through the river of mud, could see nothing but the boots of the Recruit in front of him – size nine or ten – which he used as his guide to assist his way through the narrow and nebulous embankment.

Although he could not see McGovern or Serrano, he could hear them, bickering as usual, behind at his feet. "God Damn it, McGovern, your boot is in my goddamn face! You're crushing my nose with your extra-jumbo feet!" Cried Serrano.

"I can't help it, I can't get a grip on this mud! Why dontcha back the hell up and I won't be kicking you in your face!"

"I can't back up, there's about a million people behind me! You go faster!"

"I can't go faster, there's about a million people in front of me!"

"Goddamn it, take shorter strides then, I can't take another shot to my face with your Sasquatch sized feet!"

McGovern did take shorter strides, which immediately placated Serrano. Felix shouted back to them, "Just hang in their, boys; we'll be out of this soon enough!" Saying this, he wondered, himself, how much more he could take. He was tired, hungry, and his muscles felt as though they could accept very little more abuse. All he could do to prevent himself from absolutely shutting down was to continue distracting his mind with thoughts of home.

***

The next morning, upon waking up, Felix mentally prepared himself to, once and for all, reveal to his parents the decision of joining the Marines. He wasn't quite ready, though, and remained in bed, under his covers (which, incidentally, were pulled all the way up just beneath his chin) a little longer, looking out of his window at the mixture of grey and white clouds that hung like giant bags of cotton in the sky, listening to a mourning bird that perched itself on a branch of a tree which sat just outside his window, singing its comforting, almost owl-like, melodies of 'whoo whoo ah hoo!' - something that always pleased and comforted him. He envied the fact that birds had no obligations or responsibilities. They never had to worry about going to school or getting a job or going to war. He knew that the bull session would, in all likelihood, be intense and he was not prepared for that fight; but, it was futile to hold it off any longer. As he begrudgingly arose from the bed and descended the stairs, the pungent, but welcoming, odors of bacon and cinnamon could be detected emanating from the kitchen. Upon entering, he could see that both of his parents were there; his mother, who was placing the bacon onto a plate layered with paper towels (this being done to drain the grease from the meat), and his father reading the newspaper at the table, drinking his Bustelo espresso coffee out of a mug that read, *'the difference between your opinion and coffee is that I asked for coffee.'* Felix's palms grew clammy in anticipation of what he realized would not be a singularly pleasant breakfast. He took a seat and grabbed a piece of cinnamon toast from the stockpile that rested on a serving plate in the middle of the table like a centerpiece, alongside three large bowls; one containing pieces of cantaloupe, which were peeled and cut into small slices; scrambled eggs, enough to feed a fairly sized village; and home fries, made with green and red peppers, onions and other various spices. As he spread the butter onto his bread, he began the dreaded soliloquy. "So... I have some pretty interesting news for you guys."

His father, not taking his eyes away from the newspaper,

which, ironically, displayed the bolded headline, "U.S. AND ALLIES OPEN AIR WAR ON IRAQ: BOMB BAGHDAD AND KUWAIT TARGETS," replied, "Oh, good, you got a job. You can start paying for things around the house now."

Just then… just as Felix was about to drop *his* bomb, Anthony walked in; his entry into the kitchen at that very moment proving quite untimely, as he began spilling the proverbial beans by verbally vomiting, "You got a job? When did you get a job? I thought you were joining the Marines?"

The world – the world inside the Christianson household – came to an abrupt halt for a brief moment in time and space. The sound of a glass cup breaking into pieces echoed in the distance, which, incidentally, drew very little attention. Felix's father, crushing his newspaper downward and peering over its crest, briefly lost his ability to speak. Felix's face began to feel flushed, his head felt as if it were being filled with the gasses of a hot air balloon. The look of absolute terror shown on his face and he could no longer swallow or breathe.

"Oops, was I not supposed to say that?" Fumbled Anthony, grabbing a slice of toast and taking a bite.

"What is he talking about, Felix?" Gloria inquired of Felix before turning to her younger son. "What are you talking about, Anthony?" There was a tinge of panic in her voice.

Felix could only reply by providing a look of chasmic disdain toward his brother; the kind of look that let Anthony know he was going to pay dearly once he and Felix were alone, to which Anthony responded by fixing his eyes all about the ceiling. Felix, at that point

– like someone on the precipice of a high cliff, with either the choice to make the one hundred foot jump into the ocean or face the angry mob barreling down on him - took a deep, long, breath and launched into the dreaded elucidation. "Well, I was *going* to tell you – before Mr. Bigmouth decided to open his big fat mouth – that I… I… I joined the Marines." He said, looking everywhere *but* into the eyes of either of his parents.

"What do you mean, you joined the Marines? What are you talking about?" Inquired his father, with a look of confusion both at Felix and at Gloria; Gloria's eyes, similarly, shifting back and forth as though she were sitting center court at a tennis match, saying nothing, but wearing the countenance of complete and utter consternation.

"I mean, I joined the Marines, Pop. Like, I went to the recruiting station and signed up."

"Felix -" His mother began, but was interrupted by his father's wail.

"Who in the hell said you could join the Marines?! Did you ask us if that was something you could do?!"

"Felix, what were you thinking?" His mother exclaimed.

"How dare you do something like that without consulting your mother and I!"

"Oh, Felix, what have you done? Why would you do something like that? What were you thinking?" Gloria began crying a waterfall.

"Did you sign anything? Did you sign a contract? Do you even know what you have agreed to? Do you realize there's a war going on?" His father interrogated, asking the barrage of questions, however, not actually waiting for a reply to any of them.

"Oh, my God – Oh, my God – my baby! I'm going to lose my baby, you're going off to war and you're going to die, you're going to be killed!" Gloria ranted, pacing back and forth before bending down with the intentions of picking up the pieces of the broken cup from the floor; however, she quickly stood back up to lean on the counter, bringing one of her hands to her forehead, feeling disoriented and close to a faint.

"Felix, how could you be so selfish? Look at what you've done to your mother! Just look at her! Are you happy now?" Shouted Felix Senior, making reference to his wife's malady, but not actually assisting her in any way.

"I'm glad to see that the major concern is mom and how she's taking it all. Never mind the fact that I'm the one that is actually going overseas." Felix retorted, again feeling – similar to his talk with Ronnie – that the focus of discussion appeared to somehow or another redirect its way to other people's solicitude, instead of his own.

"What were you thinking? How could you make such a decision without talking to us?" Lamented his father.

"My boy, my little baby." His mother cried in a paroxysm of weeping.

"Is there more bacon?" Questioned Anthony, shoving the

last slice of it down his throat while reaching for another piece of toast.

"You know what? I don't think you guys give a rat's ass about how I feel and what I think, you know that? I really don't." Felix glowered, tossing his uneaten slice of buttered cinnamon toast down to the table.

"How *you* feel? How *you* feel? I've got a good mind to ring your neck, you know that? Did you ever do anything in your life to remotely consider others? To consider anyone else other than yourself? You have got some damn nerve, young -"

"They'll be shooting at you. They'll be trying to hurt you. They're going to hurt my baby, my little baby!" Gloria howled, interrupting her husband's lecture.

"Mom, are you or aren't you making more bacon? Mom? *Mom*?!" Anthony wailed, impatiently.

"Anthony, how could you think of food at a time -" Gloria began.

"We're going to have a long discussion about this, Felix." Interrupted the patriarch.

"Mom, please… bacon." Whispered Anthony, gesticulating one of his hands in a circular motion around his stomach.

Felix put his hands to his face, wishing he were anywhere but there at that moment. He wished he could just disappear into thin air and transport himself far away, to a place where he could be free from this and all of his woes. Perhaps to a distant, uninhabited island, where there were no tribulations; no parents, no war. He would be alone – he and Ronnie - living off the island in peace and harmony. They would fish for their food and climb the trees for pineapples and coconuts. It would be perfectly idyllic, he pondered. There would be no one around to make him feel utterly lost and hopeless. He decided that he was done with this nonsense. "Listen, I'm going to stay at Justin's for a couple of days. It's been awhile since I've seen him and I want to spend some time over there before I have to go to basic training."

"We are not done here, young man. We have a lot to discuss." His father exclaimed, emphasizing the point with a slight bang of his fist onto the table, causing the plates and cups to clink and clank.

"I understand, Pop, I really do. I just need to spend some time with the family and my friends before I go. We'll talk about it when I get back. I promise." With that, Felix got up from the table, to his surprise unmolested, and went up to his room to pack his bags. Although he intended only to stay for a few days, he packed as if he were leaving for weeks. It's something he always did – overpack. He never wanted to be some place where he wasn't fully prepared for everything and anything.

It was about seven in the evening when Felix arrived at his cousin's apartment at Pelham Parkway in the Bronx. He rang the doorbell and was elated when Justin opened the door; it was like an instant stress reliever. "What's up, cuz? Long time no see." Justin said. They gave each other a warm embrace.

"What's up, muh boy?" Answered Felix, dumping his plethora of bags all over Justin and heading directly to his room.

"So how's things? You still going with Judith or what?" Felix said, while examining his cousin's ten gallon fish tank, which housed eight little tropical fish of all different shapes, sizes, and colors. He envied them in their protected glass encasement, being taken care of, not having to deal with the cumbersome life of a human being. Judith was Justin's girlfriend at the time, but they were always at odds with one another. If they weren't fighting about some odd thing or other, they weren't speaking at all. Justin was eighteen years old and just recently ascending from the world of drugs and alcohol. He had, unceremoniously, dropped out of high school with only a year left to graduate; however, he was in the midst of repairing the damage that was his life and now attending City College in New York City.

"Barely, barely." Justin said, taking Felix's garments out of the bags and placing them onto hangers. Justin believed that clothes should be respected that way. He thought, as soon as you arrive somewhere, you should immediately unpack your bags and hang your things. If you didn't, they would get all wrinkled and then you either ended up looking like some kind of a nomadic vagabond, or you would end up not wearing them at all, which was – to him – a waste.

"What do you mean, 'barely?' What's going on now?" Felix asked, as he sprawled onto Justin's bed.

"Arguments. You know, same old crap. Actually, we've been avoiding each other like the Plague."

"Let me ask you something. Can I ask you something? Seriously." Felix turned to Justin with a very earnest look on his face. "You've been having arguments with that girl for as long as I can remember. As a matter of fact, if she isn't consoling you - if she isn't absolutely picking your lifeless self up off the floor - you guys pretty much have absolutely nothing going on. Like, it seems to me - and correct me if I'm wrong - it seems to me, you only need her when you're down and out."

The topic was not one in which Justin was willing to converse upon. "Why don't we talk about this later? What's going on with *you*?"

"Nothing much. The usual. Drinking, spending time with my girl, joining the Marines -"

Justin interrupted. "Marines? What do you mean, Marines?"

"The Marines. You know, 'The few, the proud, the Marines.' As in, the United States military." Felix came to the conclusion that axioms were the best way to break the proverbial ice, and he had many stored in his memory bank, having collected them – in a failed effort - for Ronnie's sake.

"I know what the Marines is. What about the Marines?" Justin asked, becoming unsettled.

"I joined them, that's what." Felix replied, turning his attention, once again, to the tank, zoning in on the fish incessantly gliding round and round.

"Listen, you're kidding, right? I mean, you're way too calm for someone who just joined the Marines. You know that, don't you? You're way too calm."

"There's no use getting upset about it. It's done. Nothing I can do about it."

"Nothing you can *do* about it? What in the hell… Did they draft you for Christ's sake? They can't do that, you know. They can't draft you." Justin said, his voice elevated.

"Calm down, will you?" Felix lifted himself off of the bed, walked out of the room and started down the hallway, towards the kitchen, without saying a word. Justin followed him, breathing like some kind of deranged maniac. When they got to the kitchen, Felix opened the refrigerator door and began rifling through it. "Where in the hell is your father?" Felix inquired, pushing aside some random onions, opening a can of Vienna sausages, in an otherwise vacuous refrigerator.

"What in the hell does my father have to do with the Marines?" Justin blurted, impatiently.

"Nothing. Where is he?"

"Working, for Christ's sake. Now, what in the hell is with this Marines business?"

"Your dad really has to go shopping. This fridge is freaking barren."

"Felix!" Justin shouted. "The Marines?"

"Well, you know how I signed up for all those colleges? I got accepted to one." He said, digging into the opened can of the Vienna sausages, pulling out one of the last three.

Justin interrupted. "That's great, so why don't you go to college?"

"Can I finish?" Felix retorted, while holding up the sausage to the ceiling light and giving it a good once over.

Justin threw his hands in the air. "By all means, finish."

Felix popped the sausage into his mouth and, while chewing, replied, "Thank you… Like I was saying, I got accepted to one. Everything was going good until I got an estimate of my financial aid."

"What'd they give you? half? If they gave you half, you could get the whole family to chip in or something."

"Justin, they gave me seven dollars and twenty eight cents."

Justin's head dropped like a hundred pound weight. There was no possible rebuttal for this dismal fact.

"I didn't even tell my mom and dad until after I joined. I didn't want to burden them or anything. I felt like showing them I could make a mature, adult, decision. You know, on my own." He said, sullenly, while putting the can of the remaining two sausages back into the fridge.

Later that night, they found themselves locked in Justin's room, on the bed, reminiscing about the more pleasant things in their past. They talked about all the things they had done as kids and how much they both wished they could somehow go back in time. They deduced that they would find some kind of time machine and relive their childhood over and over… never growing up. It was a fantasy in which they both indulged very frequently; it helped them deal with the hardships that they faced, allowing them to make a great escape into their imaginations.

Felix got out of the bed, went over to the window, and began to stare out over the rows of trees that swayed gently back and forth from the cool evening breeze. There was complete silence for a while. Finally, without turning around, he said, "Did I mention my mom and dad were thinking about getting a divorce?" Felix fruitlessly fought back the tears at his own revelation, which now began to cascade down his cheek.

"What? No way. Are you serious? Why?" Justin replied in shock.

"They're always arguing about stuff. Stuff that doesn't make sense half of the time. I mean, they've been talking about that crap, divorcing, for years. About six years ago, my father told me that him and my mom weren't going to be together forever. That they were only together because of me, my brother, and sister. I felt like telling him to go to hell. I couldn't give two craps about them and their stupid fights." He headed over to his jacket and pulled out his pack of Newport menthol cigarettes.

"Since when have you started smoking?" Justin asked with disbelief.

"I picked it up during the goddamn war." He responded in a deep, grungy voice attempting to emulate a gritty war veteran. "You know how it is with us grunts. Just smokin' and jokin' when we're not layin' down some serious gunfire on the enemy." And with that, he simulated a firearm with his hands, proceeding to make machine gun sound effects, which absolutely tore him up with laughter. As he continued to chuckle, he took a cigarette out of the pack, lit it, took a long drag, held it in the bowels of his chest - with his eyes closed in ecstasy - and slowly released a plume of smoke into the air, wishing it were equally as simple to blow away his troubles and woes.

Justin, while at first in a fixed state of disbelief, gazing off into space, now bolted out of the bedroom and into the bathroom. He was dealing with his own issues and couldn't handle hearing the problems of his cousin, more specifically, the loss of his cousin; so, he sat in the bathroom to relieve himself of the pain in his stomach until he heard the phone ring. Cleaning himself up as best he could, he headed to the living room, and answered the call. "Hello?" Justin said to the caller, his voice hoarse from his emotional outburst.

It was their cousin, Rachel, whom Justin had not spoken to in quite some time. "Hey, it's Rachel. Is Felix there?"

This absolutely drove Justin insane. He and Rachel had not spoken in over a year, yet she showed no interest in speaking with him; instead, asking for Felix directly. "Felix? How do you even know he's here?"

"Anthony told me. Felix had some kind of argument with Aunt Gloria and Uncle Felix and he told me he was there. Can I speak to him?"

"Hold on." Justin uttered in disgust, relaying the message to Felix.

Felix answered the phone. "Hello?"

"Hey, cousin, it's me Rachel." Rachel and Felix were close; she spent some time babysitting Felix and Anthony ten years ago when she was seventeen, so she developed somewhat of an elder sister relationship with the two.

"Yo, Rach, what's up? I was gonna call you to -"

"Are you joining the Marines?" She interrupted. "Anthony called me and told me you were. Is this true? He told me it was true."

"That little bastard. You know, he really does have diarrhea of the mouth. Honestly."

"So it's true? What were you thinking? Why would you do that? There's a war -"

"Yes, yes, there's a war going on, I know, I know." Felix interjected. He had heard just about enough of the *'war going on.'*

"But, Felix, why?"

"It's a long story."

There was a brief moment of *dead air* over the phone wherein no one uttered a word. Felix, not wanting to express, yet again, his unrest and displeasure over the drawn out topic… especially over the phone; and Rachel not knowing exactly what to say to this grim confirmation of the facts.

"Listen, come over. Come over and we'll talk all about it." Rachel finally said, breaking the quietude.

"I'm at Justin's, though."

"Yea, I know where you are, I'm the one that called you. Just come over. I need to talk to you about this madness."

"But that's sort of rude." Felix said, although already considering it, longing for a kind of maternal connection one can only obtain from a female, especially one older than he; and, seeing as how he had no other woman in which to turn (his mother being out of the question, due to her manic tendencies), he earnestly considered Rachel's request.

"It's not rude! You're going away to war, for Christ's sake! I need to see you before you go!"

"I don't know, Rach." He said, almost yearning for her to continue insisting.

"Felix, please! I'll order pizza! Meat lovers, your favorite kind!"

"Let me think about it for awhile."

"Don't think about it. I'm ordering it as soon as we hang up, so you have to come. I'm gonna end up with a whole, large, carnivorous pizza pie by myself if you don't, then I'll hate you for life!"

"We'll see. Give me a few minutes."

"Ok, I'm ordering it right now. Bye." She hung up.

Shortly after hanging up with Rachel, Felix began packing

his things. Justin, in extreme and utter perplexity, asked him what he was doing and, without looking up, Felix answered, "I figured I'd go over there… to Rachel's… you know, since I'm going away and all."

Justin immediately began yelling, "You know what? This is insane! What in the hell is wrong with her? If you were at *her* house, I would never just call you and tell you to leave her! If you go, that will be totally messed up. I'm like in a mental crisis here and I can't believe you're going to just up and go."

Felix stopped packing and turned around with a look of bewilderment. *"You're* in a mental crisis? I've spent the last couple of hours telling you that my world is making a complete hundred and eighty degree turn with my parents getting a divorce and me going away to a goddamn war; and you're telling me *you're* in a mental crisis?" He let out a breath of utter disgust, shook his head, turned his attention back to his clothes, and resumed packing.

"Look, I realize you're going through a lot. I just meant to say that I thought we'd keep talking. I just have a lot going on, too, and I kind of need you."

Felix just shrugged his shoulders and said, "I know."

"You *know*? What do you mean, you *know*? What kind of bastard are you?"

"Hey, just relax, alright? I know it's messed up, but give me a break for Christ's sake. I could get blown to pieces in Iraq and I'd never see her again. And what was I supposed to have said to her… *no?* "

"Goddamn right you say no! You're visiting *me* for crying out loud. There's a certain kind of etiquette about this sort of thing, you know. There are unwritten rules! You can't just up and do whatever you feel like doing! When you come to visit someone, you don't just leave because someone better calls you! What the hell is so hard about understanding that?"

"Look, like I said, I haven't seen her in awhile and I'm going away soon. What's so hard to understand about *that*?" Felix said, never breaking stride with what he was doing.

Justin stormed off into the bathroom, once again; and Felix, after packing, headed into the living room to call for a taxi. After a few minutes, hearing that Justin had exited the bathroom and moved into the bedroom, Felix sauntered down the hallway, stopping at the threshold of Justin's room door. "Justin, I'm leaving." He said, being given no reply. Felix lingered by the door, fruitlessly, waiting for some sort of an acknowledgement, whilst Justin lay prostrate, sulking atop his bed; however, after receiving no indication of being acknowledged, Felix dishearteningly walked down the hallway and out the door.

Upon arriving at his cousin Rachel's place, he paused outside of her building to smoke a cigarette; he pulled one out of the pack and lit it. While smoking, he mediated on the manner in which he walked out on Justin, feeling badly for doing it so abruptly; but, knowing in his heart that Justin was not the one to make him feel at ease… not about this. Justin was dealing with his own issues – deeper issues – that prevented him from giving Felix the type of therapy that he needed at this particular moment. He felt that Rachel could provide some sort of an understanding in a way that Justin never could. She was older than both he and Justin (twenty-seven) and she had the kind of experience that Felix needed presently, as she happened not only to be his elder, but also a psychologist – albeit a school psychologist in a middle school – which was precisely the level of therapeutic intervention that he required. He took a final drag of his cigarette, tossed it to the curb, and walked inside the apartment building and up to her door, which happened to be on the first floor.

She opened the door with a mixed countenance of delight and apprehension. "Felix!" She said as she gave him a hug, leading him inside. Her dark brown hair was tied back in a bun; she wore an oversized beige sweater that covered most of her burgundy yoga pants; and, a pair of large beige socks, matching the color of her top, that were scrunched down towards the upper part of her ankles. Her apartment was like that of a museum gift shop. In her living room, there were several different imitation artifacts from several different cultures spread about. African masks hung on one wall, while Indian and ancient Chinese sculptures were positioned across the other sides of the room. Bob's Discount furniture wrapped around the living room in the form of a black pleather sectional and two matching reclining chairs of the same material, along with ambiguously living looking plants, which sat on various end tables in between. "Come in, come in." She took hold of his arm to lead him into the apartment.

"Hey, cuzzie, how's it going?"

"All is well, all is well. What's going on with *you*? The Marines, huh? What in God's glorious name is goin on with that?" She took his leather jacket and hung it onto a rustic looking coat stand that was by the door, a piece that was something out of the Dark Ages of England.

"I've been kinda asking myself that very question, over and over, to be honest with you."

"Sit, sit. Do you want something to drink? Are you hungry at all? The pizza is here, you want a slice?"

"Not yet. Just some water, thanks." He said, as he took a seat on the aforementioned sofa in the living room.

She went to the refrigerator and took out a container that housed and filtered the water. As she poured it in the glass, she asked, "So you decided this is the best thing? Is this the best thing for you?" After filling his cup, she placed the container back into the fridge, subsequently taking out a wine glass for herself, filling it with chardonnay… an Australian brand.

"I don't know if it's the *best* thing, but it's the only thing that makes sense right now."

She handed Felix the water and took a seat next to him, curling up in the corner of the sofa, cradling her wine against her chest. "I can't imagine what you must be feeling right now. I'm just shocked that you are actually doing this."

"You and me, both. So what's going on with you?"

"Me? Same as usual. The students in my school are all absolutely *non compos mentis.* I'm simply at my wits end with them all." She said with a chuckle.

"That must be pretty intense. School psychologist. Who knew my big cuz would be shrinking heads! I still remember the times when you were babysitting and putting us in head locks when we'd piss you off." He said, laughing, taking a sip of his water.

"You have no idea how much I sometimes wish that were an acceptable method of treatment." She answered with a titter, then took a sip of her wine before continuing. "Felix the Marine; I can't believe it. Aren't you so worried about the war and all? Aren't you the least bit concerned?"

"Of course I am." He said, lowering his head. "I just don't see any other option, though. I mean, I want a good future for me and Ronnie. I plan to marry her, you know."

"No, I didn't know! Oh, my goodness!"

"Yeah, well, I want to marry her and give her a good life. I can't very well do that with a minimum wage job at some Korean vegetable store. This is my only choice. The only choice that makes the most sense."

"I see. Well, of course I support you. I mean, I'm worried to pieces, but I support you."

"Trust me, I'm worried for me, too."

"Have you told Uncle Felix and Aunt Gloria?"

"I told them earlier today, but they turned it into a shit show – as they do everything else in this miserable world."

"Oh my, what happened? What did they say?"

"Nothing worth repeating. Let's just say they were their usual un-empathetic selves."

"I'm sorry, Felix. Well, they're probably extremely worried about you and just don't know how to express it."

"Forever the psychologist, huh, cuz?" He said with a dubious smile.

She smirked. "I just know Uncle and Auntie. They're from the old school. Telling you how they feel isn't their forte. I know they care, though; that much I can absolutely guarantee you. You're their first born!"

Felix sat stoically for a moment, before he revealed, "They're getting a divorce, you know."

Rachel sat quietly. It had been a rumor swirling around the family grapevine of the elder members of the family for quite some time, and she – being the eldest cousin, beating her sister Juliana (the second eldest, who was now a senior at Georgetown University) - was well aware of the unfortunate events unfolding between her aunt and uncle.

"I'm guessing by your silence that you already knew? I know you are always very well informed somehow." Felix said, with a hint of condescension. He would prefer for the strifes of his clan not to have been a source of gossip and intrigue throughout the entire family tree; but, having been on the receiving end of some very juicy rumors concerning other members of the ménage - that he thoroughly enjoyed hearing – his feelings of perturbation were quickly subdued.

"Listen, marriages have their ups and downs. They've been together for a very long time and if it's meant to be then it will be. That's not what you should be focusing on right now. Right now you should be concentrating on your own world. You should be thinking only of the situation in front of you, which is going to the military. When do you leave for boot camp?"

"Basic training will begin as soon as I take the oath, which is next week. I leave to Parris Island, in South Carolina, after that."

"So you have a week to clear your mind and get yourself ready. I mean, it's not a world of time, but at least you get *somewhat* of an opportunity to mentally prepare. Just don't waste a second of any day. Enjoy each moment and appreciate what you have here. Take Ronnie out for a nice walk and some lunch… go to a museum, a park, or whatever. Just take full advantage of whatever time you have until you go away." She said, placing her hand on his knee, giving him a warm, motherly smile, wearing on her countenance a multitude of worry lines that ran across her forehead.

Felix nodded, but did not verbally respond. He was beginning to tear and tried for Rachel not to notice; but the effort was made in vain. Upon realizing this, Rachel took hold of him and brought her baby cousin closer to her for an embrace. Once nestled in her chest, he let loose all of his emotions and began to sob uncontrollably, thinking about all that had transpired in the last forty-eight hours or so. He thought of Ronnie and the fight they had the other day, knowing he needed to see her to make up… to make things right. The last thing he wanted was to leave things a mess with her. He didn't, however, verbalize this to Rachel at the moment; instead, he just held onto her tighter, allowing himself to purge all of his emotions onto her sweater. No words were exchanged between either of them for the next few minutes; there they sat, together on the couch, in a warm and sheltered embrace, something that Felix had longed for and wished could last forever.

A few days later, Felix decided to make amends with Ronnie. The last time they had spoken it had not fared well, and this is something that burdened his mind and heart from the very moment he walked out of her door. They both possessed an abundance of very powerful feelings in regards to him going away, neither of the two conveying them to one another in the most pragmatic of ways. Generally speaking, Felix and Ronnie were well known to be very headstrong and somewhat obstinate; but, when all was said and done, none of that could outweigh the love that they felt towards each other. After smoking about three and a half cigarettes, he knocked on her door. When she opened it, their eyes immediately locked onto one another's; both of their hearts beating with the tenderness and passion of two people who absolutely adored one another. They held each other, embosomed in a tender embrace that seemed to last forever; at least, they wished it could have lasted forever. "I'm sorry about last time, babe. I really am." Felix apologized. "I realize that this whole thing doesn't just affect me. What I mean is, I know that you're going through it, too."

"I'm sorry, too, my love. I know this must be just insane for you. I know you're scared… and I am, too. It feels like our worlds are just so upside down right now." She began to tear.

"Listen, Ron, I want you to know that I love you. I love you like I've never loved anyone ever before. I want to marry you one day, when I have something to offer you. Right now, all I have are promises; but, when I get back from this thing, I'm gonna be able to take care of you and, eventually, our future little one." He said, wiping away a trickle of water from her cheek that had fallen from the corner of her eye.

They embraced once more, this time with tears pouring down both their faces. Felix wished he could be there, in her arms, forever. He wanted nothing more than for them to run off to that far, distant, land he always dreamed of… where no one would be able to find them; where they could live out the rest of their lives, just being with one another – living off of the love that they shared. This wasn't possible and he knew it. They both knew it. One can not live off of love alone, such a thing would be like having a shiny new toolbox with nothing inside; so, they held onto one another just a little longer, just a little tighter, dreaming of the day when they would be wed and of the moment when they could live the rest of their lives together as one.

***

It was in the last few feet of the final nine mile hike, up the seven hundred foot tall mountain known as the Reaper, toward the Iwo Jima Memorial (the United States Marine Corps War Memorial) at Parris Island – a majestic simulacrum that depicts six Marines proudly hoisting the United States Flag from the ground at Mount Suribachi, serving as a source of unbounded pride and immense inspiration for those who have served, are serving, and those who will soon become part of the coveted Corps – that Felix realized where precisely he was. Before that, he had been lost inside of his thoughts, pondering the journey that lead him to this very time and place. These last few cumbersome clicks would be the final enervating steps that he would take as a civilian. In just a few strides – albeit grueling strides - he would achieve greatness. There were no more thoughts of what was to come; only the here and now mattered to him. Only the here and now kept his feet moving forward, each step bringing him closer and closer to the culmination of his pledge process, his initiation, his rite of passage.

As the sound of the eighty-eight combat boots plodded onward, a single familiar voice ascended and rippled through the ears of the men. It was Private Bernard Blaze, Felix's co-combatant earlier on in the gladiatorial fighting pit. He was recovered from the brutal blow to the temples after all! Felix was comforted and pleased to know that Blaze had survived, having been able to continue on; for, all the while, he believed that he either sent the defeated Recruit packing, or the *Recruit* was packed up and shipped back home in a much more… unfortunate fashion, to put it mildly. Not merely was Blaze amongst them, but now, with mere yards remaining – bellowing from the depths of his soul a poem written by *William Ernest Henley* – he captivated, invigorated, and empowered their minds and their spirits, as he sang, *"Out of the night that covers me, black as a pit from pole to pole, I thank whatever gods may be for my unconquerable soul. In the fell clutch of circumstance I have not winced nor cried aloud. Under the bludgeoning of chance my head is bloody, but unbowed. Beyond this place of wrath and tears looms but the Horror of the shade, and yet the menace of the years finds and shall find me unafraid. It matters not how straight the gate, how charged with punishment the scroll, I am the master of my fate, I am the captain of my soul!"* The Privates, heads held high, were the captains of their souls and the masters of their fates; for, whatever may come afterwards, whatever hell they may face, their destiny –

for now - was in their hands.

The air was thick and dark with what appeared to be a murky brown film that hung in the air like an Arabian sandstorm; only the sounds of the Drill Sergeants could be heard echoing their commands to push forward. "Let's go!" From one direction. "Act like you want it!" From another direction.

As the recruits mustered up in ranks, the sounds of moans and grunts filled the air. They were exhausted – many close to falling unconscious. None of them did, though; every single one stood his ground using every bit of their being to do so. Once the platoons were lined up, they came to attention and began to report, following an order to do so from somewhere unseen by the men, who were functioning on sheer inner will. Once all platoons reported present, they were ordered to fall into a circle around the Senior Drill Sergeant who then addressed them; his words, not one of them would ever forget. "You men have just experienced three of the most grueling, intense, and gut wrenching days of your entire lives; but, you managed to get through it, not as individuals, but part of a team. You did it together. A brotherhood. This is what it means to be a Marine. This is what it means to be *Semper Fidelis; Always Faithful*. From now until your last dying breath, no one will ever be able to deny you this. As of today, and for all of your remaining days, you have the honor, the privilege, to call yourselves… United States Marines." He paused to allow these words to permeate. As he scanned the troops, tears could be seen cascading down the cheeks of these future heroes… these defenders of our Constitution, the thin line between our very freedom, our very way of life, and tyranny abroad. "Are we ready?"

A resounding, "Aye, Sir!" filled the air.

"Are you sure?"

"Aye, Sir!" The reply rang out louder than the first.

"Alright, Marines, back in formation."

"Aye, Sir!" And with that, they scurried back into their original muster formation, preparing for the Emblem Ceremony in which they were to receive the coveted token that confirms and solidifies their place in Marine lore; the Eagle, Globe, and Anchor.

Once in formation, the Drill Sergeants began, one by one, to address the men; however, this was not like any other dialogue they had ever experienced with their fearless leaders. This time, the men were being addressed as brothers. Emotions flew high as many of the men began to break down, while still remaining ever disciplined when being spoken to by their superiors. Felix stood tall and firm at attention when the Sergeant approached him, shouting a resounding, "Good morning, Sergeant!"

"Good morning, Marine." The Sergeant said in a subdued and almost intimate tone, while placing his left hand on Felix's arm and extending his other for a handshake. When the clasped hands of brotherhood interlocked, Felix could feel the Eagle, Globe, and Anchor – which was inside of the Sergeant's grip - and was instantly filled with a plethora of emotions that he was no longer able to contain. Through Felix's tears, the Sergeant continued, "Congratulations, Marine. How do you feel? You feelin' good?"

"Aye, Sir!" Replied Felix with a tremulous shout.

The Sergeant continued in almost a whisper. "I'm proud of you today."

"Aye, Sir!"

"Today is the first day of the rest of your life, you hear me?"

"Aye, Sir!"

"Through perseverance and hard work, you accomplished what very few have dared try."

"Aye, Sir!"

"You always hold your head up high, no matter what obstacles you encounter because that's what Marines do, you understand me?"

"Aye, Sir!"

"Outstanding, Marine." And with that, the Sergeant moved on to the next newly christened Soldier.

With tears of pride and joy continuing to stream out of his eyes, Felix took a glance around, noticing that Serrano and McGovern, too, were filled with overwhelming emotion. The three men caught a glimpse of one another, giving a slight nod to signify a mutual acknowledgement of achievement and admiration for the journey that had begun just thirteen weeks ago under those dark, angry, clouds and that torrential rain storm, whilst helping each other look for their bags. Felix closed his eyes and, although still weeping, managed to bring a smile to his face. There was never a time that he felt such fulfillment, such self-worth. Dignity and honor soared through his spirit… he felt as though he had wings and could fly over the highest of mountains.

***

It was about 3:07 am on a chilly Wednesday October morning and, in an otherwise silent hospital room, all that could be heard was the vital-sign monitor's steady, white noised, blips and bleeps. Outside the room, most of the lights were off, as nearly the entirety of the graveyard shift nurses were napping in the break room, with the exception of one who was barely awake at her station, balancing a pen in her hand - feigning paperwork - in case someone important happened by. Inside the room, Ronnie lay somnambulant on a reclining chair that the hospital staff most generously provided to her earlier in the evening. Draped over her legs lay a multicolored moire throw blanket, along with her Native American throw pillow - *the* throw pillow - which she, once again, held close to her bosom. The rest of clan Christianson had gone home to get some much needed rest, as they had been omnipresent – much to the chagrin of Felix - for many hours prior. The stillness and tranquility of the night was abruptly severed by the resounding alerts from the monitor connected to Felix's body, which now displayed several flat lines in a multitude of colors on the screen. Ronnie awoke with a jolt, as if struck by an electric current, and immediately jumped to her feet - at first not remembering where precisely she was – yelling frantically to apprise the nurse as to the situation. The nurse, who was, incidentally, already entering the room, depressed the code blue button, which, in turn, activated the emergency staff. After several minutes of attempting cardiopulmonary resuscitation, the doctor, who at some point made his way into the room, sorrowfully pronounced her beloved Felix's time of death.

Some moments subsequent to his departure from this world of the living - the hospital room now vacant, with only the forsaken articles left behind and all about the floor, such as rubber gloves, opened packs of jelly used for the defibrillator, &c. - Ronnie made her way to the edge of the hospital bed, adjacent to her love… her husband… placing her hand into his. She removed the drawing which lay on Felix's lap (a drawing that their baby boy had created not too long prior, depicting three little stick figures standing at the front door of a house, with the words, 'Mommy, Daddy, and Me' written at the bottom) and placed it gently on the bedside table. As she fixed her tired eyes, which were filled with tears, onto Felix's countenance, she discerned a kind of peaceful aura that illuminated around him; and, from the particular angle in which she sat, Ronnie perceived what appeared to be a faint smile adorning his face… his head held high.

Story Two

Louie & Laura

With courage you will dare to take risks, have the strength to be compassionate, and the wisdom to be humble. Courage is the foundation of integrity.

-       *Quote by Mark Twain*

The smell of *cuchifritos* - an endless assortment of fried foods - which included *empanadas* (something resembling a meat patty made of dough, stuffed with protein and fried to perfection), *rellenos de papa* (fried mashed potato, also packed with meat), and other delectable, but hazardous to one's health, victuals danced through the Spanish Harlem air on that late hot and humid July afternoon in the year 1968; which was, incidentally, one of the most unstable and tumultuous years of the modern era, what with the Vietnam War raging overseas – an extremely unpopular war that lead to incessant protests here in these United States of America - and Dr. Martin Luther King, Junior being assassinated earlier that April, which gave rise to violent riots in essentially every major city around the country. In spite of this fact, Louie's only care – his only wish - in the entire world was to devour one of those *cuchifritos* that stared at him… downright flirting with him, as a matter of fact, from the corner Spanish bakery window just a few feet away from his *spot*. As a well disciplined soldier stands his post, so too did Louie Christianson, along with his partner in crime (literally), George Trista, who served as the lookout of the operation, keeping his eyes peeled for rival drug dealers who sometimes poached the area, as well as for the long arm of the law... both equally very dangerous foes. They diligently stood their posts whilst vending small amounts of illegal pharmaceuticals to random passerby's at various times throughout the day for seven days out of the week. From where Louie stood, he could see the window to his bedroom across the street, seven flights up, inside of the Jefferson Housing Development, and wished that he could be there, on his bed, listening to Miles Davis' latest vinyl, '*Miles in the Sky*,' a personal favorite of his – something his cronies often heckled him for, calling him an old man for his musical preference; although, in some circles, Miles Davis would have been considered *up with the times...* it was the actual genre – classical jazz – in which his acquaintances jested. He didn't care, though. He loved the smooth and relaxing sounds of saxophones; trumpets; pianos; snare drums &c., whilst most all others his age were preferential to the Delfonics, the Supremes, or Stevie Wonder and the like; not that he *disliked* these other groups, he just felt a certain kind of escape from reality when Count Basie, Ella Fitzgerald, Duke Ellington, and all of the other greats undulated through his ears.

This, standing out on the corner of the street selling drugs, was something that Louie longed *not* to do. Sixteen years old at the time, he had turned to a life of dealing small amounts of heroin, the drug of choice during this particular time period, because his parents were no longer an integral part of his or his brother Felix's life - what with their father leaving his wife, their mother, years ago for another, younger, woman, then subsequently starting a brand new family (creating their youngest sibling, Julian)… and, their birth mother who was hardly ever present due to her multiple places of employment, in an attempt to make up the difference from the financial loss of her husband's untimely *exeunt*. Felix, although two years older than Louie, and the last possible option for some semblance of a proper fostering, was rarely ever anywhere to be found to provide any sort of guidance; therefore, Louie was left to steer the proverbial ship of his own upbringing - hence, the dealing of narcotics. He detested it. He resented it. It played into the typical low income stereotype that every man or woman of higher social status used as a gauge to *judge and jury* a man of color, and that is something he wholeheartedly loathed. He wanted to be better. Louie had dreams of one day going to school and getting a degree – although a degree in *what* he had no clue. Having dropped out of school after the ninth grade, he hadn't the opportunity to develop any real academic skills. He could read and write, possessing some basic, extremely elementary, mathematical knowledge (adding and subtracting with just a dab of multiplication and division), but he bailed after his first year of high school, Roosevelt High School, barely finishing the year. He thought about a trade, perhaps plumbing or maybe carpentry; but, even those skills required schooling, and schooling required currency, so he did what he needed to do to acquire these funds.

As the metallic blue Chevy Nova pulled up to the corner of East 115th Street and Third Avenue, the operator of the vehicle lowered his radio - which was playing the new smash hit *"Hey Jude,"* performed by the British Invasions' ambassadors to America, The Beatles - and gave a nod to Louie (indicating his interest in what our young protagonist possessed for sale), who then swiftly walked toward him, whilst at the same time glancing at George who, in turn, scanned left and right, keeping an eye out for anyone employed by the 23rd Precinct as a law enforcement officer, before subsequently transmitting the signal – a slight nod upwards – to convey that the proverbial coast was clear… all was a *'go'* for the transaction.

"Whatchu need?" Said Louie, darting his eyes between his customer and all angles of the street, watching for any sudden moves from either direction. He was no stranger to this scene. There were good days and there were bad; a good day being you did not end up in jail or dead. Bad days could range from no sales, to getting robbed by the would-be buyer, to getting *pinched* by the *boys in blue*, to catching a bullet from either of the former, which he was, incidentally, prepared for after witnessing many a 'bad day' around him. He gripped the handle of his .22 caliber pistol, which was nestled cozily in his grey hooded sweater pocket, as he awaited the response from the gentleman in the vehicle.

"You got that China White?" Inquired the interested party, looking at Louie up and down, from his straight, light brown hair; pellucid, hazel eyes; skin, medium in complexion, not white, but not quite brown; examining the entirety of his five foot eight frame, while simultaneously scanning the sidewalk around him.

"Yeah, I got the *H*, five or ten?" Asked Louie, referring to the five dollars it would cost to purchase the smaller bag of heroine; the larger bag priced at ten.

"Ten."

"Let me see it." Louie said, with an air of circumspection, not trusting the prospective buyer, who leered at him from the seat of the car behind his oversized aviator glasses.

"What, you don't trust me? Lemme see the blow first."

122

"You a cop?" Inquired Louie, knowing full well that, even if his interlocutor, in fact, *was* a police officer, he had absolutely no obligation to reveal such fact.

"Nah, blood, I ain't no porker. Is *you* a cop?"

"Do I look like the fuzz? I'm sixteen, man. Now, lemme see the green." Exclaimed Louie, with an air of irritability, growing impatient. Every second gone by, wasting time, talking to a prospective buyer was a second too long; it provided far too many opportunities for things to go awry.

"Alright, alright, relax, man… tranquilo, tranquilo!" Said the buyer, finishing the last two words of his sentence with a most horrific Spanish accent – he being African American - before reaching into the side panel of his car, pulling out a fresh twenty dollar bill, smiling a crooked and unsettling smile, displaying a solitary gold tooth which contained a microscopic diamond in the center. "Got change of a Jackson, young blood?"

"Man what do I look like, First National Bank?" Exclaimed Louie, ready to pull the plug, as it were… the transaction was taking entirely too long.

"I dig it, better give me two tens, then." Said the man, deciding upon acquiring two bags of the drug, worth ten dollars each.

"Now we're talking." Exclaimed Louie, pulling out the two bags of heroin, now placing his head and shoulders into the car, out of sight from onlookers, to make the exchange.

With the speed of Hermes, the operator of the vehicle grasped one of Louie's wrists, placing onto it the gelid metal handcuffs he retrieved from his waistband, locking it tight. "Gotcha, young blood." The undercover officer said with a sardonic grin, as he exited the vehicle, holding onto Louie with a vice-like grip to prevent his escape, subsequently placing him face first against the Chevy Nova to *toss* him (search him), and, shortly thereafter, discovering the firearm that was stuffed in his pocket. "Well, well, well… what do we have here? Looks like jackpot to me! My lucky goddamn day!"

George, seeing all of this transpire, expeditiously placed his hands in his rear jean pocket, clutching onto his gravity knife, reaching out to Louie with his eyes as if to indicate his intentions of obstructing the arrest. Realizing this, Louie – whose eyes intently locked with those of George – signaled an emphatic *no* with an ever so slight and undetectable shake of the head, knowing that such a precarious move would have the potential to cause the gravest of consequences. George, now releasing the knife from his grip, placed his hands to his side and watched helplessly as the Chevy Nova, now containing two occupants, the undercover officer and one Louie Christianson (bounded and placed in the rear seat as a prisoner), peeled off across 115th Street, making the left onto Lexington Avenue, then disappearing out of sight.

Six months to the day had passed since that harrowing moment in Spanish Harlem. Now, on a crisp January day at five in the morning, Louie was awakened by both the deafening bell that rang from the hallway of the dormitory, as well as the stentorian voice of the floor warden, sonorously yelling for them to get their asses up; a thing in which he and the other thirty young recovering – and some not recovering – juvenile delinquents dreaded with all their hearts and souls, not at all looking forward to leaving the warmth of their bunks. There was very minimal heat emanating from the old clanky radiator in the room; only just the scant amount necessary to keep from contracting hypothermia seeped through its tiny holes. The old wooden, only once ever whitewashed, windows prevented only but the largest gusts of wind to penetrate into the nanoscopic sized room (a room, incidentally, in which only a Lilliputian sized human being could be made comfortable); otherwise, the cubicle was, for the most part, the temperature of an Alaskan igloo at its exterior. Conversely, in the summer months, the room was a searing pan of grease, forsaken atop a lit stove; and, its occupants were the unfortunate sizzling victuals, left to be incinerated.

It was for this reason, being the dead of winter, that Louie procrastinated in unraveling himself from the warmth of his quilt, awaiting his dorm-mate, Oliver – a well mannered and even keeled young man of seventeen, who had no propensity to commit even the pettiest of crimes before, or after for that matter, arriving at BCFB, the Buffalo Correctional Facility for Boys (a juvenile correctional facility located in Buffalo, New York, for young men under the age of eighteen) – to resurrect from his slumber. As long as Oliver remained in his bunk, Louie was safe from any molestation from the floor wardens because, in the event of a forceful removal from the room, due to their tardiness to rise, the 'nefarious' (as his most unfounded reputation dictated, due to the violent nature of his crime) Oliver would be the first to receive a tongue lashing, such as it were.

Oliver was seventeen now; but, he would soon become eighteen, thereby *aging out*, no longer eligible to remain at the school for boys… instead, he would be transferred to an all adult facility for hardened criminals. His sentence of twenty-five years would not be completed for another twenty three years and – barring an unforeseeable early release for good behavior – would not know freedom until he turned forty. Growing up in extreme poverty, Oliver spent most of his days on the streets of New York City figuring out ways to make a dollar, so that he might put food on the table for he and his younger sister, Eleanor, five years his junior. A scant amount of these methods of earning were legal; however, most were not. One cloudy and cold afternoon, Oliver entered a local bodega wherein he had intentions of smuggling a few tiny items consisting of bread, a small jar of mayonnaise, and a pack of Kraft American cheese under his sweatshirt for that night's supper; that is, until he was met by the store owner at the door, who – gripping a splintering wooden baseball bat, donning the word *'punishmint'* apparently etched into the wood with some sort of sharp object imbedded into the *'sweet part'* - had absolutely no intentions of allowing the young man of fifteen to exit without paying for said items. In an attempt to evade capture, Oliver created a distraction by knocking down the potato chip stand just beside the exit, which, for a brief second or two, got the attention of the owner. While making moves similar to that of a running back on a football field, one of whom is trying to proceed passed a defender and into the end zone, he was inevitably seized by the arm and apprehended. Oliver, without thought – or, to put it more accurately, at the thought of capture – reached into his back pocket, pulling out his black and chrome colored switchblade, which he woefully used to plunge into the side of his captor, puncturing a lung, leaving him a bloody mess on the floor of the bodega. Being positively identified by several onlookers in and around the store, he was picked up by the detectives within an hour and, ultimately, sentenced to twenty-five years for attempted murder (being that the victim survived the slashing), along with various other charges, and finally shipped off to Buffalo, where he would reside until his eighteenth birthday; afterwards, to be sent to a prison for adults.

With the green, army style blanket covering most of his body, only his eyes peeking through a small opening, Louie awaited Oliver's ascent, which was traditionally just before the floor warden made his way into the room with the intentions of an aggressive extraction; however, today, Oliver sat up, post haste, and began dressing himself almost immediately after the first ring of the bell. With much disappointment, expecting, at minimum, an additional fifteen minutes of repose, Louie sat up at the edge of his bed, rubbing his eyes and clearing them of the crusty residue that resided within the caruncle before asking, "Got a hot date today or something?"

Standing in front of a mirror that rested on the mahogany dresser in which they both shared, Oliver examined his own reflection, glancing at his auburn colored hair, still disheveled from his slumber, whilst simultaneously noticing some crust still inhabiting the corners of his dark brown eyes, as he fastened the buttons of his white dress uniform shirt, flashing only a brief glance at Louie through the mirror, before replying, "Hot date? What in the hell are you talking about?"

"You're up early today. What gives?"

Rolling his eyes, now understanding Louie's inference, Oliver replied, "Can't a fella get up early? What in the hell is so wrong with that?" Oliver ejaculated, now pulling up his beige colored slacks, buckling the belt that it was still attached to (not removing it from the previous day).

"Nothing, except now *I* have to get up." Louie complained,

bringing his foot up to the bed to remove a rogue hangnail, which he noticed while procrastinating his rise from the bed.

"So stay sleeping, for Christ's sake! What's that got to do with *me*?" Oliver rebuffed, now fumbling with the knot of his standard issue, red with white diagonal stripes, tie.

"I can't... Not if *you're* getting up. If the floor warden comes in here, he'll tear me a new asshole. With you awake, there's nobody to run interference."

"Oh you're a real swell fella now, ain't you? Well, if that's your business, you'd better move your ass, kiddo. I think I hear Lucifer coming now." *Kiddo* was a term of endearment that Oliver used for all the other residents at the facility, due to the fact that nearly ninety percent of everyone else there was his junior in age. In this particular case, though, the roommates were born in the same year; but, because Oliver arrived at the facility prior to Louie, the nickname applied out of seniority. Oliver, taking hold of his toiletry bag, walked out of the room and headed for the shared lavatory down the hallway; Louie, finally extracting the hangnail from his toe – flinging and sending it to an unknown resting place on the opposite side of the room - followed behind Oliver with all of his own grooming materials.

Setting up shop adjacent to the the sink in which Oliver was utilizing, Louie, taking out his toothpaste and toothbrush from his bag, inquired, "Are you worried about turning eighteen and all soon? I mean, are you worried about aging out of here and stuff?"

"I don't know. Maybe. Hey, listen, let me have some of your Colgate, will ya? I'm all out." Oliver requested, holding up his depleted tube of toothpaste before launching it into the trash can.

Handing the toiletry over to Oliver, Louie continued. "I'd be all kind of worried if I was you. Having to leave here and go to the big house and all." Oliver, having already begun brushing his teeth, his mouth filled with suds that gushed out of his mouth, spilling down all about his chin, didn't respond, so Louie continued, "All kind of worried. I mean, I hear all kinds of the things about the big house. I hear they have this sort of initiation process. Like, for the fresh meat. That'd be you… fresh meat. I hear they like to take 'em and give 'em the real business, you know? Like… *the business!*"

Oliver, spitting his suds into the sink, subsequently washing his mouth with water, replied, "I know what they do very well, thanks. I don't need a goddamn thirdhand account from the likes of you, kiddo." He said, now washing his face with his Ivory soap bar, as Louie began brushing his teeth. Oliver continued his point as he lathered his forehead, cheeks, and chin. "And besides, I may get released. I have the hearing in a few days and they may release me to a half-way house. That's what I'm thinking. I just gotta lay it on real thick, you know? I gotta show 'em how I'm rehabilitated and all. That's what I gotta do."

Louie, now washing his mouth out, replied, "Man, nobody gets released. Nobody. I heard anybody who tries gets denied and ends up going to the big house."

"Would you cool it with the *'big house'* crap? And *Not* everybody. There are plenty of fellas that get cut loose. Plenty, I tell ya. Why, there's a kid that got released just a few years ago, as a matter of fact… before you got here. He got released just fine." Oliver explained, as he washed the soap from his face, now inspecting his countenance in the mirror.

"I don't know about any kid that got released from here, but I'm sure as hell certain he didn't go around stabbing fellas in grocery stores."

"Hey, why don't ya shut your mouth, that's a bright idea, huh? What do you know, anyways? Like I said, it was before your miserable self got here. You wouldn't know anything about it." Oliver exclaimed, gathering his things, leaving the bathroom and heading back to their room. Louie followed.

"Hey, don't get sore." Louie said, sauntering on Oliver's heels for the entirety the trip back to the room. "I'm just saying it must be hard. You must be a wreck is all I'm saying."

"Sure I'm a wreck. Whattaya think? Sheesh!" Oliver exclaimed, while taking one last look at himself in the mirror atop the dresser, thinking to himself that he could use some color on his chalky white skin. "I'm just trying not to think of it, kiddo. You know what I mean? Now drop it, will ya? before I have to sock you in the jaw or something."

Louie, leaving well enough alone, not doubting for a second the validity of the ultimatum given, completed the daunting task of donning himself in his uniform in preparation for breakfast, which was served in the cafeteria from 6am to 7am daily. The standard uniform of the day consisted of the aforementioned white, buttoned down, collared shirt; red tie with white stripes; beige slacks; blue socks; and, black slip-on penny loafers. This ensemble, with the exception of the gymnastics block and the once-a-month hiking and camping excursions, was worn throughout the entire day. During the one and a half hour gym period, the boys wore white t-shirts with the name of the institution printed upon the front in red letters, along with red, very short, shorts (booty huggers, the boys named them), also containing the facility's name, except, on this portion of the outfit, the letters were printed in white. On the trip to the woods, in which the residents embarked upon with members of the staff, the boys were supplied with hiking attire, consisting of heavy, red, sweaters and coats (also with the organization's name plastered upon each, beige cargo-type pants, and black hiking boots. In the summer, this outfit was almost its twin, with the exception of the hoodies and coats, now replaced with a t-shirt of the same color, and beige cargo-type shorts, replacing the longer pants. These garments made up the entirety of the boys' wardrobe at the Buffalo Correctional Facility for Boys. Now, seeing that our protagonist has finally completed enrobing himself, we shall follow him through the long hallway, passed the communal bathroom, down the two flights of old, wooden stairs – creaking with every step – and, finally, into the dining area.

The cafeteria buzzed with conversation; or, to be more precise, with a multitude of conversations. It was the time of day in which one at BCFB could observe and freely practice the first amendment, just so long as it did not displease or in any way ruffle the feathers, as it were, of the floor wardens that happened to pass while sauntering about with permanent scowls plastered upon their countenance. There were not many of the constitutional rights and privileges – which, incidentally, are so often taken for granted by the *free* – that were authorized by this institution that housed and secured the nearly one hundred young men between the ages of fifteen to seventeen years of age, all of whom were the perpetrators of various crimes ranging from felonious drug dealing, to arson, to marauding, to robbing, to those that yegg, and every other infraction in which a brigand commits.

Louie sat down, placing his tray of scrambled eggs, grits, home fried potatoes, and two sausage links onto the table, adjacent to Oliver and two other cronies who were grossly engaged in a heated and most intellectual discussion of the greatest import. "I'm telling you, you gotta flick the tongue back and forth to make their legs jiggle. They actually jiggle! like, uncontrollably man!" Said Eddie, a sixteen year old resident with bright blue eyes, light brown hair, and fair skin, who had a fondness for pilfering items of great expense. He especially enjoyed climbing through windows left open by inordinately trusting homeowners in the middle of the night, whilst the aforementioned tenants unsuspectingly slumbered away underneath their cozy comforters. Unbeknownst to our dear Eddie, on one fateful night in which he engaged in said infraction, the man of the house - at 3737 Pear Tree Road - had been suffering from a bout of the insomnia, deciding to roll out of bed and descend the stairs to acquire a midnight snack. Half-way down, the homeowner heard the sounds of shuffling, clinking, and clanking causing him to retrieve his son's aluminum baseball bat, which was conveniently forsaken in the corner of the stair landing. Clutching it, albeit with tremulous hands, the gentleman went forth to investigate. As the man approached the living room, much to his surprise, there he discovered our criminal red handed, as the saying goes, with several small items not belonging to him in his clutches, placing them into a medium sized trash bag. Trapping the bandit with his bat into a corner of the room, 911 was then promptly notified and - without an escape route - Eddie was apprehended and subsequently made a resident of the Boys Home in Buffalo, New York.

"That's ridiculous. I ain't never heard of no such thing in my entire life. I been with all kinds of girls and I ain't never once seen nobody's legs a shakin' before. No way." Franklin challenged. Franklin, a fifteen year old young man who – much to the misfortune of his older brother, who was the victim of an accidental, albeit fatal, gunshot wound between the eyes – was temporarily serving time at BCFB for manslaughter, being the shooter in said homicide. The hapless event occurred when the two brothers had occasion to find themselves inside of their father's gun locker, in the basement of the house, experimenting with the various firearms it contained. Lacking the proper education in the handling of guns, they both began toying around with them – playing such games as 'cowboys and indians,' 'cops and robbers,' to name a few - pointing the weapons at one another until, much to the shock and awe of Franklin (and, for a split second, his brother – whose brain ceased receiving messages subsequent to the aforementioned split second), there was a thunderous discharge, followed, very shortly after, by a removal of portions of the victim's face; thus, earning Franklin a residency at Buffalo. In a matter of three years, though, Franklin, like Oliver, would be transferred to a prison for adults, wherein the two would – in all likelihood – be subjected to the worst goings on of such a hellhole, as one might imagine.

"What do you think, Olie?" Eddie turned to Oliver in the hopes that he would provide some insight and support to his sexually deviant theory.

"I think you two clowns ought to actually be with a girl

before you start yappin' your flaps about getting it on with one, and makin' their goddamn legs shake all over the place. That's what I think." Oliver retorted without glancing up from his breakfast. Oliver, like the others, had not yet had the opportunity to *know* a member of the fairer sex in such ways, being that all of his time, prior to incarceration, was devoted to looking after his sister (who was now, as a matter of fact - since the incident - staying with distant relatives somewhere in New Jersey); and, therefore, had enough prudence to refrain from such carnal conversations.

"Oh man, you is just bein' a jive turkey. You no help at all, man." Eddie dismissed. He then turned to Louie with the intentions of relaying the inquiry to him, but instead said aloud, "Shoot, I ain't even gonna ask New Blood. The closest *he* probably ever got to getting it on was a poster of Raquel Welch, a jar of Vaseline, and a box of tissues." He concluded, explosively laughing at his own joke, the force of the laughter causing his head to tilt back.

Franklin and Louie laughed along at the mere sight of Eddie's self-fulfilled enjoyment of his own humor. Oliver, still not looking up from his food, offered a faint chuckle. Louie said nothing to rebut the insinuation because he knew it was not very far from being the truth. He had kissed a girl with the tongue just a handful of times, with perhaps a quick *feeling up* of the breasts and posterior… once or twice; however, he had never found himself with occasion to *go all the way*, so to speak. "I actually prefer Natalie Wood. She's a real fox." Louie jested, implying to the affirmative of Eddie's innuendo, to redirect the focus away from himself.

"Natalie Wood? The little girl that don't believe in Santa Claus in that movie '*Miracle on 34th Street*' Natalie Wood?" Franklin exclaimed.

"More like '*West Side Story*' Natalie Wood… the one where she plays Maria. She's a real looker in that one." Corrected Louie.

"*Maria*! *I just met a girl named Maria*!" Eddie sang.

"Aw, she don't do nothing for me, man. Not enough meat on them bones for me." Franklin offered in return.

"Yeah, I like some cushion for the pushin', myself. You got some crazy taste Young Blood." Eddie chimed in.

"Aw leave the kid alone, would ya? Quit breakin' his stones. None of you is doin' any pushin' of any kind… I think Natalie Wood is okay. She'd do just fine." Oliver declared in support of his roommate, giving Louie a wink.

"Man, you're both off your rockers." Franklin dismissively waved them off, as they all finished the remainder of their breakfast in silence.

The days leading up to Oliver's aforementioned hearing had come and gone. Today, the fate of his future would be learned; either he would be somewhat set free, transported to a half-way house with the ability to see his sister, get a job, and resurrect his life, or – in a short amount of time – be succumbed to his worst nightmare. He sat outside of the Warden's office, in a chair placed just outside of the entrance door – a chair provided solely for the purpose of stewing in one's own agonizing rumination. After what felt like ages, the old, mahogany door opened; and, out of it came one of the assistant Warden's, who motioned for Oliver to enter with a nod of the head. As the young man crossed the threshold of the office door, his attention was immediately captured by the numerous leather bound books that made their home on the bookshelves which surrounded the room. It seemed that all of the classics of the literary world were present and accounted for; Moby Dick, War and Peace, A Tale of Two Cities, just to name a very few. The office was dark and musty, only being illuminated by a very minuscule desk lamp which was situated atop the Warden's desk, a desk made of very old, but well polished wood. Although it was the middle of the afternoon, one would not be made aware of this fact once inside of the room, due to the darkened curtains, drawn shut, that covered the entirety of the large casement window, which was, incidentally, closed and locked, hence creating the musty atmosphere.

The Warden, sitting as far back as his large, leather, reclining chair would allow, glared at Oliver over his rounded out spectacles, which were slightly pulled forward, resting on the bridge of his nose. Without uttering a word, the imposing figure reached for a wooden box that rested on his desk, opening it, pulling out a large Winston Churchill cigar – clipping the edge with a cigar cutter – and, after lighting it, took numerous pulls, emitting copious amounts of smoke, all before addressing Oliver. "So, you have a hearing today, don't you young man?"

"Yes, sir; I do." Was Oliver's curt reply, not feeling a necessity to engage in excess conversation with the man whose face reminded him of some sort of a rogue Santa Claus, having a cadaverously pale countenance, covered by a beard of the same color, cheeks and nose as red as a child's toy fire engine, and a rotund stomach that pronounced itself over the desk. Anything Oliver needed to say, he thought, would be expressed to the board upon their arrival.

"Just so." The Warden continued. Also, having no desire to engage in any excessive and trivial dialogue. "Well, the way this works is, in just a few, a bunch of nice people will mosey on in here and ask you a litany of questions, to which you will return with very short and to the point type answers. Less is more… get me?"

Oliver nodded in the affirmative.

"Good… very good." The warden replied, taking another drag of his Churchill, all the while keeping his eyes planted upon Oliver.

Just then, there being a knock at the door, the assistant Warden – opening it and entering from the opposite end – informed the warden of the board's arrival. "Sir, they're here."

"That's just fine, send 'em on in." The Warden answered, placing his unfinished cigar into an ashtray, subsequently standing up from his chair and wiping some of the ashes that had flaked onto his dark, three-piece, Gimbel's department store suit.

Through the door, entered three individuals whose countenances expressed the epitome of sheer absence of emotion; void of any empathy - or indication of being alive, for that matter. As the motley crew made their way to the small conference table that stood toward the far end of the office, the Warden motioned for Oliver to head in that particular direction by extending his hand outward. Upon taking his seat on the opposite side of the inquisitioners, Oliver patiently awaited the onslaught, as the *collective* simultaneously removed from their briefcases a ream of papers, all containing information relevant to the young man's case. Once their paraphernalia was in place, one of them, directing the inquiry to Oliver, asked, "You understand that we are here today, January —, 1969, to conduct a hearing in regards to your eligibility for release?"

"Yes."

"State your name for the record." Interjected another.

"Oliver Abrams."

"Mr. Abrams, do you consider yourself to be rehabilitated from the heinous crime you so violently and thoughtlessly committed? The one in which you -" The third interviewer had to pause, so that he could refer to his notes, not knowing exactly what Oliver's crime was, before continuing, "- tactlessly stabbed a grocery store clerk?"

"Umm, yes, sir, I do believe I am."

"And why do you feel this, Mr. Abrams. What makes you feel rehabilitated?"

"Well, sir, I feel as though I've learned a real valuable lesson here at BCFB. I mean, everyone is real swell here… and they really take the time to sit and figure it all out with you. They really do. Why, I'm in therapy everyday and I can tell you, we get loads accomplished... loads! I'll tell you what, just the other day, Mrs. Janice, my psychiatrist here, says I was makin' all kinds of progress. She said to me, 'Oliver, you're really making some progress here.' Honest to God, she said that."

The warden, who was – as one might expect – somewhat incensed with Oliver's ramblings, sank deeply into his chair, his

138

face becoming flushed.

"Uh… yes, we see here that you've made some good progress in therapy… but, do you feel that you've been completely rehabilitated? That's the question on the table." Said one of the inquisitioners.

"I do, sir. I can honestly say – hand to God -" Here, Oliver held his right hand high, as one would when swearing on a bible in a court of law. "- I can honestly tell you fine gentleman that I will never stab another grocery store clerk ever again. I mean, to be honest, I was just borrowin' some food from the store to feed my little sister. That's all I was trying to do. I didn't mean for anyone to get shanked, honest I didn't. Next time, I'll just punch the guy in the gut or maybe give 'em a kick to the ol' family jewels or something like that. But no more stabbin', that much I will swear to the good Lord above. You have my word on that. Honest, you do."

The *mandem* gazed at each other with a look of perplexity, not certain of what to think or make about the prolix speech of their interlocutor, looking towards the warden for some clarity, who was now beside himself in a pool of perspiration, his hand covering his mouth to signify his bafflement; but, there being no exegesis to the disquisition, it was decided, shortly after the hearing - quite unanimously, one might add - that Mr. Abrams would, in fact, not be seeing his freedom any time in the foreseeable future.

The days following, like all of the other days during the week, was business as usual, as it were; which consisted of regular classes such as mathematics, science, English, &c. During this time, the time in which studying was conducted, one would believe that this were some kind of boarding school, which – in a sense – it was; except, instead of an institution for the privileged elite, it catered, rather, to the criminal element, albeit of the younger variety. In between classes there was, as previously mentioned, lunch, gymnastics, and recess, similar to any other phrontistery; however, there was one thing in which the boys looked forward more than anything else, and that was the monthly weekend hiking and camping trip through the woods. Every month, on Friday, in the afternoon, a select group of boys were taken – based on the their deportment during the lunar cycle – to set off on an adventure of sorts with a few floor wardens for a weekend of *roughing it.* They would trek for miles, learning about various trees, birds, and other such things of nature until they reached the campsite; once there, they would set up their tents, gather firewood and kindle; and, finally, settle in for the night. The night would pass with the lot cooking hot dogs over the fire, roasting marshmallows afterwards, whilst listening to lessons concerning any and all life topics. The following day usually consisted of more hiking, followed by fishing in a large lake that rested about ten miles from camp, and small game hunting, using makeshift traps made of wood, loose branches, and string; the spoils of which were cleaned, cooked, and eaten. It was a thing most coveted by the majority of the inmates, and most all of them did their very best to be selected.

Pinned to the wall, every fourth Thursday at 7pm, just outside the floor warden's office, was a list of twenty names of the boys who would be selected to participate in the weekend excursion; and, every fourth Thursday at 7pm, just outside the floor warden's office, were a sea of boys flooding the area hoping and praying that their names were amongst the chosen. The hallway echoed with the sounds of delight and sorrow… with the sights of smiles and frowns;

heads were held high in triumphant bliss, heads sank low in bitter dejection. The crowd, which thus far, prevented our little posse from espying the results, dispersed, finally leaving room for Louie, Oliver, Franklin, and Eddie to discover their names on the list. All four would be in attendance. Franklin and Eddie jumped up in the air with delight, high-fiving one another as if celebrating a game winning goal. Eddie then turned around, offering a pat on the back to Oliver who, while displaying more of a reserved countenance, continued to gaze at his name on the wall. Louie, who was much attuned to his roommate, asked, "You good, roomie? It's good news isn't it?"

Snapping out of his stupor, Oliver replied, "Yea, good news. Real good news." The response was accompanied with the flashing of a brief, spurious smile.

Louie could sense something was amiss. He and Oliver shared a room for nearly two months and – although Louie was far from understanding him completely (because, quite honestly, Oliver was the furthest thing from an open book), he had grown to recognize the vibes and mannerisms of his bunk mate. He was quite aware of the results of the hearing, and therefore understood and expected that there would be some negative energy emanating from his counterpart; but, this felt to him different. There was something else. Oliver was best described as a recluse, some might even venture to say a misanthrope, rarely engaging in conversation or showing emotion to excess; however, Louie had a talent for reading people and grew to appreciate his roommate notwithstanding his shortcomings… therefore, young Christianson could bet all the loose change in his pocket that there was something off, but what exactly? that, he could only conjecture. He knew better than to approach Oliver now with everyone surrounding them, of that much he was certain. Very much aware of Oliver's preference for privacy, Louie kept his feelings tucked away in his pocket in the hallway with everyone lingering around; instead, he would make his inquiry later that night when they were alone.

It had been storming relentlessly for the past three nights, this particular evening being no different, as the rain from outside pelted onto the window, creating a comforting white noise inside of the room that could lull the most irascible person into one of a lucid variety. As the two prepared for lights out, Louie decided to inquire about Oliver's aloofness earlier on in the day; however, knowing for certain that a direct line of questioning would most likely put Oliver off, he decided to ease his way into the thing. "Pretty exciting that we're going to the camping trip this weekend, eh Olie?"

"Yea, a real hoot." Oliver answered, while conducting the nightly ritual of arranging his bed for slumber, fluffing and placing his pillows in a straight line with the intentions of cradling and corralling them with his arms and legs.

"Well, I'm certainly looking forward to it. It'd be swell to get outta this joint for a couple of days. Fresh air, fishing. That's alright with me."

Oliver made no reply. He climbed into his bed and lay on his back, placing one of the pillows on his chest, staring up at the ceiling into oblivion.

Louie decided to press the issue. This beating around the bush was getting nowhere, he thought to himself, before inquiring aloud. "Hey, Olie, what's with you today? I kinda noticed you're in space somewhere… like on another planet or some crazy thing like that. What gives? I mean, I totally get that you're bummed about the way the hearing went down and all… I totally get that; but… I don't know, man, you seem… just different."

After a brief moment of silent pause, Oliver answered without removing his eyes from the ceiling. "You ever think about bustin' outta here?"

"Bustin' outta here?" Louie parroted, adding an inquisitive tone.

"What? are your ears broken? That's what I said… bustin' outta here."

"What do you mean? Like, *break* out of here? Like, as in *escape*… for *good*?" Louie asked, with a bit more volume than was required for such taboo talk as this.

"Keep your goddamn voice down, will ya?" Oliver scolded, sitting up in the bed, taking a quick glance toward the door, making certain that no voyeurs of any kind were neigh, before turning his attention back to Louie and whispering "You want the whole joint should hear ya? What in the hell else do ya think I mean, anyways?"

"Why would I want to… " Louie paused, also glancing at the door before continuing, "… *you know what*… from here? I only got a one year sentence. I'll be outta here by next summer." There was silence for a brief moment before Louie continued. "Why? Are *you* thinking of… " Glancing at the door once again and continuing in a subdued voice, "… *you know what?*"

"Who said anything about that's what I was thinking of?"
Oliver snapped. "Nobody said anything of the like! I *clearly* just
asked you if *you* ever thought of it. I never said me. Not at all."

"Well, I just thought -"

"That's yer problem. You *thought*. Do me and the rest of the
miserable world a goddamn favor, will ya? Don't do any thinking.
Whatever you do, huh?" Oliver lay his head back down, with an
exaggerated thud, onto the pillow behind his head and resumed
staring at the ceiling; then, grabbing one of the other pillows, he
placed it onto his chest, wrapping his arms around it as one would
when metaphorically sheltering oneself from an unseen foreboding.

Louie remained silent. He knew better than to go tit-for-tat
with his roommate. After a few moments of quietude between them,
Louie broke in and said, in a sort of tender tone of voice, "Listen, I
know you got it rough. I mean, not *now*; but, I know you *will* have
it rough in a few months… when you turn eighteen."

"Oh yea? What do you *know*."

"I mean, I know at some point you gotta leave this joint and
get transferred to the *big house*… sorry, I mean, adult prison. I know
that much. I know it's gotta be rough for you -"

"You think so?" Oliver interjected sarcastically.

Louie took the jab, half knowing he deserved it for that
obnoxiously obvious comment. He paused out of deference to allow
Oliver's sneering to achieve its intended result before continuing, "I
realize it sucks, I really do; but you can't seriously be thinking -"

"For the last time, nobody said nothin' about nothin'. I asked you a stupid question is all, for the love of Christ. You'd think a guy could ask a goddamn question around here. Jeez."

"Alright, alright. I'm sorry. Nobody asked a question."

"Jesus H. Christ." Oliver reached for his light switch, turning his bedside lamp off, now making the room completely dark, with the exception of the flashes of light from the strikes of lightning in the sky above.

Louie, from the midst of the darkness of the now tenebrous room, finished his thought, "I'm just saying, if that's what you *were* thinking, it'd be a pretty stupid thing to do. Damned stupid. That's all I'm saying."

"Louie… I'm about to spring up out of this bed and break your goddamn jawbone if you don't let it be."

"I'm not saying another word."

Outside their door, the scattered sounds of last minute conversations between the residents could be heard and, shortly after, the bellowing of the floor warden - giving the last call for lights out – rendered all of the voices inert. As the two settled their bodies and minds for the remainder of the night, Louie opined one final time, "*Damned* stupid."

Oliver paid no heed.

The next morning, on a sunny and somewhat mild Friday after breakfast – the deluge finally coming to an end - the chosen young men all prepared for their weekend jaunt into the woods.

Backpacks were filled with excitement in anticipation of the weekend getaway. In the lobby of the main hall, the early birds slowly filed in and gathered, awaiting the floor wardens who would lead the way. Louie, along with Oliver, Eddie, and Franklin, stood amongst the others in silent anticipation. Breaking the silence, Eddie said, "Man I am super excited, ain't you guys excited or nothin'?"

"Brother, all I can think of is about all them snakes and bears and all that other scary shit. You know all that nature shit is for you white people. Us black folk don't care too hot for being out in the woods with all those vicious ass animals that could eat us alive and shit." Franklin said, with a look of utter consternation.

"Aw, what are ya some kinda sissy or something like that? And anyways, if you're so yellow about going out to the woods, why'd you wanna come?" Eddie inquired.

"First off, who you callin' a sissy? you jive turkey! Where I'm from, a guy gets pounded out for sayin' some crazy shit like that to a brother… Secondly, I may not like all that creepy forest crap, but mama ain't raise no fool… over there is better than cooped up in here, you dig?" Exclaimed Franklin.

"Would you two cool it? A guy can't even think around here with all yer yappin'." Scolded Oliver, who was in deep thought.

"What bug crawled up *your* ass, Olie?" Franklin asked.

"The same bug that's gonna crawl up your ass when you is sleepin' in the 'scary ass forest,' you big pussy!" Eddie interrupted, tauntingly, whilst placing his finger in the general vicinity of Franklin's anus to create the feeling that bugs were compromising

146

the entrance of his rear end.

"What bug?" Oliver retorted Franklin's inquiry. "Who's got a bug? Can't a guy just sit around and think for cryin' out loud? Is that against the rules or something?"

"Something's definitely up *his* ass." Said Eddie, shrugging his shoulders and turning his attention to the others.

Just then, just before awaking the *sleeping dragon*, so to speak (as Oliver - although almost always in control of his temper, for the most part maintaining a healthy balance of composer – was seconds away from losing his cool, and no one dared flirt with the potential of his unknown), the floor wardens entered the hall and gave their soliloquy, which served more as a *riot act* of sorts. Up to that day, there had not been any unfortunate incidents on any of the prior outings; but, the speech was given nonetheless to serve as a forewarning against any possible shenanigans the young men may find occasion to cause. One ought not be too careful when it comes down to this kind of a thing; what with criminals essentially being let loose in the wild and all - albeit of the adolescent variety; however, one can never be too cautious.

The half hour bus ride left them at Buffalo Harbor State Park, an absolutely majestic place filled with a plethora of plush vegetation of all different colors and sizes, as well as a multitude of God's creatures, big and small, scurrying about. Acres upon acres of this wonderful land lay before the boys as they filed out of the bus with their eyes wide open, unable to blink out of sheer awe for the spectacle they witnessed around them. Birds of all varieties swooped up and around – some perched on branches above, singing their alluringly angelic songs while inquisitively peering at the boys below. It was perfection. Some of the newer inmates had never known such a place could exist, what with being born and raised in the slums of their particular inner cities. Some of the other boys who had the good fortune to have returned to this oasis were equally as enthralled to be present once again. One of the tourists, however, was not quite in the same state of bliss as were his comrades; Oliver was somewhere else within himself. His countenance was impassive and his focus was on something else entirely. Louie noticed. "Olie, what's up with you? You were quiet the whole bus ride and now you don't even look happy to actually be here. Ain't you glad you're not cooped up in a building for the weekend?"

"I'm happy, alright. I'm just fine. I just don't feel like talking. Does a fella have to talk every goddamn second of the day to be happy? You want I should jump through a hoop lit on fire for you, too?" Oliver replied, not quite fully addressing Louie, seemingly reconnoitering his surroundings and assessing the lay of the land, now with the countenance of a surveyor who is taking note of every minute detail within a line of property.

"Well, I sure am happy." Louie continued, ignoring Oliver's sassiness. "They don't have any place like this in New York City, except for maybe Central Park, but even that don't compare to *this* place. This is like something straight out of a fairy tale book." Louie marveled at his surroundings more in tuned with one who admires a thing of beauty, much the opposite of his dialogist.

"I'll say! A guy could get used to this!" Eddie, who caught up to the two, chimed in, placing his hands upon both their shoulders, while looking up and all around at the magnificence surrounding him.

Franklin, who had been slow to get off of the bus until he was assured - and reassured - that no lions or tigers were afoot, had also finally caught up with his pack. "I'm gonna try to catch me a big fish this weekend. My grandpa took me fishin' a few times before he passed on, so I know how to do it alright. Yes sir, we caught us all kinds of fish. Bluefish, catfish, groupers… all kinds." Said he, wide eyed and with the largest grin spread across his face.

"That all sounds real swell. *Real* swell. I just want to sit around and take in all of this. All the trees and the birds and stuff. I hear there's a super awesome waterfall by the river, I really wanna check *that* out." Louie added.

Oliver remained phlegmatic and aloof. The proverbial wheels were turning round in his head, and nothing – not even the sublimity of the eden that enwreathed him - could break his concentration. What he thought, what he was pondering, no one knew, but he. From the exterior, all that could be seen was the face of a young man – still very much a boy - that was soon to be shipped off to a facility where, in all likelihood, he would be impotently up against the gravest of circumstances. Soon, he would be a part of an environment surrounded by much older men who were of the most vile sort, and this was something he could not allow to come to pass. Sometimes, when one finds oneself in a compromising position that one knows cannot be, a sort of survival and self-preservation mode kicks in… drastic measures are then implemented. For Oliver, this was one of those times; therefore, he had begun contemplating and devising a plan to escape. He could do a stint at BCFB standing on his head all day long in the dark; but the Ossining Correctional

Facility, also known as Sing Sing? no, that was much, too much, to bear. He couldn't possibly survive in a place such as that, surrounded by the scum of the earth, the lowest of the low, most of whom were twice and thrice his age. There was no doubt about the fact that he would be prey for the animals that dwelt within those walls and could not stand the frightening idea of it all. No… something must be done. Action must be taken.

After walking the trails for some hours, gandering at the wonders and beauty of God's heavenly creation, they reached the campsite where they would pitch their tents and begin to collect firewood and kindle. Tonight, they would dine on hotdogs and hamburgers, as it was too late to fish – that task would be undertaken tomorrow. On this night, they would roast their victuals and toast their marshmallows atop the crackling fire from the makeshift fire pit comprised of large stones collected by the boys; compare stories of what they had seen along the hike; carol the songs that one would in such an atmosphere as this; and, finally, nestle in their sleeping bags inside their tents, all in anticipation of the daylight, awaiting the rays of the sun to illuminate the sky above… a sky which was now abound with the brightest stars that any of them had ever laid their eyes upon. The moon was full amongst the celestial splendor above, casting a most brilliant luminescence that gently lit the campsite like a nightlight in a child's room. After some hours, all were finally fast asleep… that is, all but one.

It was about two in the morning when a sleepless Oliver slithered out of his sleeping bag and out of the tent, ever so stealthily, so as not to awaken the others. Unbeknownst to anyone, he – earlier in the day – had taken some provisions (some hotdogs, fruit, and water) for his expected absconding, packing it all in his duffel bag.

As he sauntered along through the campsite, he cringed at every crack of every twig stepped on, which sounded as loud as a hundred foot tree falling to the ground, causing him to freeze each time, listening intently and scanning the area for movement; however, there being none, he continued to traverse along, eventually making his great escape out of the area. Before long, he found himself miles away and was, for all intents and purposes, free. Where he would go? of this he had not a clue in the world. He hadn't thought that through… not completely. What he did know, what was abundantly certain was, he had to get far, far, away. He thought to himself, 'Just continue moving forward. Somewhere down the road, I'll eventually establish some sort of foundation. I'll get a job… find some hole in the wall to live in. I can do it. I can make it.' Anything was better than the alternative.

It was about six in the morning when the campsite began to stir. The boys, as well as the floor wardens, peeled out of their sleeping bags, stretching their arms and letting out morning yawns, breathing in the fresh morning dew. The sky above was filled, once more, with dark, angry, clouds and the air smelled of an imminent shower. It was not long before Oliver's absence was realized as roll call was being conducted, which, shortly thereafter, lead to sheer pandemonium. Panic ensued as the floor wardens ran to and fro in every which direction; although not exactly having the slightest idea in which direction to run… whichever way leads one who is frantically searching for some terribly important thing they have recently lost, this historian supposes. There being no immediate way of communicating with the facility – as there were no phones nearby (the nearest being about ten miles away) and the walkie-talkies having only a limited range – they elected to set off on a manhunt.

As the rain commenced to fall from the sky in the form of a light drizzle, the floor wardens split up in all directions, taking with them each a small group of the young men in an attempt to find Oliver before having to head back to the facility with one less inmate… and possibly loss of their employment. Louie, Eddie, and Franklin paired together with one of the wardens and headed west, which was the deepest, darkest, most dense part of the forest, filled with the tallest, most magnificent, but terrifying, trees – most of which were over one hundred years in age – packed so closely together that it reduced the levels of light to the point that it nearly gave the appearance of nightfall; the scene resembled something right out of any number of Grimms' spine-tingling tales. The dark clouds above them did nothing to provide succor to the arduous task before them, which now began to unleash a heavier, steadier, precipitation, which in no way made the task at hand *money for old rope*, as it were.

For hours, in the midst of the now tempestuous storm – creating a cascading flow of streams on the craggy ground, which jettisoned in every which direction - the search went on for Oliver. Over the short-range walkie-talkies, the voices of the wardens could be heard expressing a panicked concern for the angry thunder and lightning crashing up above, pondering if, at this point, the search should be forsaken. Piercing shards of rain drops hit the ground so hard that, as it bounced back upward, it created the allusion that the storm actually ascended from the earth, rather than descending from the heavens. Shouts of 'Oliver!' could be heard in every direction… all going unanswered. At one point, the torrent was so heavy, so constant, one could see nothing in front of oneself… it was for this reason that Louie, who had traversed a path just feet away from the herd, did not realize his next step would lead him off of an escarpment, down a cliff of sorts, and into a mudslide twenty feet in depth; plunging the boy into an extremely frigid, turbulent, class-three rapid, filled with numerous high and erratic waves, inundated with extremely large and sharp rocks that had the potential to tear a human being into the tiniest of pieces.

The waves whipped Louie around like a rag doll as he struggled to maintain his head above water, managing to intake whatever oxygen he could at every afforded opportunity, all the whilst losing feeling in his extremities from the brumal waters. The prognosis appeared grim as his efforts to obtain air seemed a moot endeavor, pints of water entering his mouth in droves. Louie could see his life flashing before his eyes in between swallowing what seemed like gallons of water, entering his mouth and nose, as he fruitlessly flailed his hands and legs all about. Just a short distance away, the thirty foot waterfall – also inundated with boulders the size of automobiles – was the unfortunate culmination of the violent river he fleetingly approached. He tried desperately to grab onto anything that was within his reach, but to no avail; the waves were entirely too inconsistent to manage such a feat, whipping him this way and that. All hope appeared to be lost as Louie's innate ability – the ability for ones body to resist its own demise – now began to accept its mortality. What was once a writhing, wriggling body, was now nearly limp and listless, succumbing to the will of the churning scourge of the rapid, sending him hurdling towards the dreadful precipice just mere feet away, spelling certain doom for the young man; that is, until – just seconds before taking the banefully fatal plunge – a reaching hand presented itself by grasping tight onto the arm of the doomed soul.

Clinging for dear life onto both an embedded rock in the middle of the rapid with one hand and – with the opposite hand – the almost lifeless arm of Louie Christianson, was the prodigal inmate. Oliver, with all of his might, using every muscle fiber of his being, pulled Louie toward the aforementioned rock, lifting him to a safe position atop, laying him on his side so that the water he ingested could work its way out of his system. There being only enough room for one of them, Oliver entered the glacial waters half-way, grasping the edge of the rock with all of the strength he had remaining, his body being pulled with brute force by the rapid's momentum. "Hey, kiddo," he uttered, "you're okay… you hear me? You're gonna be okay! Just hang on tight, they'll find you. Just stay awake, okay? Just do me a favor and don't pass out, alright?"

"Olie?" Louie managed to reply, most of the water having ejaculated from his insides, still in somewhat of a daze. "Hey, Olie, we was looking for you. Hey, they're pretty sore about you taking off in the middle of the night. They're pretty damn sore about that... say, I don't feel so hot. I think I need a doctor or something."

"You'll be okay, kiddo, you just took in some water. Take nice easy breaths, don't panic. You'll be okay." Oliver said, his teeth chattering and his body convulsing from the gelid temperature of the water.

"Okay, Olie. I will. Say, Olie?"

"Yea, kiddo? I'm here." Oliver's face now pinched; his lower extremities becoming numb and immovable.

"Hey, I just wanna say… you know you're like a big brother to me. I mean it. I know I break your chops a lot, but I wanted you to know that. I sort of love you… like a big brother and all."

"I know, kid. I love ya, too. Just hang on, you're alright. Hang on."

"Okay, Olie. I will. I'll hang on."

"Hey, kiddo… listen to me, now… are you listening?"

"I'm listening, Olie."

Feeling his grip coming undone, Oliver gazed into the half unconscious eyes of his young roommate in between the voluminous drops of the violent rainstorm, now raging in every direction around them both. "I'm proud of you, little brother… you did your time like a man. You're a brave little guy, with the heart of a lion, and I know you're gonna do good things. It's up to you, though… it's up to you to be something great in this world. Be *a hero in the universe*, you hear me, little brother? Be greater than us all." He uttered these final words with a most ingratiating simper on his countenance, before being swept away and swallowed by the rushing waters.

Louie could see, materializing from in between the trees and the deluge pouring from the heavens above, the silhouettes of the search party, crestfallen impressions displayed upon their miens.

***

In the summer of July 1968, a typical day at Laura Trista's household consisted of the worst sort of abuse one could fathom – both physical as well as mental. The patriarch, Emilio Trista, spent most of his hours consuming alcoholic libations in excess and then – just before blacking out – would fly into fits of rage wherein the occupants of said household would feel his wrath in a plethora of painful and mortifying ways. Most of the time, the five children (George, the eldest; Edward and Edith, the twins; Victoria; and, the youngest, Laura) made a timely exodus when their father began his bouts of drinking, having been the victims of his outrage on numerous occasions; however, there were – much to the chagrin of anyone who could not escape the madness – some days in which the beatings and other agonizing experiences could not be avoided. Laura was somewhat of a homebody and enjoyed spending hours in her room reading the classics of literature. Her absolute favorite, pretty much anything written by Edgar Allen Poe, was her mental escape from the hell that was her reality. Unfortunately, this bore a price as she, very frequently, found herself the target of her father's fury, spending many a day on the unpleasant end of several violent blows from whatever object was closest to use as a weapon of mass destruction during his drunken tirades.

On this particular hot and humid July afternoon, Emilio's quaffing began somewhat earlier than usual, catching Laura by surprise, startling her to a jolt, when he entered her room with a brown leather belt in his clutches. "How many mother fucking times do I have to tell you to clean your goddamn mess?" He was referring to the dishes left in the sink by the male members of the tribe (George and Edward to be precise). The boys, ages twenty and nineteen respectively, very rarely cleaned up after themselves, usually leaving the formidable task of picking up the slack to the girls; however, on this particular day, that was not the case and, therefore, Laura – the only sibling who had not had the opportunity to decamp from the netherworld on that unfortunate afternoon – was left to bear the brunt of their blunder.

"I'm sorry, I didn't know there was a mess, I'll take care of it right now." She said, placing her copy of *The Complete Tales and Poems of Edgar Allen Poe* gingerly onto the bed and raising herself up, her body somewhat rigid in preparation for an imminent onslaught.

Within seconds subsequent to completing her sentence, the aforementioned belt cut through the air, landing across the rear of her midsection creating a piercing, clapping sound as it made contact with the left side of her buttock. It was only with sheer survival instinct and timely agility that she managed to contort herself just enough to avoid being struck on the forepart of her body, which only enraged him further. With reckless abandon, he whipped the young lady of fourteen, as she scrambled any way she could to avoid the painful contact of the size forty leather belt, an attempt which proved to be futile. Realizing that there was no escape, she shielded her face with her arms, tucking her body into itself to avoid being struck in the face, resulting in the remainder of the strikes being received on her forearms and elbows. What felt like hours were mere seconds until he grew tired and short of breath, finally ceasing the assault. "Now clean up those goddamn dishes, you little piece of shit." He panted before finally making an about face out of the room, bouncing off either side of the walls down the hallway, unable to maintain a straight and steady balance due to his intoxicated state. She wished he would die right then and there, but no fortune as good as that would take place on that day.

Laura remained on the floor, where the calamity left her,

attempting to catch her breath and collect herself. She wrapped her long, very light brown, almost champagne colored hair – which was now running amok all about her face – around in a bun and stood herself up like the Phoenix from the ashes. Her clothes, now stretched and torn, were removed and tossed to the side, replaced by a fresh short sleeve shirt and pair of blue jeans. As she wiped the trickle of blood from her nose, she stared at herself in the mirror that hung on her wall, just beside her old wooden dresser drawer, staring deeply into her hazel eyes, which were now bloodshot and filled with silent tears. She had been here before… this was not an inaugural beating. With any luck, her father would have tired himself out and gone to bed – passed out from the copious amounts of liquor he consumed. Barefooted, she tiptoed down the long hall and into the kitchen, so as not to arouse her tormentor. There, in the sink, she bore witness to the subject of her father's fury… one medium sized spoon containing the remnants of chocolate ice cream. Nothing more.

Once the formidable task of laving the utensil was complete, Laura treaded softly back into her room to gather a few items to take with her out of the apartment. She opened her bottom dresser drawer, pulling out a singular old tube-sock – a sock belonging to one of her brothers, as its matching counterpart became part of laundry abyss – now the repository for whatever currency she managed to scrounge up throughout the day, which at that very moment consisted of five single dollar bills crumpled up into five tiny balls. She placed the money into her front jeans pocket (not unraveling the bills, but bunching them all together into one singular ball), along with a lone house key; threw on a pair of pink socks adorned with little yellow sunflowers; retrieved her book from her bed (which fit snuggly in her rear pocket); grabbed the hair scrunchie that hung around her door knob, rolling it onto her wrist; picked up her sneakers, but refrained from putting them on to avoid detection; and, finally, made her exeunt out into the mean streets of Spanish Harlem, which, incidentally, was safer by comparison to her humble abode. She walked around for about an hour, from her apartment at East 112th Street and Park Avenue, to Central Park at around 79th Street, where her favorite place in the entire world proudly stood… Belvedere Castle. The Castle was something right out of a fairy tale, what with its majestic Gothic stone structure made of granite, complete with a corner tower, conical cap, and parapet walls, standing one hundred thirty feet atop Vista Rock, overlooking Turtle Pond (where, literally, dozens upon dozens of little turtles swam freely about).

Laura, as was her custom, sat for hours, imagining herself a subject of that gigantic castle, never once for a single, solitary, moment purporting to be of any sort of high ranking member of the aristocracy, never a queen or princess, never a lady in waiting or a high brow member of the court; she merely imagined herself one of the loyal subjects who humbly set up shop just outside the castle selling, perhaps, some spices from China or maybe sheets of fabric from the middle east. Her grim reality did not allow for such wild fantasies as dreaming above her station. Such unrealistic musing was for little girls who were already fortunate enough to have, at the very least, a sense of normalcy in their own lives. She did, however, try every so often to make the attempt at some fantastical fairy tale dream wherein she would be swept off her feet by some handsome prince, some knight in shining armor on his high horse. This Sir Arthur of sorts would trot by her kiosk of salted meats and dead chickens, hanging prominently on display by their necks for the purpose of being purchased, espying the lonely peasant girl that was her, falling instantly and madly in love, shunning his bride to be - an arranged marriage to some princess that he wanted no part of - choosing instead, true love.

When she wasn't fantasizing, she lay barefoot on the plush green carpet of the Great Lawn with the blades of grass between her tiny toes – the nails of which contained the remnants of a red polish that had long chipped away - reading her book and letting the warm rays of the sun caress her face, whilst multitudes of butterflies swooped in, zig zagging all around her. The young girl possessed an adoration for the stories of Poe, always feeling a kind of connection to the morbidity of them all. She thought of all the torment that he must have experienced and endured in order to have been able to produce such moroseness, relating, somewhat, to his life story – what with Mr. Poe's father having abandoned him, and his mother passing away shortly thereafter, at which point he became an orphan; which is precisely how Laura felt most of the time... like an orphan. Laura's mother had tragically passed away while giving birth to her youngest child fourteen years ago, since then being 'raised' by her abusive father, whose only form of affection was allowing his five children to possess keys to enter the apartment. Often, thoughts of sealing her father up behind one of his apartment walls swirled about in her mind – as in The Raven. How she would absolutely love to hear the muffled sound of his voice, pleading for help, begging forgiveness behind the sheetrock, gasping for air and eventually suffocating to death. And if, perchance, there happened a Raven upon *her* chamber door, endlessly uttering the eerie word 'Nevermore,' she would fret not; instead, Laura would simply placate it with some bird food, sending it on its merry way... no regrets and no shame. Otherwise, she and Mr. Poe lived parallel lives… close enough, she thought.

Hours passed by rapidly, the sun beginning to make its descent behind the Castle. The late afternoon July sky resembled Edvard Munch's masterpiece, *The Scream*, filled with warm yellows and oranges of the most vibrant sort; however, Laura dreaded the coming of the night, realizing that it was only a matter of time before she would have to return to her *bete noire*. She wished, with all her might, that she had the ability control the setting sun by deferring its downward climb. Alas, she could not; therefore, with much displeasure she began the dreaded trek back home. Along the way, she marveled at the lavish apartment buildings that sat majestically along Fifth Avenue. Through the large glass windows, incased in enormous stone window frames, she venerated at the magnificent residences within, descrying the foyers and their resplendent crystal chandeliers - some larger than her entire bedroom; study rooms containing mahogany bookshelves filled with an endless array of leather bound books; palatially formal dining rooms displaying priceless China on the walls; and, everything else that completed the grandeur… including the happy families which inhabited it all, gaping at the opulence with her yearning eyes. She wished with all her heart and soul that such extravagances were hers; however, there again, this sort of ridiculous imprudence was not only a waste of time, but also served to be quite dangerous to her because – when in such deep thought – she tended to lose track of time. Arriving late was not tolerated, seeing as how she and her sisters were, being the women of the domicile, in charge of preparing supper. Laura and her two sisters (Victoria, her older sister by two years, and Edith, her elder by five) were not only responsible for the cooking, but the chores about the household as well. Preparing meals, however, was one extremely essential task that, without fail, had to be completed before the archfiend grew wary. Supper and alcohol were a serious business to Mr. Trista.

It had been fourteen years, seven months, and three days since the passing of the matriarch of the household – having died giving birth to the baby of the bunch, as was previously stated; but, there was not one single, solitary second that Laura did not wish her mother to be on the other side of the apartment door whenever she turned the key (although she never actually *met* her birth giver, she would have given anything to make that so). Such utopian improbabilities were immediately contradicted and quelled when she entered the domicile, catching sight of her father, libation in hand, possessing the look of unmitigated abhorrence on his countenance, clearly in a mood of extreme displeasure about something or another not completed to his standards, to which the females of the domicile reaped the ramifications. The boys were seldom found at home, choosing, instead, to take their chances out on the street either selling narcotics, committing felonious acts, or doing whatever it took to make a dollar or two. What money they did manage to make was shared with their sisters, so that they might purchase whatever they desired for themselves, as well as whatever the household required, which – most importantly, to subdue and tranquilize the demon – meant keeping the refrigerator stocked with spirits. Selling drugs was the preferred method of the eldest of the boys, George, who, with his sidekick, Louie Christianson, did so to make most of the household's ends meet; committing burglaries and robberies was Edward's route. Between the two men of the house, the family managed to eat and had sufficient means to clothe themselves.

Laura took her place in the kitchen, joining the sisters who were already hard at work preparing dinner. Both Edith and Victoria shot her a look of discontent, knowing that her tardiness would surely arouse the Beast, who, currently, happened to be reaching for a bottle of suds from the refrigerator just feet away. Fortunately, after menacingly leering at her for a brief moment, he merely retrieved his libation before subsequently sloshing down the hall and into the living room, where he then planted himself to watch one of his favorite shows, Bonanza. Once out of sight and sound, Victoria, while breaking the raw pasta in half and placing it in the boiling pot of water, whispered, "Where on Earth were you? You are so lucky he didn't beat you senseless." She gawped a soul penetrating stare at Laura with her hazel eyes, the color of which was shared by all of the members of the tribe.

"Lucky he didn't beat *all* of us senseless." Added Edith, the matriarch by default. As a result their mother's untimely passing, Edith, the eldest of the females, was thrust into the role of mother hen to the siblings… a role in which she most definitely did not covet. "You really ought to be more considerate, Laura… honestly." Blowing a few strands of her golden bangs out of her face, which had come loose from behind her ear.

"I'm sorry, I just lost track of time, that's all. I didn't do it on purpose."

"Oh, she didn't do it on *purpose*, oh thank heavens. Well, that makes it all better now, doesn't it? I'll take that into consideration when our heads are being sent through the walls. That'll console me now, won't it?" Victoria retorted, condescendingly.

"Jesus, I said I was sorry."

"She's sorry… the hits just keep on coming, don't they?! Like a broken record, this one." Victoria continued to badger.

"Enough. This bickering isn't going to cook the food any faster, and if *he* hears you two locking horns, we'll all be in a world of shit." Edith cautioned, whilst stirring the pot of pasta sauce. "Let's just finish this dinner before *we* end up on the menu. Laura, start the salad, please." She, Edith, frequently found herself assuming the position of referee between Laura and Victoria, being the more even tempered of the three… whereas Laura was the dreamer and Victoria the cynic, Edith was the balance in between, having not the time for anything but attending to the management of the household.

Laura grabbed the tomatoes, cucumbers, and lettuce from the refrigerator, along with the salad bowl, oil, and vinegar from the cupboard, setting out to begin her task. While slicing the tomatoes, she said, "I went to see the castle at Central Park today. It's so beautiful; I wish I could live in it, even if just for a day."

"The castle… *again*? You always go there. You'd think you'd be sick and tired of that old building by now." Victoria interjected.

"Oh, I could never get tired of it. It's magnificent! I could sit there all day looking up at those great big windows, just imagining that I'm up there looking down at that old pond with the turtles down below, swimming and sunbathing… so carefree." The thought brought a smile to Laura's face as she sliced and diced the salad.

"Oh, yeah, right. Like you could be the queen or some crazy thing like that. Sure thing. All hail, Queen Laura the first! Who dares not to bow in her majesty's presence? Off with their heads!" Teased Victoria, mimicking the gyrations of a servant bowing in deference, followed by an executioner swinging his sword down upon an unfortunate soul whose head has parted ways with its shoulders.

"Victoria, you are such a kill joy, you know that? Honestly, a kill joy!" Laura said, petulantly.

Edith smirked at them both, followed by a shaking of her head while continuing to stir the pasta sauce. "Let her alone, Victoria. There's nothing wrong with her pretending to be a princess in a castle. Lord knows I wish *I* could be."

"I don't want to be a princess or a queen." Laura corrected, adding the iceberg lettuce to the salad bowl. "I just want to live in it, is all. I could live in it and not be anything at all. Just plain old me. I don't need much… just a little cot, a blanket, my book, and a few of my things."

"Sounds to me an awful lot like the homeless bum that sleeps in the train station. He's got the same set up, minus the castle. You should let him in on your deal. You two could be roomies." Victoria relentlessly mocked.

"Ugh… You are what's called *incorrigible* in the literary world. You truly are! I don't know why I even bother to share anything with you. You sincerely have no appreciation for the beautiful things in life. You'd just as soon sit in Jefferson Park all day long, smoking your stupid cigarettes and letting all the boys feel on your tits all day long, rather than taking a walk in Central Park or slipping into a museum or the library. Honestly, zero culture and zero ambition." Laura exclaimed, as her face began to flush. She hated to be teased about her fantasies, which was the very reason she preferred not to share them with anyone, *especially* Victoria. There were – in moments of weakness – times that she did invite her sisters into her reverie, but Victoria's satirizing was the consequence of such an error in judgement; and, since Edith was surpassingly occupied making sure the house was in order, it was either take the risk in sharing her thoughts or stronghold her feelings within herself in a proverbial bottle.

"*Encouragable…* yeah, I suppose I could *encourage* people to do a great many things, like I could encourage *you* to stop spending your time doing nonsense like going to castles." Victoria replied, unaware of her error in vocabulary.

"Not *encourageable…* I said, *incorrigible.* You don't even know what incorrigible means. You're so uncouth. You should pay better attention in school… knowledge is power, sis! Try and remember that."

"Whatever, brainiac. I don't need to know what all your fancy words mean. All that reading and school is a waste of time. All I want to do is to get a job and save my money to blow this joint… and if you *really* had any brains in that head of yours, you'd do the same, instead of reading a bunch of stupid books, written by a bunch of dead people." Victoria riposted.

From the the living room, the voice of the cacodemon bellowed, "Keep your goddamn voices down and finish cooking my goddamn dinner! and don't let me have to say it again!"

The girls, now standing motionless, glanced at each other in silence, with mouths ajar, until they were certain that he was not making his way in their direction; thereupon continuing to prepare supper until Victoria broke in, using a more subdued tone of voice. "Why couldn't *he* be the one that died?" Said she, while spreading the butter onto the Italian bread.

"He wasn't always like this. He was actually very… *different* once upon a time." Edith reflected, while keeping her eyes focused on her sauce, which was nearly done. Edith was only three year older than Victoria and five years the senior of Laura; but, she was old enough to remember the days before they were born, and had vivid memories of being told about the coming of her little sisters; news that, seeing as how - at the time - she was the only female, delighted her. Edith recollected how happy her parents seemed when the tiniest of the little sisters was swimming within her mother's belly and tried to hold on to those feelings whenever things were at their bleakest. Although now, nearly fifteen years later, she could find no good reason at all. The man she once knew was something else, something dark and wicked… capricious and malevolent. The complications during delivery caused Marguerite Trista her life, changing the course of events for the family forever.

Laura, keeping her silence, just listened. Having no memory of her mother, she hardly felt it appropriate to interject in conversations having to do with her; instead, she took the plates from the cupboard, put them in their places along with the utensils and drinking glasses, wishing with all of her heart and soul that the place she set for her father would be for naught (fantasizing, often, that he had fallen into a drunken coma, unable to don his presence at the table); but, such high hopes almost never came to fruition; for, outside of alcoholic beverages, eating was his next best divertissement; and so, with great misfortune for the young women, when the food was ready to be consumed, Emilio took his place at the table and, as he customarily would do on any and every other occasion, complained about the cooking – comparing it to the late Mrs. Trista's – thereafter, barking his expectations for the remainder of the day, which were never at all different from any other given day. All the while, the girls remained taciturn, only speaking when spoken to, limiting their replies to one or two words. Grave lessons were learned when – on previous occasions – this particular routine was not adhered to; either one or all of the girls were corrected in the form of a Richter Scale-type backhanded slap. Emilio wasn't an especially Brobdingnagian sized individual; as a matter of fact, one might even venture to say that he was below average in stature... vertically challenged, if you will. What he lacked in vertical loftiness, he made up for in girth; although he would not be considered portly so much as thick and broad, especially about the shoulders, chest, and arms. In any event, his anger – the vexation that lived deep in his now blackened heart after the loss of his wife - made the volume of his physical being a moot point. Although the words were never uttered by her siblings, it was clear that the blame for the loss of Marguerite Trista lay with his youngest offspring, our little Laura. This was acknowledged by all of the brothers and sisters; and, even though not a one would ever verbally admit such a thing, the feelings were secretly mutual amongst them; only Emilio allowed it to manifest into the world of the conscious.

When dinner was complete, all but Laura (who had a bit of

her supper still unfinished on her plate), immediately arose from the table to begin clearing and washing the soiled dishes. This unfortunate act of tardiness in finishing her meal was met with a startling strike to the side of her face from an open hand slap, which sent the five foot three, ninety pound, girl flying through the air, landing her onto to the floor, her body hurling approximately six feet away from the dinner table. "You little shit! You think you're better than anyone else here?!" Shouted Emilio. "Dinner is over!" The girls, who had already commenced washing the dishes, stood frozen by the kitchen sink, unable to turn around, torpefied in fear at what was transpiring now behind them.

Rising in a state of stupefaction, fixing her hair and adjusting her clothes, she replied, "No."

"What the fuck did you say?" He roared, standing above her, posturing himself for a second blow.

"No, I don't think I'm better than anyone else here." She clarified in a soft monotone, lips quivering, her eyes staring directly into his, fighting back the tears with all of her might.

With that, he took hold of her plate, smashing it onto the ground, some of the shards making contact with and cutting her bare feet. What food was left uneaten by her now lay between her toes, as well as the floor and the lower cabinet doors. "Now clean all this goddamn mess up off the floor before I make you lick it up with your fucking tongue. You understand me?!" He growled, making an about face out of the kitchen, now heading into the living room with a fresh beer from the refrigerator in his talons.

The sisters, once assured that their father was a safe enough distance away from the kitchen, rushed to help clean up the aftermath. No words were spoken. No one dared to make a sound for fear of his return, and for fear of being the next victim of his tirade; although, to be quite honest, not one of them denied the fact that Laura was the catalyst of his fury, knowing full well that when *he* was done with his meal, *everyone* was done with their meal. The mighty dictator always had the last word and, apparently, the last bite; so, it was with much perplexity and displeasure that her sisters swept up the fragments of the broken plate and uneaten portions of food. "What in the world were you thinking? I mean, really, are you suicidal?" Whispered Victoria, emptying the first round of the forsaken aftermath in the garbage can.

"Laura, I honestly don't understand you sometimes. You know very well that he hates when we don't finish our food by the time he's done." Edith added, as she vigorously scrubbed the floor with a sponge, on her hands and knees.

"I wasn't hungry. I couldn't very well finish eating if I wasn't hungry."

"Well you'd think that's something you could've told me before I served you. Wouldn't you agree?" Edith lectured sternly.

"I suppose." Said Laura, until Edith – stopping what she was doing to peer into Laura's eyes - expressed her extreme dissatisfaction with the reply; which, in turn, caused Laura to make a minor adjustment to her answer, resubmitting her reply to a somber, "Yes."

Such was the typical day in the life of Laura Trista. Typical days turned into typical weeks which, in turn, became typical years. Two years of abuse in every which way… fathomable and unfathomable. It was only a few days before Laura's seventeenth birthday when a most horrific turning point occurred on a somewhat chilly and overcast autumn day. Her route from school to home was always the same; she would ride the Six Train to Lexington Avenue at 96th Street, preferring to take the walk and glance at the storefronts, rather than exiting at the 116th Street Station, even though it was miles closer. The additional thirty minutes that it took her to get home was worth it, providing her with an escape from the grim reality that was her existence, albeit merely prolonging the inevitable. As she passed the stores, she imagined owning some of the various items that were displayed prominently in the storefront windows. One establishment, which had for sale a multitude of second-hand dresses, exhibited a white gown that, when looked at in a certain light, sparkled most brilliantly and seemed made for a princess. "Much too fancy for me." she thought to herself; an opinion, incidentally, that never seemed to stop her from gazing at the dress every single day, secretly wishing for it never to be sold, wanting always to be able to pay it a visit whenever she passed. As she expelled her customary sigh before bidding the dress adieu, she continued on her way toward the abyss.

The crisp, clean, outside air entered her nostrils and it pleased her, filling her with a kind of peace and tranquility in which, normally, she was without. On any other given day, smells of smog, mixed with other variants of filth, undulated through the New York City air; but not today. Today was as though the Earth were freshly bathed with the intoxicating aromas of chamomile and lavender and it was good. Laura wished she could remain out there forever, but would settle for a few moments more, continuing to take the long way home. As she approached Park Avenue, just before traversing underneath the elevated train tracks, the rumbling sound of the Metro North Train whipping by caught her attention. She wondered, at first, where it was headed; but instantly realized that the destination was irrelevant, wishing with every fiber of her being that she were a passenger, regardless of its terminus. As Laura emanated from under the bridge, she caught sight of her apartment building located in the Taft Housing Development and, looking up, gazed at her window three stories above, emitting another bemoaning sigh. The familiar feeling of revulsion filled her soul, suddenly making everything appear bleak and hopeless… lifeless and dark. It was at this point that, everyday, thoughts of making an about face and going somewhere, anywhere, else ran rampant through her mind like a rush of water from a tumultuous rolling rapid. The mephitic fragrance in the lobby of the building in which she domiciled, coalesced into a distinct odor that only could be found in the *projects*. It was an amalgam of homemade sofrito (a Spanish seasoning containing garlic, cilantro and other herbs and spices), marijuana, and a blend of canine - as well as human – urine and fecal matter. The elevator, to her displeasure, served as a sort of hot box for the aforementioned fusion of scents; thankfully, though, she needed only to endure it for a short time, as the elevator ascended to the third floor.

She fumbled for her key, which lay at the bottommost point of her book bag and, once retrieved, slid it into the cylinder lock, turning it counter-clockwise, gingerly unlatching and opening the front door. With eyes and ears on full alert, as well as a developed sixth sense to his presence, she tuned intently for any sign of the resident Beelzebub, who seemingly had the distinct ability to unsuspectingly soar through the air, as if he were the Lord of Flies himself. Hearing no evidence of his being in attendance, she removed her shoes by the doorway – as was the custom of the household - and proceeded down the hallway towards her room. From the threshold of her room, she could see that his bedroom door was ajar. Warily, and on the tips of her toes, she crept ever so softly towards his room with the intention of reconnoitering her father's lair, praying to the sweet Lord above that he was either not at home or in a state of unconsciousness caused by his bibulousness. There, at the doorway, she stood frozen in absolute horror; for, from the ceiling fan that Mr. Emilio Trista installed many years ago (turning a once dull and somewhat standard light fixture into a pleasant and functional piece, at the behest of his lovely wife), hung her father's lifeless body, his face blue from lack of oxygen caused by the noose wrapped snug around his neck. "Nevermore." She impetuously uttered to herself.

***

The harmonious sounds of the Staple Singers, 'I'll take you there,' rang out from a passing car on a cool September afternoon in 1972, with menacingly dark clouds hovering overhead, threatening an imminent downpour. George Trista, now serving as point man for the *spot,* kept his hazel eyes glued to the aforementioned passing vehicle for any possible indications of bluebirds, *fuzz,* looking to make a *collar* – an arrest. Seeing no sign that the automobile in question was *hot,* as it rolled away northbound down Third Avenue, passed East 115th Street, he gave a quick glance over to his old partner, who stood watch approximately twenty feet to the rear, using the portico of a building as cover. They both exchanged nods to acknowledge each other's visual check-in. George managed to stay off of the radar for the entirety of Louie's stay at BCFB; therefore, now that he and his compatriot were reunited – someone George trusted implicitly – a sense of security and contentment filled his chest, giving him an air of reliance that was not had prior to Louie's return. Unfortunately, this sort of sense of fortitude would prove inadequate on this particular day, owing to the fact that - from a 1970 Cadillac, brown in color, carrying in it four occupants from a rival narcotics gang, one of whom having in his possession a black M1918 Browning automatic rifle - shots suddenly rang out, hitting their intended target, one Mr. Trista, multiple times about the body. Shielded by the columns of the building, Louie managed to evade the showering of ammunition and could only watch in absolute trepidation, as his comrade toppled like timber being cut in the forest, hitting the ground within seconds, breathing the last of his breaths micro-seconds later, one of the rounds managing to pierce his now expired heart.

***

The funeral home was far from overflowing; just a few close friends of George's (mostly of the seedy variety… a delegation of local hooligans wearing their crew flags – bandanas - in the color representing their troop, all of whom brought with them various articles of gang paraphernalia to place inside the coffin, alongside George's corpse). Also in attendance were his siblings, Edith, Edward, Victoria, and Laura who were, as a result of their father's untimely demise, now tenants in a Bronx apartment located in the confines of the South Bronx, cared for by the sister of the late Mrs. Trista, their aunt. Tardy in arriving to the Ortega Funeral home was George's *business* partner and best friend, Louie Christianson. After delivering the gang's esoteric salutation to his associates present at the wake, Louie made his way to clan Trista, expressing his condolences for their recently departed brother. After a brief dialogue with the tribe, he took a seat adjacent to Laura and, not uttering a word, took hold of her hand while gazing at the coffin which housed the deceased. He was always very fond of Laura, and she him. Being such a close friend to George, Louie always thought himself a member of the family, growing close to them all; but, it was always Laura who caught his fancy. He knew the grim tale that was Laura's life and, in spite of its moroseness and morbidity, held an affinity for her nonetheless. Similarly, she possessed a fancy for Mr. Christianson; having had somewhat of a crush on the now twenty year old young man for quite some time – what with her heart proverbially skipping a beat whenever her eyes locked with his. As they sat in silence, hands tightly clasped, they thought of times past and times yet to come. They both, having experienced their own versions of perdition, wanted nothing more than to be free of the tribulations that plagued their young lives up to now, and tacitly - through the sensation that two beings feel when hands become interlocked, similar to that of an excess amount of air flowing into one's nostrils, subsequently rushing down one's chest – expressed this desire and heartfelt emotion to one another. She lay her head on his broad shoulders, shedding a tear; not a tear of sorrow, however, but one of joy. For the first time she felt safe; soon, he would become her protector and she his charge... they would eventually build a life together. Not very long after the tragic death of her big brother, Laura, for the first time in her young life, would finally experience a sort of glorious delectation. Approximately eleven and a half months later, Louie Christianson and Laura Trista were united in holy matrimony in a Manhattan family courthouse on a lovely spring day with Edith and Victoria in attendance as their witnesses (Edward unable to attend due to his incarceration); and – one full earth cycle around the brightest star in the sky later - gave birth to a five pound, seven ounce, baby boy named Justin Christianson.

Story Three

Juliana & Robert

Prejudice is a burden that confuses the past, threatens the future and renders the present inaccessible

- *Quote by Maya Angelou*

Dear Justin,

I received your letter today and I must say, I feel like hanging myself. You have to be the most morbid person in the entire world. I don't particularly enjoy knowing that you feel the world is - how did you so eloquently word it? "A lonely waiting room for the afterlife." Why don't you join a club or even a fraternity? You shouldn't just sit on benches, by yourself, writing letters to me. Don't get me wrong, I enjoy hearing from you; it's just that you'll never make new friends or experience the wonderfully sublime things this world has to offer that way.

You remind me of my dear Robert. Ever since he's graduated from NYU, he feels this sort of emptiness, like he's all alone or something. I keep telling him that he simply needs to get adjusted and adapt to the new chapter in his life. He really needs to move on. Really, Justin, moving on is a very natural part of human nature. Caterpillars become butterflies, Justin, they really do. You're like a soul that hasn't accepted its detachment from the body after death. It just wanders around in purgatory, wondering what in the hell is going on, instead of getting its ass up to the pearly gates. You have no idea that your life has just begun. Carpe Diem, my dear little cousin. Seize the day!

To paraphrase Mr. William Ernest Henley, you are the master of your fate: you are the captain of your soul! The dark part of your life is over now. You need to realize that. Your life starts today! Move on, Justin. Move on to bigger and better things. Experience all the beauty there is out there. Explore, write… whatever! Just don't sit around and become a fossil. You've got a whole life to live and before you know it, you'll be old and pruned and it will be too late. Travel the world damn you, see what the globe has to offer. Just don't forget to send me a lousy t-shirt or postcard or something, okay? I love you, Justin. I know everything will be alright. Take care and write me again, soon.

-   Juliana

(1991 AD)… Juliana, after vigorously rubbing her eyes with the tips of her thumb and index fingers of her left hand, placed the ballpoint pen down onto her ivory white writing table that, incidentally, took up a significant portion of her tiny Georgetown University dorm room, folding the letter into thirds before placing it into the envelope, subsequently affixing a stamp onto the upper right hand corner. She would send the correspondence out before leaving Washington, DC for New York City, which, as it would happen, was in an hour or so. The confidence that exuded throughout the letter did not transfer over onto her countenance, as was apparent from the deep, dark circles beneath her hazel eyes, appearing as though she had gone into the championship rounds with Iron Mike Tyson; and, her usually fair, rose tinged, skin was now bilious, bordering on a yellowish-green. Robert, her boyfriend, had not been quite the same since graduating from New York University with his bachelor of science degree in economics, discovering that such levels of schooling, nowadays, held the equivalent to that of a ninth grade education, albeit even from a prestigious institution such as NYU. Contributing to his melancholy was the fact that he could not secure employment with the numerous firms in which he interviewed, leaving him no choice but to consider moving out of his studio apartment in White Plains, New York, to make a prodigal son's return to the three-bedroom domicile currently still inhabited by his parents, located at Co-Op City in the borough of the Bronx. Needless to say, this is a thing that sent Robert into a reprehensible clime of the doldrums… a region that, when once nestled there, was nearly impossible to ascend. Juliana packed a small duffel bag – just a few shirts and a couple of jeans; an extra pair of black and white converse sneakers; a fist-full of panties and socks; and her hair and make-up products – subsequently departing the campus to the Metro North train station where she would catch the one thirty-five, in order that she could be at her dear Robert's side during his time of need.

***

(1983 - 1988 AD)… Growing up in the Bronx - Co-Op City to be more precise - for Robert, had not been the dismal, trepidatious, experience that most residents of that particular borough experience for two reasons; one, Co-Op City was considered a haven wherein the demographic make-up consisted predominantly of elderly Jewish folks, all of whom could be found, on any given day, planting themselves all about the spacious grassy grounds, resembling - from his parent's three bedroom apartment that sat fifteen stories high – flocks upon flocks of osprey in respite. They sat on their lawn chairs ostensibly by the hundreds, creating an exceptionally non-threatening and most placid atmosphere of a retirement community; and, two, Robert was fortunate enough to have both his parents present under the same roof – as opposed to the broken family structures that were slightly more omnipresent in that particular geographical location - and was always provided with a circumambience of love and support, being given every possible opportunity to succeed... or at least, provided with the tools that one needs for such an endeavor. Originally from the South Bronx (this location being a truer representation of what one might conjure up in ones head at the mention of this borough through another's lips), his mother and father worked diligently day and night - and everything in between - to break free from the bowels of that hell, settling into this oasis of sorts. Upon their initial arrival, they found that they were one of the first African-American families to discover this whole new world, so to speak, and – at the onset – were a bit taken aback at the egregious welcoming – or lack thereof – that they received. It wasn't quite a matter of any type of physical confrontation which plagued their minds, so much as the racially motivated innuendos which flew freely out of the mouths of the natives, who were less than thrilled at the advent of the newcomers. Numerous and frequent calumnies of acquiring public assistance to be able to live amongst the more fortunate working class was an especial favorite; often masking the contumely directed at Robert with audaciously passive-aggressive affronts... one such barb, in sum and substance, was how his parents were so very lucky to have been able to utilize government funding to secure their apartment. This was, by the by, a complete farce. Robert's father was employed by the New York City Transit Authority as a motorman and his mother was a director at a reputable law firm in Midtown, Manhattan; however, such things were to be expected back then, in an era filled with ignorance and misguided prejudices stemming from a lack of parental guidance, as well as social education, and failed to break the young man's spirit… most times.

The years that had come and gone provided many onerous tests of Robert's character and that of his will. He frequently struggled to check his inner most impulses and desires to literally beat back his tormentors; those whose small, uneducated, minds gave them occasion to call Robert out of his name, appallingly replacing it, instead, with variants of the root word, *nigger.* "Hey, little nigg"; or, "Look everybody, the little nigglet is here." Sometimes these young hooligans would get creative, utilizing words that they could only have acquired from either an older generation of clueless denizens or perhaps some cinematic presentation of *Roots*, in which the moral of its tale was apparently lost upon the mindless lot. "Get over here, *coon*, and fan me with your notebook, I'm hot" or "Hey, are your parents *Uncle Toms* or something? Why the fuck did they move around here? Don't they know they ain't white?" One particular day, on a chilly March afternoon after school, five middle school-aged young boys – one of whom happened to be our dear Robert - disembarked the school bus while engaging in a heated argument regarding a matter of the utmost importance, as a 1983 Cutlass Supreme, emanating 'Maneater,' by Hall and Oates from its speakers, awaited the cargo from the bright yellow conveyance to unload.

"Man, there is no way that Spider Man can whoop Iron Man. No way. Iron Man has all kind of weapons *and* he can fly." Andrew, a very corpulent young lad, stated to the group, moving his fiery red bangs away from his heavily freckled face.

"Motha Fucka, don't you know that Spider Man has super strength because he was bit by a radioactive spider? He ain't ordinary… and his webs is super indestructible." Answered Matthew, a lanky boy with skin as pale as untouched snow, who, having a propensity to pronounce certain consonants with a protruding and pointed pink tongue, caused a projectile of saliva and food particles (containing, incidentally, bits of his undigested lunch of tuna fish and corn chips) to fly from his mouth and onto his interlocutors.

"Dude! *Say* it, don't *spray* it!" Scolded Brian, a vertically challenged little tyke, barely standing at four feet tall, with blonde, bushy hair that encompassed most of his physical being, now shielding his face with both of his hands in an attempt to prevent any of the aforementioned shrapnel from entering any of his orifices.

"Guys, none of that stuff about Iron Man and Spider Man even matters because *everybody* knows that Superman can beat every single one of them." Interjected Robert, confident in his claim.

"Aww man, what are you even talking about?" Matthew broke in, quite perturbed. "Superman ain't even in this conversation because he's *DC Comics*. That's a whole different universe from *Marvel Comics*!"

"Yeah, stupid ass. We ain't even talking about *DC*." The portly one, Andrew, shouted.

"Hey, man, take it easy. What's with calling me a stupid ass? It's just my opinion, that's all." Snapped Robert.

"Well it's a fucking dumb ass opinion." Retorted Andrew, now turning his body in Robert's direction in an aggressively posturing manner, mere inches away from his face.

Robert extended his hand outward - similar to that of a running back attempting to avoid being tackled - to reclaim the social distance that was taken from him by Andrew and replied, "Dude, go and eat a Twinkie or something, you know you get all bitchy when you haven't eaten." Robert took exception to his opinion being railroaded and, furthermore, failed to appreciate Andrew's pugnacious approach in the matter.

"Oh yea, well at least my family wasn't slaves, fucking stinky ass nigger!" was the *out of left field* reply given by Andrew, which had no bearing or connection to the topic at hand, completely stunning the entire coterie.

Most days, this kind of verbal assault would be allowed to slip by, owing to the fact that one must pick and choose one's battles; for, if one were to skirmish for every slight received, life would be an endless, bitter war with little to no hope of coming to a resolution in one's foreseeable lifetime... however, this wasn't one of those days. With the acceleration of a Peregrine falcon, Robert pounced mercilessly upon his prey, knocking him to the ground, delivering blow after blow to the left and right jaw - and temples - of one Mr. Andrew Wojcik, while vociferating, "What did you call me, white boy?! Say it again... say it again!"

"Fucking stinky, fucking ass, fucking nigger!" was the less than eloquent reply from his calorically challenged, dyspneic and bloodied, opponent in between the strikes to the head.

The pugilists rolled to and fro, exchanging strike for strike, flipping and flopping, twisting and turning, causing a crowd of fight fans to gather around, whilst Matthew and Brian stood helplessly amongst them in unmitigated amazement at the sight of their two chums engaged in a bare knuckle, mixed martial arts match that could have rivaled any of the professional sort. This contest would end up with no victor; for, the long arm of the law appeared, mercilessly putting an end to the clash of the tiny titans. The arrival of the 45th Precinct officers, like a can of bug spray to a midge, caused the audience to take off in every which direction; therefore, all that was left of the brawl were the original players, two of which – the combatants – were being held by the collar of their shirts and given the riot act, as it were.

"What are you two little hoodlums doing scaring all the old timers with your bullshit?" Scolded one of the officers.

Never breaking eye contact with Andrew, Robert – in between his gasping for air – replied, "Nothing officer, it's nothing. Just a misunderstanding is all. Nothing else."

"Is that true, slim?" The other officer asked of Andrew. "All is well between you two retards?"

"Like he said, officer, just a misunderstanding." Answered Andrew, also depleted of oxygen, now fixing his eyes down upon the ground.

"Well it better be, because if you two meat-heads make us come back here, its gonna be a very different outcome, believe me." Warned the officer, before releasing his vice-like grip, allowing the combatants to go free upon their own recognizance. Such was the way in which things of that nature occurred, for Robert, when the proverbial shit hit the fan during those days in Co-Op City; it was all good until it wasn't… an unfortunate way of life.

A few years had come and gone since that day, Robert now in the ninth grade and attending Truman High School, which was the zone school for students residing at Co-Op City; but, make no mistake about it, Truman – in those days of yore – was linear to any of the top notch private schools during the years in which Robert received his education therein. Being an honors student in mathematics, as well as in science, all within the very first year, he established himself as an intellectual scholar, receiving grades no lower than an A (With the exception of that singular time in which he was given a B+). This paltry grade, that of the B+, occurred only once and was owed to the fact that his academic strength in the areas involving the arts were less than superior… he could write prose just as well as the next fellow; however, he could not wrap his head around poetry, anything not involving concrete facts, or things which could not be proven and tested; ergo, Shakespeare never stood a chance. One would not be too far off in accusing dear Robert of being a stoically unromantic individual, which is the point being driven home in the particular matter at hand. Be that as it may, what he lacked in romance, he more than made up for in other, more pragmatic ways; such as, loyalty to those whom he cared for deeply – which could, very well, be envisioned as somewhat of a romantic notion, if one pondered on the thing long enough.

One example, solidifying the aforementioned point, comes to mind in which Robert displayed a sort of chivalrous loyalty by defending the honor of his high school acquaintance's beau. It was an unseasonably warm October day, at around three in the afternoon, shortly after class was let out for the day, when Robert's fealty was put to the proverbial test. Truman High School, as was previously mentioned, served as the zone school for young men and women who resided in Co-Op City. Now, one must understand that students living in Co-Op City, its grounds being rather spacious, either lived very near to the institution or, conversely, at some distance. Those whose abodes were at a stretch either rode a conveyance home or, if not unnerved by somewhat of a hike, would set off on foot – which, at the furthest most point, could amount to a half-hour walk, depending upon how sizable ones strides happened to be. Robert, preferring not to be imprisoned inside of a bus, filled with unruly and – in some cases – noxious smelling human beings, often chose the latter. On this particular day, as Robert trekked home, along with his friend, Thomas - as well as Thomas' love interest, Rachel - a group of approximately ten, perhaps even more, nefarious young hoodlums crossed their path. As most adolescents do (especially those who find themselves in large groups and having far too much idle time), these *would be* gangsters began to heckle and chant at the three. "Oh, well, now would you look at this! What have we got here?" Yelled one of the thugs. "I see you two got yourselves a slave?" He continued – now with a raised voice directed at Thomas and Rachel (who, this historian neglected to mention, were of a lighter skin color, in comparison to their young African American companion, which is to say that Thomas was of Anglo-Saxon heritage, and Rachel of Puerto Rican descent on her mother's side of the family) – making reference to Robert, who – being somewhat accustomed to such juvenile and ignorant statements – was willing to let the barbarians be; therefore, continued walking, offering no retort.

"I seen a sex video like this, boys!" Interjected a second thug. "What we got here is called a cuckold. They scraped this nigger out of the gutter, so he can fuck the white slut while her man watches!"

This, Robert would not tolerate… as was alluded to before, he possessed a sort of chivalrous romanticism that prevented him from allowing such a slight upon the fairer gender, in this case, Rachel. A woman's honor was at stake here, and it could not go unpunished. In a move that could only be rivaled by the mighty Greek demigod, Achilles – as portrayed by a strapping Brad Pitt in the cinematic presentation of 'Troy' - Robert leaped into the air, cocking back his right arm whilst, simultaneously, balling up his fist and, as he descended from above, extended his aforementioned right arm with the force of a cannon – fist still closed tight – connecting with the nose of one of the thugs, splitting it in half, breaking the bridge instantly, much to the absolute stupefaction of Rachel and Thomas, not to mention the apodeictic dismay of the *Axis Powers*. This spectacular move, only witnessed, at any other juncture, solely in the ring of some professional wrestling match, was followed by a roar of "oooo's" and "ooohhh's" from the crowd of on-lookers around them. The small victory was short lived, however; for, after the initial shock of the thing wore off, the remaining nine or so goons wasted no time avenging their fallen comrade. Within a matter of mere seconds, Robert and Thomas found themselves, much to their disapprobation, at the fundament of a pile of especially enraged associates of the fallen collaborator, receiving numerous kicks and punches to various parts of their bodies, all the while a vexed Rachel could be heard screaming at the top of her lungs and seen wildly, yet quite fruitlessly, slapping, with all of her might, at the backs of the pack of wolves, her diminutive hands having an effect equivalent to that of a gnat incessantly buzzing around a herd of elephants.

The beating, which seemed to go on for hours, ended just minutes later as the sounds of police car sirens could be heard approaching from the distance. How Robert and Thomas arrived home was an anecdote only Rachel would have had the wherewithal to narrate, due to the fact that the boys lost all memory of any happenings to have occurred somewhere in the middle of the thrashing, what with having been wailed upon repeatedly about the face and head to the point of mild amnesia. According to Rachel, a few good samaritans aided her in bringing her champions to the apartment in which she domiciled, which was, incidentally, a bit of a distance from where the two of them were pummeled. Once there, she nursed them as best as she could by placing warm compresses on their bruised and battered foreheads, gently patting the open wounds that the two sustained in battle with peroxide water. Moments subsequent to this, a voice could be heard expressing sheer trepidation and bewilderment. "Oh my God, Rachel, what in the hell? What happened? Who are these people?" That's when, right then and there, Robert saw what appeared to be an apparition - an angel descended from heaven – hovering high above him. Like Aphrodite herself, a vision of absolute perfection, absolute flawlessness, looked down upon his bloodied countenance while simultaneously interrogating her sister, who just so happened to be the elder of the young lady making the inquiry about the madness going on in the living room at the present moment.

"Juliana, relax. Stop screaming. This is Thomas, the guy I told you about a million times, and his friend from school, Robert." Rachel replied, accidentally abandoning a soiled wash rag over Thomas' face, as she focused her attention on her irate younger sibling, explaining the tale that led them to this instance in time.

"Well," said a now subdued Juliana, after learning the entirety of the tale, "we had better get our weekend warriors cleaned up and out of the house before daddy comes home and finishes them off… and us for that matter. You know how he would feel with boys being in the house… albeit maimed ones." As she tended to the wounds of the star struck Robert, who – not for a single, solitary moment – took his eyes off of her hazel-green eyes, which made him ponder the warm waters near a tropical island, gently undulating against the white sands of its beach. Her light brown hair fell gently across portions of her face, cascading down to the tips of her shoulder as she leaned over to tend to his scrapes, causing him to imagine a cascading flow of drizzling sweet caramel… smelling equally as sweet, he thought to himself. It was love at first sight. On that day, one of the worst days of his life, he bore witness to the most winsome creature he had ever had the great fortune to lay his eyes upon.

Juliana Christianson, back then, attended the Walden School, located at 88th Street and Central Park West, in New York City. Walden was considered a progressive high school and, oddly, the students were allowed to address their educators by their first names to enhance the wholistic atmosphere of the institution. The idea of this unorthodox kind of learning was to remove any barriers between student and teacher, so that the root of the lessons would be the focal point… and it worked; therefore, was not questioned; that is, with the exception of anyone outside the safety of the borders of the building, which is to say, anyone who was not connected or associated in any way, shape, or form with the school. Most of the time, this was anyone that Juliana conversed with on matters of importance, a time when she exercised this free spirit, so to speak, during any such aforementioned discussions. During these intense dialogues, young Miss Christianson would make her point abundantly clear in a manner which not many interlocutors were willing to accept or tolerate. Her father, Julian Christianson – her namesake, minus the 'a' - affectionately referred to her as a 'tough cookie,' a term of endearment that she welcomed with open arms; although, to the patriarch, this was not always meant to be the complement in which his youngest daughter received it. Her elder sister, Rachel, was more of an observer and less of a dialogist; thus, she typically bore the brunt of any unpleasant situation without so much as a peep; instead, internalizing it for storage, or armory, if you will, in her cerebellum to be used at a later, more tactically advantageous, opportunity.

Growing up, Juliana was known as *Juliana the super genius* or *Juliana the bookworm*. As far as anyone could recall, she gravitated towards the quest for knowledge. Many members of the immediate and extended family predicted she would become something great… first woman president? First woman to land on Mars? Perhaps a renowned scientist who discovers the cure for every disease under the yellow sun? And all of this was solemnly declared by the ripe old age of six years old… commencing in the first grade and right up to Walden (at the point of this chronicle), she remained right on course to being a model student. Superior student. Her grades never slipped below an A, in spite of the mental anguish it caused not only her, but everyone who had the misfortune to be within sight and sound. There were a few times when, after studying for hours on end, she would collapse out of sheer exhaustion from the hours upon hours, days upon days, months upon months, of rigorous reading, writing, and calculating. This minor setback, merely serving as a speed bump on a residential street wherein one simply slows down just enough to avoid serious damage to their vehicle, but quickly accelerates once they are clear of the obstacle, never managed to alter her course; full speed ahead and onto the next task. It was on these grounds that the world stood still, as it were, when it was discovered that she and Robert had become an item. No one, the exalted and omniscient Nostradamus included, could not have predicted such a coming... to even conceptualize, if only but for a fleeting moment, that the girl whose only love, only passion, her dear, sweet devotion to education, would have made room for that of another would surely have been perceived as a delusion of grandeur; but, somehow, Robert accomplished this feat, penetrating the unbreakable force shield around the heart of the young woman, and they became an item of exclusivity shortly after the previously journaled melee that lead to their initial meeting. *C'etait le destin*, if the reader will permit.

The unforeseen relationship was not without its challenges; some within their control and some not. One of the most difficult, not within their sovereignty, were the provocations the two had the misfortune to endure when out in public. The slanderous comments hurled their way by onlookers who took exception to a bi-racial couple so openly showing affection in public – such as they frequently did - was a perennial and cumbersome phenomenon. These displays of tenderness in the open were not in any way meant to offend, but unconsciously brought forth by the true and very real emotions felt by the young lovers as they happily strolled about, holding hands and delivering to one another tiny pecks to the lips here and there... much to the chagrin of certain pedestrians who happened to cross the path of our teenage sweetheart's Xanadu. In most cases, stares and muffled snide, untutored comments were the worst of the spurns, which grew to become commonplace and somewhat white-noise, heard only in the bottom-most levels of their consciousness. "Can you believe they do it right out in public for everyone to see?" or "They obviously have no shame;" or *"Her* parents must be beside themselves;" or "I'm sure they hide the silverware when *he* comes over," to reproduce but a few. There was a time in which Robert would not have had the temerity to prevent himself from pouncing on these beings of lesser cognitive abilities, knowing that such opining gave the greatest offense to his *querida*, which, to our knight in shining armor, was a most sinful offense of cardinal proportions, as has already been established; however, through the gentle squeeze of Juliana's silk-like hands that were lovingly intertwined with his own, it was esoterically reminded that he was the better man, and he need not entertain the mumblings and ramblings of those lacking the mental wherewithal to discern that the mere shell of a person, the color in which the epidermis lies, is not what determines the being's worth, but it is the soul that dwells within that is the true essence of who we are… and it is this soul – unlike the flesh, which eventually rots away into nothingness – that transcends all things tangible, living everlasting.

One early Saturday afternoon, Juliana and Robert sat quietly in the living room of her parent's place – miraculously with the blessing of the man of the house, having the choice to either accept the union between Juliana and her love, or deal with the ramifications of engaging in a battle of the wills with his baby girl… a skirmish he acknowledged was a sure lose/lose scenario for him. As was their custom, Juliana being unavailable during the remaining six days of the week due to her obligatory compulsion to study ad nauseam, they sat to movies, snacks, and essentially taking the form of vegetables. Perched upon the couch and in front of the television, together they enjoyed Kung Fu theater on channel five, which was currently airing

'The Return of the Five Deadly Venoms.' As the supernatural skills of the martial artists projected from the television set, Robert bore a deeply pensive countenance, not at all giving the slightest attention to the movie, which was unorthodox due to the fact that, besides pepperoni pizza, drizzled with garlic powder and red pepper flakes, watching the spectacularly acrobatic, although quite unrealistic, moves of the Buddhist Monks displayed in these programs was a singular favorite of his. Juliana, who had just then made a comment about ordering out, perhaps – as she imagined was jocularly apropos – some Chinese food, noticed his look of consternation and inquired as to its cause. When he failed to reply, she – who, at that moment in time, was resting her head on one of his shoulders – gazed up at him, realizing that, although his body was present, his mind appeared to be a thousand miles away.

"Robbie." She called out, receiving not so much as a blink of an eye. "Robert!" She repeated in a more commanding tone of voice, removing her head from his shoulder, now sitting straight up.

At this more forceful attempt at grasping his attention, he was snapped out of his daze. "Yea, babe, what's up? You don't like the movie?" Asked he, completely unaware that he had already been espied not giving one iota of attention to the film.

"The movie is just fine. What are you thinking about?" Her brows scrunched together inquisitively.

His brows, in return, as if in startled response to hers, ascended and arched in the opposite direction. "I'm not thinking of anything. I'm just watching the movie. You okay?"

"Me? I'm *perfectly* okay. Are *you* okay?" She responded, fully aware of the volley that was going on.

"Why wouldn't I be okay? Why? Do I not *look* okay?" He was savvy as to the stupidity of the question and was also supremely conscious that this was becoming a fast-paced ping-pong match, but procrastinated in his forthcomingness nonetheless.

Juliana was done with this game of back and forth. "I don't know, you tell me. You're staring off somewhere into space. I asked you a question and tried to get your attention for like an hour, but you just kept staring blankly ahead like a freaking zombie. Like, you didn't even hear my voice. What were thinking about? and don't say *'nothing'* because I know you definitely were thinking about something."

"It's noth -" he began, but quickly put a screeching halt to his intended locution, hesitating for a brief moment to collect his thoughts. "It's really *not-a-thing*." He finally replied, breaking up the root word into three separate words, hoping this would appease his interrogator into ceasing and desisting the current inquisition.

"Are you thinking of another girl? Is that it? Is that what you're doing?" She said, now with raised voice, not really believing that to be the case, knowing full well that Robert was not capable of committing such an act of atrocity, nevertheless using it as a war-craft tactic of sorts… as a method of extracting from him the information she wanted. His life was devoted to two things, his studies and *hers-truly*; and, without a shred of doubt on his end, he knew her devotions to be one and the same. It was due to this concrete, inarguable, fact that he only need respond exactly in the way that he did, which consisted of a sideways half-glance and scrunching of his lips, along with a disapproving shake of his head... no verbalization necessary. She continued, "Babe, you have to be able to communicate with me. That's how grown-up relationships work. If we don't learn how to trust and talk to one another, it's not ever going to prosper... *we* will never prosper."

He knew she was right; but, merely knowing that one speaks the truth does not always motivate the other into baring their soul. He tried to stall. "I know that. I *always* communicate with you when something is bothering me. I don't want to trouble you with this one, is all. It's nonsense. Not even worth a second of your time. Honestly."

"First of all, not *always*, because, technically speaking, that would include right now, which we can clearly see isn't happening; secondly, nothing you say – nothing that is on your mind – would bother or trouble me... not in the least; so, cut the bullshit and tell me what the hell is going on in that head of yours?"

"I'm just... I'm just sick and tired of dealing with all the bullshit." He said, finally caving in.

"What bullshit? What are you -"

"The bullshit." He interrupted. "Just all of it. All of the looks we get when we're walking together out in public; the racial comments; the way people stare with faces of fucking disgust, like they'd lynch me if somebody went and told them that it was okay to do it."

"Babe, what's bringing this on?" She leaned into him, gently placing her hand on his knee, caressing it back and forth with her thumb. "Why are you -"

"Because I'm tired of it, Jules. I'm sick and tired of it."

"I know you are; I am, too. But what can we do about it? Are we going to tell off everyone that stares at us or beat up everyone who makes a rude remark? We have to just ignore them and live our lives."

"Who's *we*, Jules? There is no *we*. *You* aren't the one they're looking to hang from a tree if they had the chance. *I'm* the one they truly can't stomach. *I'm* the one who they don't want in *'their'* neighborhood, dating one of *'their'* neighborhood girls."

"I understand that -" Juliana said, now gently taking hold of his forearm.

"Understand?" He interjected, obstinately breaking free from her touch. "What do you understand? What could you *possibly* understand? All my life, all I've ever known is the contempt that people, *your people*, feel when I walk by or enter a store or whatever the case may be…. thinking I'm gonna snatch their purses or steal something from their stores… what do you understand about *that*?"

"Okay, first of all, they're not *my* people. I think you're forgetting that I'm half Puerto Rican."

At this, Robert rolled his eyes up, practically into his eyelids. "Girl, you are half white and half *even whiter*. There's nobody that looks at you and sees anything but your snow white skin and your emerald green eyes."

Juliana chuckled at what she assumed was a comical, satirical, break in his anguish and, in thinking this, began to apply a caressing touch against the back of his head, to which he responded by shaking her off and standing erect from the couch. "I'm serious. This isn't a joke, Juliana."

"Babe, I don't think it's a joke. I was laughing at your silly '...half even whiter' comment. I don't want to fight, I just want us to enjoy our one day off before we return to our weekly grind. Please, babe, sit down and lets not ruin our day." She implored, motioning for Robert to return to her side by patting the forsaken space on the sofa that was abandoned by him.

"Look, I… I just need some time to myself. I just need to be alone and think right now." He declared, with a look of angst on his countenance, passing both of his hands over the top of his head, subsequently gripping the back of his neck, feeling a tension headache coming on.

"Seriously, babe? You're going to seriously let this ruin our day?"

"Hey, I'm sorry my personal issues of being black is ruining your day." With this comment, Juliana reacted only by sinking her body all the way back onto the couch, folding her arms across her body whilst shaking her head, fixing her eyes onto the floor, saying nothing. Robert then continued, "You know what, I can't even begin to explain this to you. This is *exactly* why I didn't want to get into it. This is *exactly* why. I knew you wouldn't get it. I *knew* it. You could never understand what I'm feeling… what I'm going through. How could you?" He inhaled and exhaled, looking up at the ceiling before continuing. "Listen, I need to get out of here."

"Where are you going?" She inquired, not altering her posture, her eyes still locked upon the floor.

"I don't know… just out." And with that, he grabbed his blue Levi's jean jacket and stormed out of the front door.

Once outside the apartment building, the fresh, brisk air slapped him in the face like a disciplinary blow from a scorned parent; and, once exposed to the oxygenated air, he almost instantly regretted the squabble with Juliana. He knew very well that the feelings which dwelt inside his chest – feelings similar to that of a volcano, whose boiling lava is set, at any given moment, to eject its lethal scourge upon the Earth, along with all the inhabitants – were not, in any way, directed towards her; she, unfortunately, was simply collateral damage at that point. And, truthfully speaking, in his defense, he did make an attempt at deflecting her inquiry… more than once, if memory served him correctly. She pressed him, in spite of his denials that there was something on his mind. She egged him on, wanting to know what he was thinking; therefore, it would stand to reason that she had a fault in the matter. Yes, that's it, he was not a completely guilty participant in the thing; she was part owner of the contretemps. This is what ran through his mind as he walked around the large, sinuous, path that jutted alongside a part of the Hutchinson River; which, by the by, gave off a pleasantly gentle and soothing aroma of the marine life that dwelt within its waters.

He often walked this path when he wanted to clear his mind of any burdensome thoughts that plagued his mind. When he was younger, he would ride on it for hours with his bicycle, all by himself, fantasizing that he was an astronaut, and his bike a rocket ship, that would lead him on all sorts of adventures to far and distant worlds. He wished for those days again as he traversed along the winding road, gazing at the rows of dark green, agreeably sweet smelling, pine trees, along with the picturesque American Maple trees, standing proud and tall above him with their brown, red, and yellow leaves cascading down onto the floor that lined the path in which he roamed. He watched as the squirrels and birds scurried about, dipping and dodging around him, on the hunt for nuts and berries to be stored for the long winter ahead, and marveled at the creepy critters that crawled passed his feet, their backs mounted with provisions, swiftly and with great agility wishing to avoid being squished under his boots, a wish he merrily granted. Nature. It all made sense when looking at the world from their prospective. No race, no religion, no politics. Just the unadulterated, natural beauty that was truly a paradisal representation of God's great heaven above… man was the only real flaw, he concluded. The excerpt, '*Man, the most selfish of all animals, the most personal of all creatures, who believes the earth turns, the sun shines, and death strikes for him alone, - an ant cursing God from the top of a blade of grass,*' from one of his favorite novels, *The Count of Monte Cristo*, came to mind. Man, with his prejudices and his rules and his laws and his contradictions. A plague upon the earth is what they are; just a microbial germ that infests and destroys the beauty and innocence of the First through the Fifth days of Creation – the Sixth day, the day in which the animals and humans were forged, was clearly a misstep on *His* part… the animals were the exception, the humans a clear error in judgement. After mere seconds of having such blasphemousness thoughts, Robert quickly apologized to Him, sealing the apology with numerous signs of the Cross, for fear that such postulations would surely earn him a corner office in Tophet, with a clear view of the Acheron, Cocytus, Phlegethon, Styx, and Lethe… a thought that made him shudder.

As Robert continued to saunter the path, a group of young men – known collectively as 'the bad white boys,' a name bestowed upon them by the few people of color that made their abode in Co-Op City in those days – began to make their way towards him. Coming to the conclusion that it was too late to alter his course, Robert internally battened down his hatches, preparing for a worst-case scenario confrontation, as his sympathetic nervous system entered into 'fight or flight' mode, his adrenaline causing his heart rate to increase and beads of sweat to emerge from the top of his brow. The 'bad white boys' were well known for unleashing hell upon their prey, mostly to people of the darker shaded persuasion; and, thus far, never had to answer for their criminalistic behavior, due to the fact that no one had the nerve to drop the proverbial dime on them, which is to say, no one told on them. As they drew nigh, their evil smirks became distinctly visible, which made their sinister intentions abundantly clear. One thing was for certain, they were not looking to make a friendly acquaintance with the likes of Robert, and if the situation were more favorable for a Sun Tzu-style tactical withdrawal of some sort, he would gladly, without any form of hesitation, have preferred that option. Alas, retreat was not to be, as he was outnumbered seven to one with his back to a fence that lead to the river; withal, to make matters significantly worse, he was currently being flanked on all sides by the advancing platoon… the only way was forward.

"Well, well, well… if it isn't the black part of the zebra!" Shouted one of the antagonists, causing the rest of his cronies to burst out into hysterics at this less than witty asseveration.

"Yea, where's the white half?" Added another.

"The good half!" Shouted a third. Again, they all fell into a fit of laughter, resembling a pack of wild hyenas cackling and ululating before devouring their kill.

"Yea, where's that fine piece of ass? that white girl we always see you walking around with?" They continued to poke and prod.

"In the sack with a nice, wholesome, white guy if she knows what's good for her!" One of the brigands replied, referring to Juliana, whom they had seen with Robert on previous occasions... this last gibe being uttered whilst he licked and bit the bottom of his lip at the thought of her, as though she were a tasty dish.

"Man, if she *really* knew what was good for her, she'd be riding *this* white stallion." One of the others added, while gyrating his crotch back and forth, simulating a most gruesome sexual innuendo.

Angered at the fact that their remarks drew not the slightest reaction from Robert, the larrikins began to intensify their affronts with pushes and shoves; some of them throwing whatever objects lay before them on the ground, such as rocks, twigs, &c., giggling all the while. "You deaf, monkey? You need us to throw you a beating or something?" An ignoramus inquired, following up with a shove from his opened palm to the side of Roberts head, commonly referred to as – utilizing the vernacular of the 1980s - a *mush*.

"I think we oughta teach this spade a lesson, huh boys?" Said one of them, cracking the knuckles of his fist.

"I think you're right." Another replied, subsequently followed by a round-house style kick to the chest of Robert, who was abruptly sent plummeting to the ground, gasping for air. This act of barbarism was coupled with a few kicks to the legs and stomach by the lot.

Robert continually attempted to pick himself up from the ground; however, every attempt made by him was met with some strike or another, sending his battered body back down once again, furthering their kicks, pushes, and punches to various portions of his person. What was actually only a minute or two, felt like hours to Robert… when would it end? Would it ever? 'No,' he conceded, coming to the conclusion in his mind. If not this physical drubbing, the lambasting would certainly never cease; therefore, why fight? why not just submit to the inevitable? There was no hope for him… no hope for humanity. The best, most pragmatic solution, he concluded to himself, was to surrender; surrender his body and surrender his soul. Just then, just before he thought his physical being could not possibly endure another strike, he began to see – one by one and two by two – the 'bad white boys' go down like pins in a bowling alley. As if angels were sent from heaven, descending upon the Earth to serve as his protector, he witnessed Thomas and some of his allies taking hold of the chavs, placing them in various World Wrestling Federation headlocks, along with other similarly agonizing mixed martial arts holds, resembling a mighty python squeezing the life out of whatever had the misfortune to be in its grasp; which, eventually, once released from these painfully compressing positions, sent them scurrying in different directions in an *every man for himself* withdrawal from the battlefield – aided along with taunts of, "Yea, that's right! you better run!" and "Do something now! you pussies!" in addition to other similar catcalls from the two cheerleaders and moral supporters of the blitzkrieg, Rachel and Juliana, the latter rushing to her downed prince who had received multiple, but minor – for the most part – battle wounds (it would be learned later that he had, in fact, incurred a hairline fracture in his left ankle).

"We seem to keep finding each other in these precarious situations, friend!" Said Thomas, with a triumphant smile, as he grabbed hold of Robert's arm, aiding Juliana in raising her fallen warrior from the floor.

"You know how I love these midday beat-downs." Robert replied, taking hold of Thomas' arm, returning the smile, wincing and groaning all the while, grabbing on to his rib area as he was being hoisted to his feet, favoring his right leg, as his left felt the pain of the above mentioned minor fracture.

"Yes, for sure… puts hair on your chest!" Thomas joked.

Robert laughed, but quickly groaned once more, clutching his ribs. "Don't make me laugh, it hurts too much."

"Is it broken? Are any of your ribs broken?" Worried Juliana, gently feeling around for any sign of severed bones; although, other than an obvious indication – such as an actual bone protruding onto, or out of, his skin – she would not have the slightest inclination of what a shattered rib or ankle bone might feel or look like.

"I don't think so. I think I'm just banged up. I'm fine." And with that, after bidding thanks and farewell to their confederates, the two, Juliana and Robert, took refuge at the customary place of convalescent bandaging and recuperation, the humble dwelling place of Miss Christianson.

It wasn't for a few years, about three years to be exact, until Robert was finally able to discuss his inner turmoil with Juliana. All the painful and confusing thoughts that ran amok in his brain about who he was and how he felt about it all finally surfaced. Throughout the years, a range of emotions swirled around in his mind about who he was and *why* he was. Why did God have to make me Black? he often thought in anger and resentment. Why couldn't I have white skin and be done with all of the hatred, the resentment, the sideways glances, and the whispering when walking down the street of an *exclusive* neighborhood? Done with all of it, he wished he was. For the rest of his life, he would have to carry the burden of the color of his skin, and the thought of this was almost unbearable. He wanted a *normal* life – whatever that actually was.

It was a pleasant night in September, the gentle breeze brought with it the smell of fresh cut grass and the odoriferous scent brought forth by the warmth of the Hutchinson River, as they sat by a bench, *their* bench, overlooking the water. At around the time they first became an item, Robert had carved their initials, R.S, Loves J.C., along with a heart – as best as a heart can be scribed with a small pocket knife - into the wood of the bench, which had thus far stood the test of time. Many a day and night were spent on that bench; many a kiss stolen; many a debate had; many a quiet clasping of hands. Tonight, as they sat pacifically – her head situated upon his shoulder – he concluded that he would, finally, share with Juliana his animus towards the cruel world, the tragedy that was his reality, the thing that he had been sheltering in the deepest, darkest, parts of his brain… a repression of epic proportions in his world. With only some slight trepidation – fearing that the topic possessed the potential to conjure more of a kind of commiseration, rather than true understanding to his plight, the mere thought of which he loathed, not desiring to be felt sorry for; but, instead, to be completely and totally empathized with - he began his colloquy. "I wanted to tell you something. Something important."

She lifted her head from his shoulders with a look of consternation and stared intently into his eyes. "What is it? What's wrong?"

"It's… it's just something that's been on my mind… my heart… for a long time. I've… I've never really talked about it. Not really. Not the way I *really* feel. I mean, I tried… a few years ago, I tried to talk about it, but I just couldn't. I didn't know how." He stammered, overwrought with years upon years of pent up fervor.

"Talk to me. Tell me. Oh my God, you're trembling, Robbie. What is it?" She inquired, placing one of her hands upon his back, gently rubbing it in circular motions in an attempt to soothe him.

As he made an attempt to bring forth the words, emotion took control; tears began to well up within his dark brown eyes, eventually breaking through the duct and, ever so slowly, falling down upon his ebony skin, a skin which resembled the richness of fresh cocoa. Juliana solicitously took hold of his face, bringing it down onto her chest and kissed the top of his head. A waterfall of heartache and grief began its descent, Robert now engaged in an uncontrollable sob.

"Shh, it's okay, my love. Shh. It's okay." She reassured, as she gently rocked him back and forth, as a mother would a child in distress.

Robert sat up and, after taking a few breaths to calm the waters of his soul, wiped his eyes whilst peering out onto the river with its serene little ripples, which the seagulls undulated upon as they patiently waited for a herring or two to happen by. "I love you, Jules. You know I love you with all my heart and soul… but, you don't know what it's like. You don't know what it's like to be me… or anyone like me. To be a black man in a world where – no matter what advancements society has made or adversities it's overcome – no one accepts you… I mean *truly* accepts you. It's like, you're either dealing with people who detest you or people who just *tolerate* you. The people who detest you… well, sometimes I actually prefer those folks because you know where you stand with *them.* The people that tolerate you… man, you just never know what you're gonna get from those types. Those are the ones that smile in your face and make all kinds of chit chat about this, that, or the other; but, deep down inside, they hope you leave real soon and they hope you don't date their daughter… and they *really* hope you don't move into their neighborhood. Either way, you're not accepted. You're not wanted. You have no idea how lonely I am. Not the kind of lonely where you want to be around everyone, not that kind of lonely. It's the kind of lonely that can't be cured. It's the kind of lonely that never goes away because every step you take, around every corner, everywhere, there's someone or something that reminds you that you're not wanted."

"Is it about the stupid *bad white boys* that time? Robert that was three years -"

Robert interjected, "It's not about them… well, it's kind of about them; but, they're only one little example of what I'm getting at. It's all the things and all the people *like* them. It's the stares that we get when we walk down the street, or in the park, or in the stores, or at the movies, or wherever. It's about the fact that, no matter what I do or where I go, I know what they are thinking."

"Who? What people?"

"Everybody, Juliana! Everybody! You *really* don't get it, do you? You really don't get it. And you know why you don't get it? Because you're white, so you have the luxury of not getting it."

"How many times do I… I am not fully white! I'm also Puerto Rican from a *very* Puerto Rican grandmother. And I have made mention of that many -"

"It doesn't matter if you're Puerto Rican, Jules! Look at you. Light brown hair, hazel eyes, skin whiter than the untouched snow in winter time. Unless you walk around with an *'I am a Boriqua'* shirt on, with an arrow pointing up at your face, there's not a person alive and breathing that would think you were anything but a very pretty white girl…. and even then, they'll probably think you borrowed the damn shirt from somebody! Furthermore, you're not Juliana Gomez, or Julian Sanchez, or Juliana Ramirez. You're goddamn Juliana *Christianson*… how Puerto Rican is *that*?!"

"I can't help my name, Robert, now can I?" Juliana rebuffed, taking offense at his chiding, feeling her culture was being brought into question.

Robert knew he overstepped, so he inhaled a deep breath and exhaled slowly. "I'm sorry. I didn't mean to come at you."

She put the palm of her silken, white hands on top of his, knowing that Robert's intentions were not to injure her in any way. She knew that his heart was in turmoil and she quickly adjusted her countenance to that of a tender leman, broken hearted for her love, wishing that she had the ability… the power… to take hold of his pain and toss it into the Hutchinson River for the seagulls to devour. They sat quiescent, as a flock of Canadian geese – who happened, also, to be residents of Co-Op City, much to the chagrin of any pedestrian who, perchance, took a stroll along the grass where heaps of their green and white excrement lay, ending up all over the bottom of their shoes – flew overhead, heading toward a tiny island that sat in the middle of the river which bore the name of the birds which soared above, Goose Island.

"Robbie, I wish I had the words… I wish I had the power to make it all better… to take away the pain. You're right, I don't exactly know how you feel or what you're going through; but, your pain is my pain, just the same way that your joy is my joy." She paused, gently taking hold of his face, bringing his eyes to hers. "I'm here for you, in good times and in bad times. Don't ever feel that you can't come to me… that you can't share what's in that hard head of yours. People don't always have to experience someone's pain to be empathetic towards it, babe. I don't have to be a beautiful black man to feel your hurt; I only have to love you with all my heart to feel it just as much."

"I know." He said, as he smiled and kissed the top of her forehead. "I know you love me and I know you're always gonna be there for me. And I know when I'm down and out, you're always gonna be there to pick me up, like you always do. I just wish the world was different. I wish it wasn't so full of bullshit that doesn't matter, where a person's skin color has nothing to do with how someone judges you or accepts you. Imagine… just imagine a world like that. I mean, I get it, there are lots of knuckleheads out there doing things they shouldn't be doing and acting like they shouldn't be acting; they're disgusting people and I despise them just the same as the next person; but, what in the hell does that have to do with being Black? I've seen people of every color, race, religion, height, weight, shoe size… I've seen all of them be just as bad; so, honestly, what does it matter what the color of their skin is? Seems to me it's a *class* issue. Seems to me you have *low* class people and *high* class people; and, honestly, that has nothing to do with anything but the *kind* of person you are. You're either a good human being or a bad one; it's as simple as that… it's as simple as that."

"Lord knows I agree with you, love. Lord knows I do." She said, returning her head onto his shoulder. "But, love of my life, this is an issue that mankind has struggled and dealt with from the beginning of time. There has been prejudice and racism since the creation of man. It's who we are as a species… some of us just sort of rise above it by educating ourselves and believing that, after we pass from this world, we will be judged by our actions and are rewarded for our achievements in this place, here on Earth. It's not for us to wish things were different or to sit and wonder and worry about what other people are doing or not doing… even though we know it to be unjust… it's not for us to say or make judgment about that; that's not our job… not our purpose. We just have to be the best people we can be until our fleeting moment here on this little planet comes to a conclusion; then, when our time is up and we're called… then that's when we will finally be happy, truly happy. No more doubts, no more worries, no anguish, no pain. Until that day, you'll just have to be contented by the notion that I love you for everything that you are; a beautiful, strong, intelligent, *classy* man." She concluded, smiling up at him and he down at her.

He heard her words and understood them; but deep down in his heart, he knew that his woes would continue to have a dwelling place in his soul. The ugliness of the world assuredly had not reared its wickedness for the last time; and so, he would, without doubt, continue having to search for that succor within Juliana, and in himself, to push forward in this brutish world; he would attempt to make the absolute best of his life, in spite of its blemishes, and pray to God for better days to come. They sat together for another hour before returning home. In spite of all their worries and troubles, the little blue planet continued to turn; homework was still due and studying had to be done. The hour passed with little conversation; both enjoying the serenity of the water and the innocence and tranquility of the birds who spread wide their wings, gliding carefree across the blue expanse.

***

(1991 AD)… The Metro North train arrived at Grand Central Station at around five thirty-eight. As Juliana traversed the hallway that lead above ground, where she would soon meet her dear Robert, she beheld the beauty of the concourse, with its tremendous arched ceiling and *Beaux-Arts* design which personified the essence of French neoclassicism, along with a mixture of the Gothic and Renaissance periods that she fell in love with while studying European Arts at Georgetown University. She always thought to herself how much she would positively love to visit France and bear witness to some of that amazing architecture one day. She decided that she and Robert would, without a doubt, have to make such a trip very soon. As she continued down the hall, where all of the small businesses displayed their knickknacks through the windows, she happened by a coffee shop, which filled the air with an intoxicatingly sweet odor of coffee beans from all over the world, combining to create an indescribably delicious scent that she could not resist. She entered and bought herself a cup of Cuban espresso coffee that danced on her tongue like the rumba, filling her insides with delight.

As she sipped her java, which, incidentally, was sweetened with a little milk and one sugar, she continued out of the station and onto Forty-Second Street, where the bustle of New York City was in full swing, as a multitude of people could be seen going to and fro in all different directions. A father and mother, along with their two children, walked briskly westward toward the majestic Stephen A. Schwarzman Building – also known as the *main branch* of the New York Public Library, where one could literally become lost in all of its charm and splendor. Juliana spent many a day in that library, pretending she was its caretaker, imagining that all of the literature was hers to do with as she pleased, always enamored by the intoxicating aroma of the thousands upon thousands of books that dwelt in that repository of happiness. In another direction went a couple holding hands, perhaps heading to a trendy restaurant for a nice dinner of lobster, penne alla vodka, and some quiet cocktails; something she planned to do forthwith, just as soon as she and Robert were together. The couple seemed in love as they made their way passed Juliana, stealing kisses from one another and possessing a particular twinkle in the eyes… a twinkle that could only be achieved when one is truly bewitched by a person who holds the proverbial key to their heart. Juliana smiled and shyly broke her stare.

In between it all, she spotted a yellow taxi which pulled up to the curb in front of her. The rear passenger door opened and its occupant, still inside, leaned forward, handing the driver the currency owed for the fare. As Robert stepped out of the cab, he spotted the love of his life who now, with a smile beaming so bright that it could have lighted the darkest of rooms, waved and started toward him. Meeting her halfway, his countenance a reflection of the euphoria which filled his heart and soul, they entered a warm and tender embrace. He picked her up off of her feet, twirling her once around in a complete circle, before planting her back down where they remained for a few moments more, interlocked in each other's arms, simply gazing into one other's eyes, not uttering a word… their two hearts, beating together as one, was the singular language in which they spoke. Not a single care in the world entered their minds, or their souls, as the crowd of people scurried all around them carrying on with their day.

Story Four

Selena

*"I leaned my head back to take her all in. As I beheld her beauty,
I wondered if I could ever possibly truly love someone other than
Judith. I was wondering if that were ever possible because,
one day, I'd like to love again. I knew, though, at that moment,
I couldn't be. I had too much work to do rebuilding myself. I
needed to get reacquainted with myself and it wouldn't be fair to
Selena, or anyone else for that matter, to start something in which
I couldn't commit... I wanted to tell her just how perfectly stunning
I thought she was. I almost did, too, that is, until I changed my
mind. I didn't want to ruin anything by speaking. Sometimes
words, any words, can spoil it for two people who are looking up at
the stars. Maybe I'd tell her a little later, I'd tell her that she was
a gorgeous person- inside and out; I'd tell her how, every time she
called me, she brought my spirits up. I'd tell her how much I loved
that she was always happy and if I were ever able to love someone
else, it'd be her..."*

-        *Justin Christianson, Excerpt from 'Moving On,' Written by
J.L. Caban*

It had been a long and tumultuous career. Twenty years.
Twenty arduous years, filled with joy, heartache, sadness, some
more joy, some more heartache, some more sadness. One could,
at this point, with the utmost ease – however cliché it may appear –
insert a quote… *THE renowned quote*… from Mr. Charles Dickens',
A Tale of Two Cities, "It was the best of times, it was the worst of

times…" because it literally was, at least it was for Selena. Her send-off, or *walkout,* was one of those best of times. She was leaving this confounded place for the last time; after today, she would no longer be an active member of the Police Service, dealing with the tribulations of New York City. At forty-one years old, she had finally made it to the proverbial finish line and would be done, once and for all, with the *job,* along with all of the cynicism and despondency in which it is unfortunately associated. As she climbed into her black Ford Escape, her colleagues – many of whom she no longer knew because, as time goes by, guys and gals either retire, *vest-out* early, get *jammed up,* or pass away – were beginning to trickle back into the Precinct, with only a handful yet waiting for her to pull out of her parking spot and drive away. As the car began to pull off, she gave a final wave to the one or two stragglers that remained and started on her way home. She half smiled, the feeling still very surreal that she was, in fact, now officially a retiree. As she headed up the New York State Thruway, thoughts began flashing through her mind… a collection of memories that had been stored in her head and placed into a corner entrepôt deep in her cerebellum; that is, until this moment.

As the vehicles on the highway zipped passed her at speeds comparable to that of the Daytona 500, she thought of her youth and how much she always admired Police Officers. Growing up in the Pelham Parkway area of the Bronx, she had many opportunities to come in close contact with the Police Department; some experiences were pleasant and some were less than favorable; however, all things being equal, she always held an affinity for them. There was a time, when Selena was about thirteen years old, that the detectives found occasion to bang on her door. It was the kind of banging that, prior to one even having any idea who was on the other side, alerted one to just *exactly* who it was by the sheer manner of the thunderous pounding, which sent a resounding echo throughout the entire apartment. The investigators were searching for one of her friends who had run away from home, not having been heard from in quite some hours. The two officers of the detective squad, who were dressed in suits and overcoats, one wearing a beige fedora with a small red feather sticking out of the brown band that wrapped around the, incidentally, smart looking hat, warned her that withholding information would bring forth the gravest of consequence; and, furthermore, if she had any knowledge as to the whereabouts of the runaway, she had better 'fess up… or else. Selena did, in fact, know of the young girl's whereabouts. Selena did *not,* in fact, divulge the information. She was no rat.

There was another time – a time when she was around the age of fourteen and found herself playing hooky from school - that came to her mind. She, along with a few of her cronies, decided that watching the boys playing handball (as well as participating in a few of the matches, herself), while smoking marijuana and cigarettes, as well as drinking forty ounce bottles of malt liquor and Brass Monkey, was much more important than attending class. Out of nowhere, much to the stupefaction of the truants, officers of the law arrived onto the scene and began chasing the fugitives who, in an *every man for themselves, you can't catch us all* manner, made a mad dash in every which direction. Selena, being one of the unlucky, was apprehended shortly after the mass exodus attempt. As the officer took hold of her by the arms with a sturdy, yet somewhat surprisingly gentle grip, she initially jerked forward with the intentions of breaking free from his clutches, to which he responded by rigidifying his hold upon her, still, quite unexpectedly, not in such a way that discomforted her; it was just enough to render her immovable. "Come on, kid," he implored, "it's over. Let's not fight now, okay?"

Seeing as how she was at a loss for oxygen, having not the stamina to flee from her captor, she settled into his grip, causing the Officer – Officer Newcamb (she could see this was his surname from his silver nameplate beneath his badge) - to retract the squeeze from her arms. "That's better. There's a girl." He said, relieved that the internee accepted defeat, not wanting any part of furthering the pursuit. "Listen, kid, I'm trusting you here. I ain't gonna slap the bracelets on you, but you gotta promise me you ain't gonna take off on me."

"I'm not, Officer. I'm not." She assured him, still attempting to catch her breath, her chest rising and collapsing from the incessant inhales and exhales that, at the moment, she could not bring under control.

"Okay, now. You promise, right? If you break your promise and I have to chase you, I'm gonna be pretty angry… and you don't wanna get me angry, kid. You hear me? I'm trusting you over here, get it? I'm trusting you."

"Officer, I swear, I'm not going to run."

"Okay, sweet deal. Let's go, then."

She was, thereafter, taken back to school and handed off to the dean of students; but, before the Police Officer's departure, he turned to her and said, with a timbre of sincerity, "I ain't never seen you before and that's a good thing. I coulda taken you to the precinct and held you there until yer parents picked you up, but you seem like a good girl that just got caught up in a bad thing. Those guys you was hanging out with today are my regulars, and I can tell you they ain't going anywhere but down. Listen, kid, there ain't nothing for you out there in those handball courts but trouble. Stay in school, go to college, become something great."

"Thank you Officer Newcamb. I know that you're right and I'm going to take your advice… I really am. I appreciate you not taking me to the precinct and all. I really do. My dad would've skinned me alive if he had to walk into a police precinct to get me, so I want to thank you for that. I really, really do." Selena said, with the utmost sincerity; for, her father would most likely have, indeed, rendered her rear end inutile for the purposes of sitting had he been asked to retrieve his offspring at the police station.

"Alright, kid, you're alright. The name is Scotty, by the way. You take care of yourself, now. Don't be afraid to give a wave if ya ever see me around. And just so ya know, I'll be keeping my eye out for ya, so ya better behave!" Warned Officer Newcamb, wearing an endearing smile on his countenance before walking out of the dean's office. That, incidentally, was the last time Selena had ever seen him; which, as he worded it, was *a good thing.*

She had always been fascinated by the *men* in blue (this historian purposely singling out the aforementioned gender; for, at that time, it most certainly was a boy's club, as it were, comprised primarily of males). One other day, in particular, that came to her mind, in which she felt this sort of sense of intrigue towards the protectors of life and property, was inside of the pizzeria on

Eastchester Road and Mace Avenue, approximately two years after the aforesaid interaction at the handball court with Officer Scotty Newcamb. Through the door of the pizzeria, in waltzed two larger than life Officers – figuratively, but not far from literally. At a stroke, Selena was mesmerized, as they both stood at least six feet tall, towering over everyone they passed. These giants entered the establishment, instantly drawing everyone's attention by their mere presence; their eight point caps, complete with shiny sliver metal cap devices, donned their heads; the gold collar brass indicated the precinct in which they hailed and was attached to the collars of their powder-blue uniform shirts; the dark blue pants, creased down the center were held up by their leather gun belts, which showed signs of wear and tear from the grinding years of service on the streets. As if royalty had graced a hamlet of common folk, these men commanded attention and authority and Selena liked it. It was as if the pride that exuded from them somehow projected onto her, causing her chest to expand, her heart to palpitate, and her chin to ascend up high, as they made their way passed her and up to the counter to order their slices of pizza.

As the gendarmes waited patiently for their viands of mozzarella cheese, tomato sauce and dough, she continued to gaze at them in awe… from eight point cap, to the .38 caliber revolver resting in its swivel holster, to the black combat boots containing scuff marks that only accentuated the mystique of these Brobdingnagian gentlemen, she marveled at them. As if in possession of a sixth sense, one of the Officers turned his head in her direction, looking down at the wonderstruck girl - quickly assessing her threat level, as any well trained graduate of the Academy would do, never knowing the who, what, when, where, and how of a thing until it has been scanned and vetted (this skill being accomplished in mere seconds) – and, subsequently, once it was determined that she posed no threat of any kind, delivered to her a warm, benevolent, smile. Like butter on hot toast, she melted within her shoulders, utterly enamored in the officer's beguiling essence, returning the smile with proverbial stars in her twinkling eyes, staring reverently into his.

Selena, incidentally, had not always had the most pleasurable of experiences… such as the time - she being approximately eighteen or nineteen years old and accompanied by a gentleman friend of around the same age (his name escapes this chronicler at the moment; but, thankfully, it bears absolutely no relevance to the account at hand) - upon returning from a nightclub, and now about a mile or so away from her neighborhood, the front driver's side tire to the vehicle in which they traversed was unceremoniously torn open due to an unknown sharp object which had lodged itself within the rubber, depleting the wheel of its air. As the cavalier (Selena's aforementioned unnamed associate) proceeded to exchange the dilapidated tire for a fresh one, a blitzkrieg of some five or six patrol cars, all with lights and sirens blazing, promptly surrounded them, followed by an outpouring onslaught of swarming blue uniforms with their pistols bearing down upon the two unsuspecting youngsters, causing Selena's poor companion to require a change of his Fruit of the Looms ascribable to his body's inability to constrain its bowels. As it turned out, some concerned citizen had called in what she perceived to be a *GLA,* grand larceny of an auto, giving the precise description of not only the car, but of Selena's hot pink tube top shirt, incidentally accentuating her well endowed bosom; form fitting Express jeans; and a pair of DSW black platform pumps… as well as her comrade, whose hair was gelled to perfection, donning a white button-down shirt from the Gap; faded blue, boot-cut jeans from the same establishment; and, a pair of black Doc Marten shoes with yellow stitching around the sole. All of this being explained to her once the situation stabilized, guns making their way back into their holsters. As was already foretold, it certainly was not always the most pleasant of encounters experienced by our young protagonist; however – nevertheless – she held a fascination with the post of local law enforcement, longing to be a part of the brotherhood, as it were, and short of an absolute declaration, Selena's mind was made to do just that. On January first, in the year two thousand and one, she became a sprocket of the *Finest*.

***

It was a mere eyebrow raising transmission at best, nothing more, when – at 8:51 in the morning, approximately five or so minutes after the initial collision - the police radio broadcasted the limited details of the first airplane crashing into the North Tower. "Oh shit, did you hear that? One of the towers got hit by a plane." Selena said to her partner, Kenneth Lockwood, with her two-way radio planted onto her ear – as if in doing so, she would somehow have the ability to hear the garbled chaos more clearly - listening to the clamorous bellows of Officers stepping over each other's voices in a futile attempt at relaying information.

"Ain't da first time and probs won't be the last." Answered her partner, in his Long Island twang, with an air of inanition. Not much could rouse Lockwood out of his insouciance. "Got bombed back in ninety-three. Fuckers set off some kinda car bomb in da lower parking garage in one of dem buildings. Crazy bastards. Didn't work, though. I mean, the bomb went off sure enough; but, it didn't knock da buildings down. Those fuckin' buildings ain't goin' nowhere. The architect built 'em to withstand the worst shit ever. I mean, actually *built* da fuckers to withstand plane strikes, if ya can believe dat. Modern technology, I'll tell ya, boy." At this, the thirty year haggard veteran, who had seen and experienced just enough to compromise the integrity of the bulwark that protects ones mental and spiritual fortress - something in which ten years of psychotherapy could not put a dent - continued to read his newspaper, the sports section, vacuously taking small sips of his lukewarm coffee and large pulls from the cigarette that rested between his calloused fingers.

"Yea, but what about all those people. I'm sure there were a lot of people who got hurt and probably even died with the impact. They're saying it may have been a big plane... like, a commercial airliner." Selena commented, with an tinge of worriment in her voice.

"Population control, kiddo." He replied, only slightly looking up from his chronicle. "Everybody can't live... there's a food shortage, don't you know? Just imagine if everybody in da world lived... nobody ever died, nice and tree-huggy, da way you like it. Just imagine! La-dee-da, la-dee-da, look at all of us humans livin' and never dyin'! Look, look! Millions and millions of people, now fightin' over all da resources in da world. Now what? Huh? Answer me dat, Mrs. *Kumbaya*, Mrs. *let's all get along and live forever*! Thanks ta you, now grandma can't have her tea and biscuits, because it all ran out. And do ya know why? Well? Do ya? I will enlighten you. It's because, again, thanks ta you, all da other grandmas who shoulda been croaked, are now livin' forever, eatin' all da crumpets... drinking all the Earl Grey. Get me? We all gotta die sometime, and today… well, today was dat sometime for a bunch a' people. Now, if you don't mind, I'd like ta finish readin' my paper, if dats okay with you." He concluded, shaking his head, burying his face back into his tabloid.

"Ugh… You are so low rent, you know that?" Selena said with utter disgust, looking out of her window, continuing to listen through the muddle of radio transmissions.

What they didn't know, what no one could have predicted, is that – approximately seventeen minutes later - the South Tower would be similarly struck by yet another commercial airplane, thereby ruling out any semblance of an accident and confirming the intentionality of the event. The towers had been struck as an act of terrorism, sending the bewildered citizens of New York City into a whirlwind of panic, including Officers Selena Martin and Kenneth Lockwood, as well as all the rest of any and all persons employed by a 911 activated profession. The precise events that followed cannot be specifically described, in any way, to anyone that was not present during the time period in question; and furthermore, at the explicit request of Selena, before this history was transcribed, it was somewhat forbidden to be shared. *'Anyone who needs a play-by-play account of what happened, or needs to know what we all went through, can watch a documentary… don't ask me about* it,' she would say to all those who asked; therefore, out of respect for her wishes, all that this author will convey is, for weeks – for months – what was seen and experienced by all of the men and women during those endless, cataclysmic, hours can only be equated to Sybil's guided tour of the Underworld given to Aeneas.

Eventually, after some time, things returned to *'normal.'*

People continued to rob, burglarize, assault, and commit acts of felonious mopery; so, as it stands to reason, the Police had to continue their pursuit of these villains of society. Hence, *normal.* And so, too, did Officer Martin resume her duties, having caught a burglar responsible for previous acts of the same – as well as committing a home invasion in which the knave tied up his victims (the victims being a husband, wife, and two small children) and several firearms possession charges, a multitude of which were used in the many robberies that were also perpetrated by this singular cancer to humankind. Selena also had occasion to nab a rapist that violated three separate victims on three different occasion; a bandit who robbed multiple grocery stores at gunpoint; as well as a slew of other criminals, all within a span of five years. The entirety of these arrests (or *collars,* as it were) occurred over a five year period, earning our protagonist a spot on the coveted Anti-Crime Team – an undercover, precinct level, plain clothed unit that sought out the worst of the worst on the streets of New York City. This transfer of assignment, considered a field promotion of sorts – not so much financially, but more in terms of prestige - in such a rapid time frame caused much friction amongst a few of her peers. Some of the jaundiced individuals used the pretense of Selena being too young on the job… just a 'piece of shit rookie' who needed more time on the street to have been given such a coveted position, a gripe that she completely understood, having the humility and deference to comprehend the validity of the argument that a neophyte being presented with the salient post was a somewhat taboo notion; that is, until, on one particular evening, she happened to have need for the lavatory and, being in close proximity to, and using, the restroom in the *muster room* (a place where, at certain times of the day, all of the Officers working a particular shift would stand in unison and receive their assignments), overheard a conversation being had by two of her colleagues, both of whom were discussing the abhorrence they felt about the subject at hand.

"Can you believe that shit with Selena Martin going to Anti Crime? I mean, jeez, what the fuck's *that* all about?" Said Officer A—, with a countenance expressing that of pure loathing.

"Come on, bro, you know *exactly* what that's about. *Everybody's* talking about it." Replied Officer B—

"Yeah, I know what it's about... she's a hot piece of ass and the Anti Crime Lieutenant wanted to get her nice and close." Rejoined Officer A—, while gyrating his hips back and forth, simulating the thrusting of sexual intercourse... intercourse, this historian believes, he very rarely experienced, but that is not for the narrator to say, one way or the other.

"Oh yeah, you know it, brother. Hey, you can't hate the guy... if I was him, I'd want that smokin' hot little bitch close to me, too." Officer B— added, while precipitously taking out a pen from his shirt pocket, commencing to graffiti on one of the posted wanted flyers taped onto the wall.

"Yeah, I ain't mad at him. The problem is all these bitches gettin on the job and fucking their way into these positions, *our* positions. It ain't fair, you know?"

"Brother, you are preaching to the choir. She's just another porcelain doll that'll stand around looking at her freshly done nails, while the rest of her Team is rolling around the floor trying to put a guy in cuffs. Guaranteed she's gonna just stand there and do nothing. I bet ya… you watch." His drawing, that of a penis, which included all the appropriate anatomical portions - from the head, to the shaft, to the testicles, inundated with wild strands of pubic hair - all pointing in the direction of the wanted individual's mouth, was nearly complete.

"Who you tellin'? Man, that's the way it is now. When I got on the job, these slits knew their place. You shoved 'em in a scooter car with a pack of parking summonses and sent them on their way to the other end of the precinct confines. That's the way it was, I tell ya. And you know what? they liked it. Sure, they may act like they was all *o-pressed* or whatever ya call it; but, let me tell you, they like being subservient to us men. That's a fact." Contended Officer A—.

"Ah, those times are long gone, my friend… long gone." Asseverated Officer B— standing back to admire his work; then, realizing he neglected to daub the chin of the wanted individual's flyer with the depiction of dripping semen, went back in to correct the omission.

"Yes, they are. Yes they are. We better get out on the street before the Sergeant and Lieutenant realize we ain't out there. I'm hungry as all fuck anyway. Let's hit up that taco spot." Suggested Officer A—, licking the top and bottom of his lips at the thought of his suggestion.

"Yeah, good call. My stomach is all kind of fucked up today, but the taco spot sounds lovely. You're in a world of trouble after I finish eating, though. My ass is blowing out world ending, apocalyptic farts today." Officer B— guffawed.

"Wonderful."

Selena listened with disheartenment as the two Officers left the muster room. She lingered a few moments before exiting the room, just to be sure that they did not espy her and realize that she had been listening to their soliloquy the entire time. Is this how people viewed her? she pondered in despondency. All the while she believed that people were genuinely happy for her… that they acknowledged all of her hard work, appreciating the tenacity she displayed on the streets during *heavy* jobs, jobs in which – if need be – Selena's hands would be the first placed onto a *perp* in aid to her fellow Officers. She simply could not fathom the idea of her being thought of in such a negative aspect and considered relinquishing her new assignment, returning, once again, to routine patrol. She ascended the stairs to the second floor, now standing just outside of the Anti Crime Lieutenant's office, with the intentions of doing just that. After about a minute or so, contemplating on what excuse she would conjure up to give him – knowing that the truth was not, in any way, shape, or form, an option (not wanting to appear to be a victim of any kind) – she thought better of it and descended back down the stair case, three flights down to the basement, where the female locker room was located. As she sat on the bench in front of her locker, Selena further contemplated about what was said between the two Officers in the muster room. After some doubt and second guessing of herself, she came to the conclusion that her stalwart will was far superior to that of a bunch of ignorant male chauvinistic pigs, and that she would not allow their daft opinions to ruin a wonderful opportunity for her; an opportunity that she wholeheartedly earned with blood, sweat, and tears… literally. There were many days that she came home with cuts, scrapes, bruises and the like, chasing the goblins of the Earth, making a name for herself out on the street. The local criminal element grew to know her and, whenever they caught a glimpse of her coming around the proverbial corner, would make an about face to traverse the opposite way, not wanting any part of her tenaciousness. She knew she deserved this advancement and would not let the likes of the two clowns dissuade her. "These assholes don't pour milk on my cereal." She imparted to herself as she slammed her locker shut.

On her first night out in the new assignment, Selena felt out of place, as a bald actor would in a revival of Diane Paulus', 'Hair,' being that she was the sole female in the auto. Her attire not helping her to feel any more at ease, choosing to don her patrol uniform pants, full gun belt (what would be typically accoutered by a uniformed officer), and standard black work boots, which is the antithesis of what would normally be worn by a member of her new unit. A typical Anti Crime Unit consisted of four service members, all in regular street clothes, so as to blend in with the average, everyday people in the neighborhood; although, in all honesty, anyone with two eyes (or one really good one) could see the Crime Unit rolling down the street with their black, unmarked, Chevy Impala – the standard Police vehicle, minus the lettering which advertised the Agency - traveling at five or ten miles an hour (patrol speed), in addition to their very distinct colored wristbands (placed on their persons to indicate to other members of the police service their identities in the event of a confrontation between themselves and the uniformed variety), wrapped around their wrists, which could be prominently seen as they dangled their arms out of the car windows that were rolled down on hot days; as well as their puffy chests, this being owed to their bullet proof vests fastened securely around their front and back torsos.

The four occupants of the car consisted of three Officers

(which included Selena, O'Reilly, and Vicente) and their Sergeant (Bucknell); therefore, she felt somewhat timorous and overwhelmingly intimidated, being of the female variety surrounded by nothing but the quiddity of testosterone. Being outnumbered by the male persuasion hadn't normally been the greatest concern for her because – as a whole – the Department, as previously mentioned, was primarily an *all boys club*, a fact in which, after five years, she had grown accustomed; however, these were close quarters, inside of a car filled with four men for eight hours, which could invariably be cause for consternation to anyone in her shoes, what with discussions of '*hot chicks*,' detailing exactly what they would do to them if they ever got the chance – which, incidentally, none of them ever came remotely close to getting; chain cigarette smoking, filling the inside of the vehicle with plumes of nicotine clouds that latched onto the fibers of her clothes and hair; and, *hot boxing*, a diabolical business wherein one or more of the bastards would fart and subsequently lock the windows, creating a painfully frowsty atmosphere, forcing the powerless victims to inhale and digest the toxic, noxious fumes.

Her first night as a member of the Team, however, was a memorable one. It was about one or two in the morning, half-way through her *tour*, or shift, and all was '*the Q word*' (literally referred to as such), which was the esoteric equivalent of the actual word, '*quiet*' – as no one dared, for motives superstitious in nature, utter the actual appellation during their tour of duty (due to the fact that, at least one to three percent of the time, in utilizing the forbidden aforementioned word, something tragic subsequently occurred) – when suddenly, as they approached the intersection of Third Avenue and East 170th Street, *all be damned* broke loose, as an armed young man - about twenty years of age or so – barreled out of a convenience store, holding in his left hand a silver nine millimeter pistol, firing it into the establishment. Upon spotting the Officers, who were now exiting their car, beginning the foot chase, the malefactor placed the gun in his rear waistband and sprinted with the velocity of Jesse Owens in the opposite direction to evade capture. Within a few mere seconds, Selena, who just so happened to be the sprightliest of the Team, by far, found herself within footsteps of the assailant and, as a lioness in the midst of the jungle pounces upon her prey, she leaped and tackled the armed robber onto the sidewalk. The crook attempted, in vein, to remove his pistol from his waistband with the intentions of using it to put an end to our heroin's life here on Earth; however, immediately after taking him down to the ground prostrate, with one arm across the bandit's rear shoulder blade, she rendered him immovable on the floor. With the swiftness of a gazelle, she then used the other hand to remove the firearm from his control, tossing it far from his reach, subsequently placing his two wrists behind his back, handcuffing him with little to no resistance, as the perpetrator had heretofore expended all of his oxygen in flight, having saved no gas, as it were, for a brawl.

Upon arriving at the *Station House*, or Precinct, the Team lead the perpetrator to the Desk Sergeant to begin filling out the pedigree card, which contained all of the prisoner's relevant information, as well as the charges being filed against him, when three or four Officers happened to pass through the area. One of them, we'll call him Officer C—, seeing Selena *toss*, or inventory search, the jailbird (which consists of removing from his person any and all objects which may be a danger to himself or others, or that which may damage property in the cell in which he was shortly to inhabit) – gibed, "Bet she was a statue when they got *that* guy, probably freshening up her lipstick."

The Officers who were sauntering with Officer C— guffawed and prepended their own fallacious and snide remarks. "Yeah, this is probably the only work she's done all day." Added Officer D—.

"For sure, I'll bet they even let her have the collar, too! Didn't do a damn thing to earn it, but she'll sure as shit get the credit for it." Officer E— presumed.

"Hey, assholes…" interjected the senior of Selena's Team members, O'Reilly. "She was the one who bagged him, just so you dickheads know. She chased the mutt down, floored him, got the gun away, and slapped the bracelets on before we could even catch up. So why dontcha shut your traps and keep walking… and while yer at it, since yooze clearly have nothin' better to do, why dontcha go get us a couple of coffees... There's a bright idea."

The cretins discontinued the bantering, continuing to move along, not wanting any part of O'Reilly, a crafty twenty-five year veteran of the police department, who had seen his fair share of the Greatest Show on Earth – the job and everything that encompasses it - as was dubbed by the gendarmes of his time. Selena shot a quick smile to her guys and they returned the gesture. From that point forward, she felt a comforting sense of belonging. She knew, right then and there, that she had found a home within that little subculture. She was now a part of the Team and they were part of her.

Not all of the days that followed were quite as eventful. There were days, and sometimes even weeks, when absolutely nothing happened at all, especially during the bitter cold months of winter. Once the temperature dipped below freezing, not a soul could be seen for miles, as the Team would practically drive in circles, having nothing else to do, for hours on end. That being established, these times, these *down days*, in a manner of speaking, were a recipe for disaster; for, it is when one is in such a state of respite that one is most likely to be challenged; when one is not on one's guard and not, in any way, prepared for a worst case scenario situation of any kind that calamity strikes. And so it was, on that day, when not a sound could be heard for miles, as large flakes of snow - equal in size to the feathers of a snow goose - gradually fell from the dark grey sky, that their police radios resonated with the eerie sound of indistinguishable screams for help from a then unknown Officer. Frantic replies of, "Give us your location! What's your location?!" sounded over the air, imploring the Officer in peril to indicate to everyone where precisely he was, so that they could provide immediate assistance. Selena and her Team listened helplessly awaiting that crucial missing bit of information, so that they too could provide the succor needed.

Finally, after what seemed like an eternity, a location of Washington Avenue and 173rd Street was given over the radio, in between the screams and the distinct shuffling sounds of a physical struggle that one grew accustomed to distinguishing when one had heard enough of it throughout one's career. With lightning speed, she and her Team sped to the scene of what would turn out to be plenary bedlam. After climbing five grueling flights of stairs, spilling out onto the fifth floor hallway, what they laid their eyes upon was nothing short of the pure horror and madness in which one might witness while viewing a Halloween feature film. Blood stains, bright crimson in color - in the fashion of some sort of abstract painting - could be seen smeared all about the floor and walls as they approached the entrance to the apartment. On the other side of the door, they could discern the crashing of objects, along with the mad ravings of a male voice shouting, "I told you not to mess with me! I'm invincible! I told you! I warned you!" The voice grew ever closer to the entrance, indicating his imminent egress until, ultimately, before anyone could react, the door flew open, exposing the maniacal figure and owner of the aforementioned crazed voice, coated from head to toe in scarlet gore, breathing and growling like a wounded wild animal, with a thick coagulum of saliva sticking to both corners of his mouth, all the while clasping onto a large samurai sword, also saturated in blood (whose life fluid? no one knew), and possessing a black firearm (the firearm belonging to the now deceased officer who originally called for help over the radio) tucked into in his waistband, leaving only the handle to the gun visible. The Team scattered to the left and right (O'Reilly dashing to the left, Selena and Vicente scampering to the right) of the door to create distance between themselves and the menacing two hundred and fifty pound figure that stood six feet and several inches tall.

The perpetrator looked left and then looked right with a demonic countenance, contemplating on who his next victim would be, unceasingly inhaling and exhaling like a man possessed by Lucifer himself, wearing a most unsettling grin across his face, something resembling Heath Ledger's interpretation of the sinister Detective Comic Book's Joker. Making his choice, he pivoted left, advancing towards the elder of the Group, O'Reilly. As the beast rushed toward the Officer, wielding the sword with ninja-like skills in a sort of figure eight type of motion, O'Reilly reached for his sidearm, extracting it from its swivel holster, letting loose all six bullets of his .38 caliber revolver, striking his adversary all about the arm and shoulder, albeit and unfortunately opposite the extremity gripping the deadly weapon; therefore, the mammoth of a man, whose momentum continued to drive him forward, was unaffected by the bullet wounds he received, aided, most assuredly, by the copious amounts of cocaine apparently dwelling in his blood stream – some of the residue which could be seen in and around his nose - pressed onward, managing to plunge the sword deep into the stomach of O'Reilly, between the exposed, open space separating the bottom of his bullet resistant vest to the top of his pants buckle. Within seconds, sixteen shots rang out from across the hallway, all coming from the black, nine millimeter Glock 19 being clutched by Selena, striking the villain with every egressed bullet, center mass upon his back, dropping him to the floor, causing him to abandon his grip from the handle of the sword, leaving it planted well inside the guts of her partner, who now, too, took to the floor in a seated position, both of his hands gripped onto the sword, mouth slightly open, head draped forward, and countenance blanched without life.

Officer Patrick O'Reilly, posthumously promoted to the rank of first grade Detective, was not only a partner to Selena, but a mentor. His loss weighed heavily on her heart; for, his guidance was immeasurable… his absence would be felt in ways that one could not put into words. As she stood there in full dress uniform (shiny leather shoes, pressed ceremonial blue trousers and matching blouse, white shirt, blue tie, white gloves, and eight point cap with a shiny brim) at his funeral, she reflected on the lessons he had taught her during all of those *down days* in the car… lessons that she would not only never forget, but always make certain to pass on to the younger rookies in the future. O'Reilly was the first person to support her when no one else would; something in which she would be eternally grateful. He would be missed, immensely.

***

As she sat in the office alone, awaiting the arrival of the Captain, Selena glanced around the room, which was inundated with crime statistics plastered on every wall, along with wanted flyers of local gang members scattered about. Pie graphs, line graphs, and reports, placed into voluminous binders rivaling Leo Tolstoy's, 'War and Peace,' were spread about the desk and stacked upon shelves that wrapped around the office, and she wondered if he, the Commanding Officer of her new precinct, actually had the time to read it all. There were no personal photographs of any kind anywhere around the office. Not a single, solitary, sign that the C.O. had a family or anyone that he cared for, which she thought was a bit lachrymose, but not uncommon for a young, high ranking Officer; there were many executives within the Department without relationships of that nature. She wondered what kind of Commander he would be; there were all varieties. There were the younger ones, such as this one in particular, whom we shall soon make acquaintance, who hit every test perfectly, managing to achieve the rank of Captain in the first eight or nine years - these kind almost never having a real pulse of the men and women in which they have charge, often with unrealistic expectations of the cops, sergeants and lieutenants, most times leading to an entire precinct's moral decline – and there were the older kind, completely clueless as to what was actually going on around them… dinosaurs, if you will, still stuck in the world of *yester-year*.

234

Footsteps drew nigh and, finally, after waiting in that office for almost an hour, the Commanding Officer of the precinct, Captain Shannon, glided in. "Sorry for the wait, Sergeant. It gets crazy here in the summertime, as you shall very soon find out." He remarked, not yet looking at her, while placing his police radio on its charging base behind his desk.

"That's alright sir, I haven't been here that long." Replied Selena… now *Sergeant* Selena Martin. Some time after the incident with O'Reilly, Selena put all of her time and attention into preparing for the Sergeant's exam, spending an average of eight to ten hours a day studying the vastness that was their Patrol Manual – a thousand and something pages of endless rules and procedures, its soul objective being to drive one mad with boredom. Her diligence was rewarded when, one sunny autumn afternoon, she retrieved a correspondence from her mailbox sent to her from the Police Department, opened up the envelope which contained the result of the six hour exam, and discovered that she had received a score of ninety-seven. Shortly after receiving the letter, she was promoted and shipped off to her new command (the rules stating that once one is promoted, one may not remain in ones current command; the reason being to avoid any favoritism one might have for their cronies or, conversely, to avoid any retribution one may wish to impose upon those that one does not care for).

As he took a seat on his leather chair, a chair resembling something that one would find in the office of a high powered CEO of some Downtown corporate firm, he – still not making eye contact with her – rifled through the multitude of reports and all of the boundless paperwork that lay all about his desk. "Yeah, it's a goddamn madhouse out there." He said, directing his dialogue not to Selena, but to the aforementioned paperwork. "Every time I tried making my way into the command, something or another popped off. Never a goddamn moment's rest. Ah, here it is." In his hand, he held a folder which encapsulated Selena's entire career as an Officer and, upon opening it, began briefly perusing over the papers that dwelt within. As he scrutinized the plethora of documents, she sat up restlessly in her chair, leaning slightly forward, attempting to espy said documentation. "I see here," he continued, "that you effected over three hundred arrests as a cop, seventy-five percent of them felonies. Good, very good." He flipped through some more of the papers. "Your sick record is impeccable and your civilian complaints are within reason... considering how active you were, I'd expect that there'd be some complaints here and there... goes with the territory, isn't that right?"

He spoke aloud, but more to himself than to her, still not offering so much as a peek in her direction; however, she threw in a sort of reflexive, "Yes, Sir" just the same, so as not to have him think she were not fully aware and alert to his commentary.

"Just the person I was looking for, it seems." He continued. "My Crime Sergeant just got transferred to the Vice Squad, and I'm in need of a new one... a new Crime Sergeant, that is. It was slim pickings until you got here; I had very few options before that. Goddamn Sergeants I have in this command aren't worth a damn, worse than some of the cops around here, you know what I'm saying? You'll do nicely."

Selena's heart sank. She had absolutely zero interest in becoming the Anti-Crime Sergeant. First of all, she *just* recently was promoted and felt that such a position had to be earned, the way in which she had earned the Anti-Crime spot as an Officer, doing her five years on regular patrol, paying her proverbial dues before accepting such a distinguished position as this… and even in *that* case, if the reader will humbly recall, Selena had received a less than supportive endorsement by her peers. Secondly, she was not entirely sure if this type of assignment was the direction in which she wanted to take at *any* point… not in five, ten, or twenty years down the road. It was one thing for Selena to be a part of a Team, it was an entirely other matter to have a Team of her own, where Cops would be looking to her for direction, for guidance. With over nine years on the job, she knew that, as a regular Officer, before being promoted, she could hold her own in such a demanding role… that was far from her concern; but, now as a Supervisor, would she have the skills needed to be responsible for others in a specialized unit? Of that, she was less than confident. Starting out as a regular Patrol Supervisor would be far more ideal for her, less responsibility, she thought, before finally responding aloud, "Sir… Captain… I really appreciate the offer. I *really* do. It's just that… well I thought… what I mean to say is, I'd prefer to start slow. That is to say, I'd prefer to get my feet wet before jumping in the pool, sir."

The Captain, now placing the papers onto the desk and – finally – meeting his translucent blue eyes stoically with hers, inquired, "Are you telling me that you're *refusing* this assignment, Sergeant?" His voice cold and sharp.

"Sir, *refusing* is such a harsh word." She rejoined, holding her eye contact firmly with his; her tremulous voice, howbeit, somewhat revealing her timorousness. "I'd just like to start slow, maybe do a few years as a Patrol Sergeant. Then, after putting in my time in uniform, I can think about taking a team."

A few moments ago, she wondered as to why this man would not give so much as one glance her way; now, she wished with every fiber of her being that his penetrating, laser beam-like stare, which sent a glacial-like chill down her entire nervous system, would cease and desist. She thought of a million and three places she would rather be at that moment… anywhere but there in that office would do just fine, sinking into her seat as though it were quicksand. "Now, listen here, *Sergeant*, maybe I didn't make myself too clear. I wasn't *asking* you about what your feelings on the subject were. I'm *telling* you what you're assignment is gonna be. You understand?"

With her mouth slightly agape, jolting up in response to his commanding tone of voice, she now sat completely erect in the chair and replied, "Yes, sir."

"Now, I'm not such an unreasonable person." The Captain said, with a more tempered tone of voice, reacting to her precipitating display of deference. "If at any point someone else comes along that's qualified to run the Team, then I'll reassess at that time. That is, if you still don't want the gig… but, as for now, you're it."

"10-4, sir, I understand."

"Well, now that *that's* settled, why don't you take the rest of the day off and come back tomorrow at 1720 hours when your new tour starts. We have two other Sergeants working today, so you can go end of tour now."

"Yes, sir. Thank you, sir." Said the freshly appointed Anti-Crime Sergeant.

***

She could feel her heart thrashing against her chest like the incessant beating of a war drum before an imminent attack on a formidable foe. It was as though she were flying, her body soaring through the air, as she sprinted down the street in a full-on foot pursuit, attempting to apprehend the scoundrel who had, just moments earlier, assaulted an elderly woman aged in her seventies, whilst simultaneously pilfering her scantly filled purse which, incidentally, consisted of three dollars and seventy-three cents; five butterscotch sucking candies; some cut-out coupons for tunafish, butter, and orange juice; and, her New York State identification card. Being significantly more volant than her Anti-Crime cops, Selena lead the pack with the speed of a pronghorn and the gracefulness of a deer. The chase found her leaping over a three foot high fence, sliding across the trunk of a slow moving car in the middle of Second Avenue – all of the vehicles, as it happened, failing to yield as she raced across the street – continuing down 120th Street where, using every last bit of her nearly depleted vigor, she leaped with all her might, corralling the ruffian around his waist with her arms. As they both began to fall forward towards the ground, her hold around his midsection began to give way, her arms sliding down, descending from his waist towards his claves where she managed to squeeze with all her might, locking his legs together, just before making contact with the pavement. In a last ditch effort to retain his freedom, he wriggled out of her grasp, and planted his size ten foot into her face, between her nose and mouth, before scurrying to his feet in an attempt to flee. Scrambling to stand, not yet feeling the pain of the blow to her grill, she sprinted after him and, using her momentum from behind, gave the outlaw a vigorous shove to the back of his shoulders, which sent him barreling forward, causing him to lose his balance and sprawl across the floor, subsequently pouncing on him the way in which a wolf would a sheep; at which time, Morales, Jackson, and DiCarlo – finally - caught up to them, placing the brigand under arrest. Selena, *taute de suite,* rolled over to lay on the sidewalk, allowing Jackson to place the handcuffs on the perpetrator and, with every fiber of her being, endeavored for dear life to catch her breath, breathing in and out, laying supine, like a wounded animal that had been hunted down and shot, now, parenthetically, feeling the pain of the kick to her mug. DiCarlo extended his hand, taking her by the forearm to aid her in standing up. "You good, Sarge? You need an ambulance?" He said with a jovial snicker, meaning no ill will as, for the last five years being his Anti-Crime Sergeant, she had more than proven her worth as their leader and partner. Anti-Crime Sergeants – the ones worth their weight – were less like supervisors and more akin to being merely another member of the Team. On paper they were the superior Officers; however, once out on the street with the Team, they were an integral cog in the machine, engaging in any and all activities expected of the collective.

"Screw you, DiCarlo!" She said in between her gasps, taking hold of his forearm and hoisting herself from the floor. "Where was *your* fat ass when I tackled the mother fucker to the floor?" DiCarlo, who was not morbidly obese by any means, did possess somewhat of a protruding belly due, no doubt, to his fondness for fast foods.

"She got you there, DiCarlo. It musta' been the extra cheese on your bacon cheeseburger that slowed you down this time." Jackson, the tallest and youngest member of the Team, standing at about six feet tall, teased.

"Fuck you, Jackson, I was one step right behind you, I just

didn't wanna cut you off and trip you or some shit." Defended DiCarlo.

"Wow, DiCarlo, that's gotta be the worst load of bullshit I've ever heard. And I've heard years of *your* bullshit." Morales, the senior-most member, whose hair resembled salt and pepper grains… more pepper than salt, chimed in.

"Oh, don't even get me started on *you* Morales. Believe me, you do *not* want me to tear into *your* old-ass! Some people age like fine wine, while you're aging like spoiled milk, mother fucker!" DiCarlo raged.

"Alright, alright, boys. Let's get Mr. Wonderful here back to the command." Selena interrupted, referring to the prisoner who was to be transported to the Precinct for processing, just now finally catching her breath, patting her slightly bloodied countenance with a napkin she retrieved from her pocket.

"Yeah, let's get this scumbag, who apparently is such a big tough guy, robbing innocent old ladies, to where he belongs… in a nice stinky cell." Rejoined DiCarlo, leading the prisoner towards the unmarked police car.

"A cell is too good for the likes of this piece of dog shit. We should tie a cinderblock around his ankles and dump this guy into the East River. That's what we *should* do." Morales added.

"Yeah, like, Cosa Nostra style!" DiCarlo asseverated with a snicker.

"Man, what the hell do you know about the Cosa Nostra,

bro?” Jackson remarked, knowing it would get a rise out of DiCarlo, who always claimed to have 'loose ties' with the Organization, always taking much offense to the fact being put to question.

“I know enough, trust me… how many times have I told you about my exploits? A billion and one times, I think? I'm practically a connected guy.” DiCarlo uttered this last sentence in his best Brooklyn-Italian accent.

“Oh, you're connected alright, you're as connected as a loose, live electric wire laying in a puddle.” Exclaimed Selena, causing everyone to laugh, including the perpetrator.

“What the fuck are *you* laughing at, mutt? You're goin' to jail!” DiCarlo exclaimed to the prisoner. And with that, the jailbird was placed into the car and taken to the command.

In the office – a drab and dank space in the basement of the Precinct, but made suitable with a sofa and throw pillows; a few plush chairs; a decently sized television set complete with cable, a village style Turkish area rug; and, a large lavender and vanilla candle that Selena purchased from 4ever5CandleCo - her Team processed their arrest paperwork, as she reached into the communal Team humidor (which housed a plethora of cigars), pulling out a chocolate flavored one, giving it a whiff – eyes shut with delight - first inhaling from the open tip, then sniffing along the stem, before finally lighting. The first puff was always the best, so she cherished it and released the initial plume in a slow, overelaborate stream of delight, whilst falling into a seat on one of the plush reclining chairs. After each pull of her cigar, clasping and rolling it between the forefinger, middle finger, and the thumb, she held it before her eyes, goggling at it as though it were one of the eight wonders of the world. It relaxed her. Made her feel free.

A shrill voice impeded upon her vibe. "Sarge, one of these days we're gonna have to get you a *real* cigar." Commented DiCarlo, screwing his face with displeasure.

"Bite me, DiCarlo. This *is* a real cigar. It's got tobacco leaves and *everything*." She answered, clinching the cigar between her teeth, taking a drag, watching the tip turn bright orange, while simultaneously releasing some of the smoke between both sides of her mouth.

"I wouldn't exactly call *chocolate* a real cigar flavor, madame Sergenta. I mean, it smells like a goddamn Godiva store in here." Joined Morales, half glancing in her direction from the computer monitor.

"Yeah, can we at least get another humidor? Your M&M flavored cigars are messing up my Ashtons. I like my cigars to be *complex*, not *complicated*." DiCarlo scoffed, laughing at his own joke, or what he *thought* was a joke.

"Leave the Sarge alone," Defended Jackson. "I like it, Sarge." He said, turning towards her. "It's very… aromatic."

"*Thank you,* Jackson. It's nice to find a guy who can appreciate the good things; and, by the way, DiCarlo, now you know exactly what to get me for my birthday, since you don't want my deliciously flavored cigars messing with yours, you can get me my own humidor! Make it a nice one, too… not those cheap, bullshit ones. Maybe made from a nice Spanish Cedar, with a glass top, and hygrometer on the outside? Yeah, that sounds about right. As a matter of fact, I saw one on-line for about three hundred beans, a steal if you ask me! Don't let me down, I'll be looking forward to it." Selena gibed, shooting a wink to Morales and Jackson.

"Aww shit, you see, DiCarlo? you do it to yourself all the time." Jackson teased.

DiCarlo said nothing, but the flushed look on his countenance gave away his embarrassment.

As her men continued their work, she sat and reflected on her conversation with the Captain that first day in his office after her promotion. Little did she realize, when she made it abundantly clear she wanted nothing to do with the position of Anti-Crime Sergeant, that – five years later – she would not want to be anywhere else. She had grown to love her guys as their leader and protector; being anything other than this was inconceivable to her now. She watched as they typed away at the reports, along with sealing up the property needing to be vouchered, and felt a sense of pride; both, in them and, even more so, herself. Not many women had achieved what she had in those years of yesterday, especially as a supervisor, possessing a Team of her own… it was an achievement worth beholding. Only one thing could alter the current events of her life as they were; and that *thing* was another promotion. Selena had long wished to attain the rank of Lieutenant, which was considered to be a junior executive on the job; and, had Selena been merely a Patrol Sergeant, she most definitely would have taken the steps required to do so long ago. The only downside, that is, the only variable that caused her to refrain from even taking the exam, was the fact that, once promoted, she would have to say farewell to her Team. Once elevated from

Sergeant to Lieutenant, she would have to change commands once again, similar to the way in which she was transferred from her original Precinct as an Officer subsequent to her first preferment. The thought always disconcerted her, which was the very reason that she avoided the test like the plague, year after year. These thoughts deluged her mind like a wave crashing down upon a child's sand castle, as she sat in the office, puffing away at her chocolate flavored cigar.

A few weeks had come and gone when the new Anti-Crime Lieutenant summoned her into his office, which was not altogether out of the ordinary. It was common for a newly assigned Crime Lieutenant to make acquaintance with his Anti-Crime Sergeant as well as all of his other Special Operations supervisors. It was, however, unorthodox for him to have shut the door upon her entering, which rarely ever signified anything positive; it was enough, at least, to raise a proverbial eyebrow. "How are you feeling, Selena… it *is* Selena, isn't it? Everything okay?" He asked, as he shut the door. While passing her on the way to his desk, he placed his long, bony hand on the middle of her back, just above her buttocks. As he continued to traverse passed her, he allowed the hand to glide along the side of her hip, which caused Selena some apprehension, sending unbidden chills throughout her body, which shot down the length of her spine.

"Fine, sir." She replied, still standing, somewhat frozen, awaiting permission to take a seat.

The liberty was not yet granted, as he planted himself in his swivel chair, behind his mahogany desk, all the while never removing his dark brown, almost black, eyes from her chest area, which displayed just a hint of cleavage from her size thirty-four, c-cup, breasts. Having recently arrived to work, she had not yet changed into the attire in which she would accouter herself while actually out in the street, fighting crime. She wore a fitted, white, buttoned down shirt, which tucked into her Forever 21 blue jeans, also fitted, accentuating all of her curves. "Good, that's good. I love that shirt you're wearing. Nice fit." He said, now taking a full inventory of her body.

"Thank you, *Lieutenant*." She said, emphasizing his rank, in the hopes that it would snap him out of whatever perverted notion that happened to be spanning his cranium.

"No problem… no problem at all. Do you workout? You *must* workout… with a body like *that*?" He continued to flirt, biting his bottom lip in between comments. "Man, you *do* have a little body on you, don't you? You must do a lot of cardio, huh?"

"Uh… not really… umm… was there something you needed, sir?" Her heart rate increased; she began to feel her cheeks and ears become febrile and flushed caused by a mixture of anger and embarrassment.

"Yeah, yeah… listen, have a seat. I just want to introduce myself and get to know all my Team's supervisors." Selena gladly sat, using as much of the desk as possible for cover and concealment. "So," he continued, "you're my Anti-Crime Sergeant, huh?" He said, rolling his chair slightly to the left, to acquire a more advantageous positioning for peeping purposes.

"Yes, sir, I am." She kept her answers short, not wanting to prolong this infelicitous meeting any longer than was absolutely necessary.

"Well, that's a first for me! I've been all around the city on this job and I'll tell you, this is the first time I've seen a chick in the spot… I mean, good for *you*! I'm sure you *did what you hadda do* to land the gig, huh?" He said, accompanied by a deviant chuckle, along with a venereal wink. The innuendo, she was certain, did not imply that doing '*what you hadda do,*' as he so eloquently phrased it, was in reference to her hard work, knowledge, and experience. The implication that she had slept her way to her post infuriated her, but she said nothing, hoping that this harrowing conference would mercilessly come to a climax, post haste; however, much to her absolute vexation, he continued, "So… you like this spot? I mean, are you happy doing what you're doing?" She could see that his eyes were now directed between her legs, towards her crotch area; to which she instinctively crossed them to thwart his aberrant stares at her womanhood.

"Yes, sir, I am happy with the spot. I have a good Team. They do good work." Selena felt the beads of cold sweat against her, now overly heated, forehead trickling down onto her brow.

"Hmm. Okay. I mean, the thing of it is, I see in your folder here that you were looking for a transfer back to patrol. I see it right here on a yellow sticky note. I was assumin' you weren't happy or something." He was referring to a sticky note in which Captain Shannon had placed in her personnel folder on her first day at the command, indicating, in sum and substance, her initial displeasure with accepting her assignment of Crime Sergeant, a feeling which was long forsaken by her.

"Oh, no, sir… that must have been put in there by Captain Shannon. I originally told him I wasn't interested in the gig, but that was almost six years ago now. He must've forgotten that thing was even in there."

"Captain *who?* Oh, *Shannahan,* right! The *old* C.O." Captain Shannon (not Shannahan, as the Lieutenant mispronounced it) had, months prior, been promoted to Deputy Inspector and was no longer in command at the Precinct. "Heard he was a hell of a guy… hell of a guy. The good ones always go quickly, don't they?"

"They really do, sir."

"Sure do. Listen… uh… so about your Crime Sergeant spot… the thing of it is, there's this note in your folder… obviously it was before I got a chance to speak to you… the thing of it is, I have this guy that'd be perfect for the spot; he's an old buddy of mine… Richardson… from my old command. I already spoke to the C.O. about it, who happens to know him, too, seeing as how we all came from the same precinct."

Selena's countenance dropped like a ton of cinder blocks. "Sir, I don't understand. Are you… are you replacing me?" Her voice shuddered just a bit.

"Well, look, I mean… you know how it is. I'd just feel more comfortable with someone I'm familiar with. I've known Richardson for a good long time and he's really a decent guy. You'd *really* like him, I'm sure! I mean, the guy is ripped from head to toe, musclebound type; he's like the goddamn Rock… you know, Dwayne 'The Rock' Johnson? Except he's got hair – real good hair. You'd go nuts for the guy, all the *chicks* dig him… real lady

248

slayer! I'm sure you would jump on his bones with the quickness, you know what I mean?!" He said, slapping his hand against his lap, replicating the same sniveling chuckle and wink as before, this time displaying his yellow, jagged teeth and swollen gums.

"Sir, I'm sure I don't. Excuse me, sir, but I'm very comfortable with my Team. We have a chemistry, we work well with each other… and the activity is there... I mean, if you need more from my guys, they'd be more than willing to -"

"Oh, yes, I see the activity," he interjected, "and I know they are a solid bunch of guys. I know all about it. That's why I'm hookin' my boy up with the spot. Man, he wouldn't have to do a single thing! A ready made gold mine, your guys are! All's he'd have to do is slide on into your spot!" He exclaimed, ejaculating the same giggle as previously mentioned, before clearing his throat, shrugging his shoulders and adding, "Listen, if the note wasn't in the folder -"

She interrupted, "I'm sorry to cut you off, sir, but I already told you that I'm not looking to leave the position… the note must've been left there years -"

"I got that, Sergeant, but like I said, had I *known* that when I made the call… look, Selena… it *is* Selena, isn't it?" He asked again and, without awaiting her confirmation, continued, "Look, Selena," he paused to slide his eyes, once more, towards her cleavage, "maybe there's something that we can do… you know… maybe to make a deal? I'm sure my guy wouldn't mind if I found him something else – some other Team. I'd *hate* to disappoint him and all, but if you and I worked something out… if we came to some kind of…

understanding…" His last words lingered in the air like the odor which emanates from a passing of gas through an unwashed anus.

"I don't know what you mean, sir. What kind of understanding?" Selena knew full well the intended implication to which the Lieutenant alluded.

"Now, listen, Selena… you seem to be a smart *little* girl. I think you know full well what I'm trying to say. You scratch my back and I'll scratch yours, get it? *Quid pro quo*, you know?"

Selena sat in bewilderment, not believing that this was actually happening. She had heard about it many times, but could not believe that it was her reality at this moment in that office. For nearly fourteen years, she had fought for and earned everything she had ever gotten on the job, all without ever resorting to or relying on her gender – especially not by way of sexual extortion. A sense of shame overwhelmed her, not certain where the blame lay… had she done something wrong? Did the fault lay in her? Should she have not donned such revealing attire? It took but mere seconds for her to snap out of her stupor and realize that she was not, in any way, the culpable party in this fiasco of epic proportions. She had just met this man; he had no clue, not one iota of an idea, as to her work ethic or value. What is more, he, in all likelihood, did not care one bit. "Sir, I don't know what to say." She uttered, her eyes fixed onto the floor.

"Say you'll consider the deal. Matter of fact, hows about us getting together after tour? We could swing over to my place for some drinks and whatever else. You look like you could use a nice drink and maybe a good massage. I happen to give really good ones, just so that you know… *really* good ones." He averred with a sardonic grin, holding up his skeleton-like fingers, the knuckles of which appeared as though they had been overly cracked, gesticulating the motion of a massage, and, once again, biting his bottom lip.

"I don't think so." She said, coldly, still staring at the floor.

"I'm sorry? You *don't* think so?"

"No, I don't think so. That's not going to happen." Now lifting her head up and glaring directly into his pupils like a laser beam fixed onto its target.

He shifted in his seat as though he were sitting on needles, now with a look of indignation upon his mien. "Now look, Selena… I thought I made it clear… I assumed we could come to an understanding." He continued to shift back and forth in his seat.

"No, there's no *understanding*. The only understanding I have is that you think I'd stoop so low as to fuck you – it *is* what you're inferring, I assume… for me to fuck you to keep my spot? *Quid pro quo*, right?"

"Well -" is all he could muster, as his face went from carnation pink to ghostly white in a matter of seconds, discomfited at her declaration.

"Listen… *Lieutenant*… I have no intentions of doing anything remotely of the sort. That is something that will absolutely never, ever, happen… and I'm beyond offended that you actually think that you could even pull something like this with me… you *do* know - I'm sure you are *fully* aware - that sexual harassment in the workplace is -"

"Whoa, whoa, whoa, let me stop you right there, *Sergeant*! I, in *no* way, shape, or form, meant to imply that sex was a nexus to the position. It's clear from this note in your folder, the one that your old C.O. placed here, that you were no longer interested in it. That much is clear. I only meant that maybe you and I could get together for a drink to talk things over... to see what options we had! It's *clear* to me now that my advances are *not* welcomed and I will, of course, cease this conversation, which I currently see is making you feel *uncomfortable*." The Lieutenant now paraphrased the patrol manual, which stated, in a proverbial nutshell, that if one's flirtatious behavior was not *wanted*, then one must stop said behavior forthwith. He was proverbially covering his rear-end by making it appear as though he had no knowledge of her discomfort before she verbalized it aloud.

"Right. So am I safe in assuming that I'm no longer the Crime Sergeant?" She said in monotone, losing all semblance of emotion, blank faced, and awaiting the final blow of what was sure to be an affirmative to her somewhat rhetorical question.

"I'm really sorry, but the wheels are already in motion, as I indicated. The C.O. already approved the transfer and we promised the gig to my guy, who, incidentally, will be here by tomorrow. I really wish there was something I could do... really."

Selena could very well have filed a complaint and gone – as it were – the whole nine yards; however, she considered all the stories told by, and about, other women who had experienced similar situations and the fate suffered by them as a result of filing such a grievance. In the end, it never turned out well for the complainant; most of the time these crestfallen individuals would, ultimately, wind up on some unwritten 'black list' that essentially blocked any chance of ever landing another appointed position again; therefore, hushed she remained.

***

Selena's next five years flew by in the blink of an eye. Before she realized it, the time for retirement had come nigh. She tried recalling, as best she could, all of the many moments in her career, both pleasant and execrable alike, but could only recollect a handful; all the rest were a haze… a distant memory. From time to time, she would reconnect with some old acquaintance she knew from one of her former commands, which aided her in remembering a thing or two, here and there; other than that, her independent recollection was almost null. The handful of memories in which she was able to bring forth would serve as the most precious to her, holding a most singular place deep within her heart. These times, in particular, would always be treasured. She remembered O'Reilly, which almost always brought a tear to her eye. A prayer card with his picture hung inside of her locker, and she spoke to it many times, often asking for advice or sometimes merely sharing a thought or venting her frustrations; but, always, whether she spoke to him through the card or not, a loving pass of the fingers over his image was given before taking to the streets. "Watch my back, will ya, old man?" She would always say, before closing her locker door.

Selena also remembered the two Officers in the muster room; the simpletons, Officers A— and B—, who claimed she would be the type of Anti-Crime cop that stands idly by, looking at her nails, whilst the men did all of the work, alleging that she received her accolade by fornicating her way to the position. That always made her laugh out loud, realizing how so very mistaken they were, and how so very many people would also laugh them right out of the command whenever spewing that kind of slanderous erroneousness; anyone who knew Selena knew that she was a force to be reckoned with, and there was not a cop on the job who wouldn't take to the minacious streets of New York City without her at their side, or not want her *on the back* of the most perilous of situations.

There was also the memory of Officer Scotty Newcamb, so very many years ago, when she was only fourteen years old, the one that caught her playing hooky at the handball court, that entered her mind. His words, "… Stay in school, go to college, become something great" played inside her head like Antonio Vivaldi's 'Spring,' and it warmed her heart to think of him. She did stay in school, getting excellent grades, making honor roll several times; she did go to college, Mount Saint Vincent, in Riverdale, New York, majoring in English and receiving a grade point average of 3.8… Magna Cum Laude, incidentally; and, although her wish – once upon a time – to become a writer (perhaps the author of the coveted *great American novel)* never came to fruition, she did become something great. She always thought she would cross paths with him, maybe at a special assignment or something of the sort, and be able to show him what she had become… to thank him for his kindness and those influential words; but, she never did see him again. She hoped he was alive and well, long retired, and living by a beach somewhere sipping a Mai Tai.

These visions all flashed through Selena's mind as she descended the stairs from her locker room into the vestibule, where the Members of the Service of her command awaited to celebrate her *walkout*. Many of the faces were not familiar, but all knew her. As she passed her fellow brothers and sisters in Blue, all gave their best wishes. Chants of, "Congrats, Lieutenant!" "Good luck, L.T.!" "Way to go, Lieutenant!" "Take care, L.T.!" "We'll miss you, Lieutenant!" could be heard, as she walked out of the building and to her car.

The New York Thruway was unusually light on her way home. She wasn't complaining, though. The only thing she longed to do at that point was fill her bathtub with hot water and lavender oil, light her 4ever5CandleCo. candles, turn on some light jazz, close her eyes, and soak. The very thought of that eased the tension around her neck and shoulders that had built up over the last twenty years, as she exhaled with delight; but, nothing made her more contented… more at peace - as sun made its descent in the distance, painting the sky with strokes of magnificent oranges and purples - than pulling into the driveway, as the solid oak door to their beautiful Victorian home flew open, watching as her two little boys, Joseph and Joshua – with their brown and black spotted beagle, Ernest, hot on their footsteps - stormed towards her car, arms wide open, with screams of "Mama! Mama!" whilst her husband, Justin, awaited her at the threshold, cradling baby Josie, the newest member of the Christianson family, in his arms.

Story Five

Memoirs of a Broken Hearted Gentleman;
Introducing Jasper Loring

Human nature is not perfect in any shape, neither in good nor evil.
The profligate wretch has his virtues as well as the virtuous man
his weaknesses.

-   Madame de Volanges to the Presidente de Tourvel, excerpt
from 'Les Liaisons Dangereuses,' penned by Pierre Choderlos de
Lacios

They said to keep a journal; so, it dawned on me, as I sat on the floor in my bedroom, leaning against my twin sized bed, with the black 9mm pistol pointed to my right temple, that I should get up off of the hardwood floor and make the inaugural entry. It seemed such an apropos moment to begin the chronicle; moments from shattering my skull into a million pieces all about the tiny room which, I'll have you know, incidentally, barely fit the microscopic bed and the even smaller metal chair - albeit a very charming chair, having the most intricate of designs… sort of a floral pattern resembling roses with thorns swirling all about; quite beautiful actually. Next to it stood a matching metal table, identical in design to the pretty chair, which I frequently use to place my whiskey-on-the-rocks at least ten times a day. At least, I think it's ten times a day. I sort of lose count after the seventh or eighth glass. I drink to the point of excess and incoherence very often – which is to say I drink to this particular point of intoxication everyday. From the look on your countenance, I can tell what's swirling around in that brain of yours; I mean, I know what you're thinking… you think I'm some kind of alcoholic who probably needs to go to one of those anonymous meetings, or some crazy thing like that. Well, you are highly mistaken, I must say. I don't have a drinking problem; as a matter of fact, drinking helps *solve* most of my problems… And before you get all Doctor Oz on me, telling me some crap like, *don't drink to forget your problems because you might see them double,* I've got absolutely no time, whatsoever, for any of that nonsense. Whether I pound them down or not, my struggles and strifes exist; therefore, I do not care to buy into the whole *Friends of Bill W.* mumbo jumbo.

I'm not what one would call a happy sort of fellow. I like to use the term melancholic when describing my personality. Manic Depressive was the diagnosis of choice once upon a time; but, the 'Diagnostic and Statistical Manual of Mental Disorders' changed the name of this disorder to Bipolar, which doesn't have the same charming ring to it, so I decided to go with melancholia… this simply would be the best way of describing my disposition… my temperament, if you will; but, more importantly, there's almost a romantic chime to it, wouldn't you say? Not romantic in the traditional sense, as in a romance novel wherein two people are kissing, hugging, and making love to each other all over the goddamn place; no, I'm referring to a kind of tragic romanticism of the Shakespearean variety, a thing possessing all the elements of sorrow, pain, and death, something that really gets the ol' proverbial juices flowing. Anyway, before I continue off into a tangent, as I frequently tend to do, I was telling you about making that entry… I placed the gun on the bed and headed over to the table and chair to have a seat; I grabbed the journal - a white, four inch by eight inch reporter's notebook containing seventy pages, the only thing I had readily available in which to write – and made an entry.

Dear Diary...

I lined that out and began again.

Dear Journal...

Better change it back to diary. Journal sounds so stiff, unfeeling, very dry. After I blow my brains out, I'd like for it to sound more intimate. I lined it out once more and began yet again.

Dear Diary...

Even better, I thought, how about 'memoir?' That really has some pizzazz... very upper class. It'll knock the socks off of anyone who happened to be snooping around, looking through my personal effects, having the great fortune of running into this masterpiece.

Memoirs of a Broken Hearted Gentleman...

December 7th, 20-

Today I want to kill myself again. I just don't see the reason for living. Why on God's green earth am I even alive? No one loves me. No one cares. I just want to be done with it. God, please forgive me and let me into heaven, even though suicide is a sin. I'd really appreciate it. Just so you know, God, I recited – in advance - a few Hail Mary's and Our Father's as penance, anticipating your forgiveness, I hope that wasn't too presumptuous of me. To anyone who finds this entry – and along with it, presumably, my carcass – please phone my mother and father at 212- (the remainder of the number withheld from this chronicle due to the probability that one or more of you may attempt to dial it out of sheer curiosity or boredom) *and give them the bad news.*

Much appreciated, Jasper Loring.

Post Script: By the way, today is my twenty-ninth birthday; so, if you do find this entry along with my dead body, do be a sport and wait until tomorrow to make the notification to my parents, as I do not wish for the day of my birth – a much happier moment in time - to be, in any way, associated with my quietus. Thanks a million.

I sat there with the pen hovering over the notepad, wondering what else I could possibly add; perhaps some little tidbits about my life, in case whomever is tending to the mess I'd left behind becomes bored out of his or her miserable mind, waiting for the authorities to arrive. As I read over what I had already penned to paper, I felt a sense of embarrassment. It was sort of ridiculous. First and foremost, what was supposed to be a memoir entry – for some God only knows reason - transformed into a suicide note. Secondly, in no way, shape, or form did it come remotely close to what I was truly feeling inside. It's like when you have an awful dream, a nightmare, and you wake up in a puddle of sweat, your heart pounding a million beats per second... at first, you think the dream is reality; you feel as though everything you saw, everything you smelled, everything you tasted, was actually happening... that is, until you try explaining the dream to someone. It is then, at this precise instance, that you realize what a complete and total idiot you sound like. You hear and see the detached, uncharitable tone and countenance of the person on the other end of your soliloquy, realizing, at this point, that you are truly and utterly alone. The person has not one inkling of empathy towards you or your pathetic dream; and, furthermore, the person looks at you as though you've got a huge pile of human dung splattered all about your face. Trust me, I've experienced this first hand and I know exactly what I'm talking about… you try and share your stupid dream with someone and just see how well that works out for you… go on, try it. I'll wait here until your done.

One time, a few years ago, I had this insane dream that I was on some sort of locomotive that was traveling through a kind of a desert. I found myself – at the onset – atop of the train, jumping from car to car (like in those insane action movies where the hero and the villain have this ridiculous skirmish on a moving train at speeds upwards of two hundred miles an hour), apparently looking for an opening, so that I might enter the conveyance. Once I found the opening, which was located at about the third or fourth car, I entered. Upon gaining access inside, it seemed that I was in a traveling haunted house of sorts. There were various body parts, hands, fingers, feet, eyes, &c, scattered about the floor, the car saturated in a deluge of blood everywhere. Along the walls, there were openings secured with iron bars, resembling prison cells, that were filled to capacity with the most terrifying beings of all different kinds. Human they were not, more like supernatural beasts or something. I couldn't exactly make them out because it was very dark and – as in all dreams – there was haze, making it somewhat difficult to decipher what, exactly, they were. I could only make out their silhouettes, which bore frightening shapes… it was not humanoid, that much was for sure… and I could smell an unmistakably putrescent odor, unique to that of death, emanating from the aforementioned cells.

As I continued to traverse through the train car, I could feel the hands of the prisoners, the ogres, reaching out in an attempt to grab me, most likely with the intensions of devouring my body whole. The fingernails on one of the creatures, faintly making contact with my epidermis, were as sharp as knives; but, strangely I felt no pain, even though I noticed that my arms were sliced here and there. Pushing forward, the sounds of gut-wrenching screams could be heard, both in the far distance and, strangely, all at the same time, directly right in front of me. Desperate to escape this insanity, I began to search for an exit; however, each time I opened a door – a door that seemed to appear from thin air - it lead me to yet another train car filled with much of the same carnage. This went on for what seemed like days, until, finally, I spotted a ladder which lead to the top of the train car – where the dream initially commenced. As soon as I reached the top, I could see that yet another train, headed in the opposite direction, happened to be passing by; so, I jumped with all my might and somehow managed to land on it safely, a pretty bad ass move… a *tour de force* right out of that movie, The Matrix, with Keanu Reeves. As I glanced at the former conveyance, which was now at somewhat of a distance, I could see a creature, with some sort of pitch fork, coming out of the same exit opening that I had just crawled out from, seemingly very put-out that he hadn't the opportunity to dice me into itty bitty pieces. This is the moment wherein I had, mercifully, awoken from the nightmare. Judging from the look on your countenance, it seems that I was correct in my assessment of just exactly how the telling of a dream such as this would be received. You can't say I didn't warn you.

Later that day, after the whole memoir entry thing, at around lunchtime, I met one of my acquaintances for a drink at a local bar, not too far from where I reside, and I made the mistake of sharing that particular dream with him. As we sat there, in a booth off to the far edge of the bar, he with his Tom Collins, garnished with a maraschino cherry, and me with my whiskey and cola on the rocks, I told the fellow my dream. When he wasn't absolutely tearing himself up with laughter, along with obnoxiously gratuitous asides, he attempted to tell me about some pointless and unrelated dream of *his*, as if I cared one bit about he and his painfully irrelevant nightmare; a nightmare in which he was engulfed in water and apparently drowning… boo hoo, honestly. I sat there, most begrudgingly, staring through his oddly shaped skull – something resembling a Neanderthal's cranium, you know the kind… pronounced brow, sunken eyes, elongated head - as he continued to spew useless, downright stodgy, and lackluster conversation at me, wishing to Christ above that I had not agreed to meet with this complete buffoon. I would have departed post haste had it not been for the second round of spirits in which he most thoughtfully purchased… everyone is good for something.

I reached into my pocket - as I continued to nod my head up and down like that of a bobblehead doll affixed to an automobile in motion, feigning attention, and, quite truthfully, lacking any interest, whatsoever, in his dialogue about some absurd happenings at his place of employment - and pulled out a pack of Marlboro cigarettes. As I placed the cancer-stick in my mouth, I patted around for my lighter to no avail; luckily, the old chap had one at the ready, which he ignited, holding it towards me, and I leaned in for a light. Yet another reason, I thought, not to take the tall, very sturdy, Tom Collins glass to his face to bring an end to this God forsaken, egregious, discourse. Instead, I sat, continuing to listen to him drone on and on. His voice was unpalatable and his conversation was vacuous, but a gulp of my drink helped to dull my senses, allowing me to pay some attention to what in the hell he was saying to me. "I'm telling you, Jasper, you simply *must* head over to that exhibit. It's all the rage. I can't go two steps in the office without someone or another bringing the thing up, so I'd be damned if I didn't slide on over there and check it out for myself."

He was talking about this limited time only exhibit being displayed at the Guggenheim, an art museum in New York City, on 5th Avenue, between 88th and 89th Streets, across from Central Park, that specializes in impressionist, post-impressionist, early modern, and contemporary art… very awe-inspiring stuff which I happen to like very much, if you must know. The thing of it is, I just don't like talking about it – or even thinking about it - as if it were some kind of gimmicky, en vogue, *kill yourself if you don't see it* thing. I couldn't care a goddamn less if the entire world thought a particular thing was '*all the rage*,' as this moron so eloquently worded it. I would downright refuse to be even remotely associated with it under those insufferably conformist circumstances; although, to be absolutely honest with you – in this case - I kind of *wanted* to see the miserable thing, seeing as how I love art. I love the arts in all its forms, to be completely transparent with you. I love art, music – *real music* (like classic jazz and classical chamber music), and old novels from like the seventeen and eighteen hundreds. There's something very rustic and nostalgic about all of that stuff, in my personal opinion. I'd love nothing more than to be able to have lived during those times – minus the plagues and croaking at the median age of thirty-five, that is. Other than those two pretty crucial downfalls, I'd like to have experienced those time periods. I'm pretty sure that the people that *did* live back in those years of long ago, hadn't the slightest appreciation for it; of that, I'm certain. No one ever appreciates anything they have, when they have it. No one is ever satisfied. If you're poor, you want more money; if you're rich, you want more society. It's just the way it is. That's life. "Yes, I've been meaning to check that exhibit out. I'm really busy, though. I don't really have a lot of time." I replied to my acquaintance, taking a long drag of my cigarette and directing the exhale into his general vicinity; he offered a few of those clearing-of-the-throat sort of coughs in return, as my plume of smoke entered his nostrils.

The waitress came by to check on us. "Hello, boys, everything alright? Can I get another round for ya?" She asked in the most succulent Irish accent. An absolute dream, she was, with her golden blonde hair – albeit bleached, but still very sexy - tied up into a pony tail, her fair skin reminiscent of a sort of velvety cream, and her translucent, Caribbean sea-blue eyes which made my heart skip a beat as I dared to meet them with my own.

I smiled as I ordered a third drink, doing so for the sole reason of getting another good look at her, and maybe work in some of my charm. I've been told, incidentally, by many a member of the opposite sex – and, as it happens, some of the same sex - that I have a magnetic personality… that there's just *something* about me which intrigues them to want to know more. The problem is, when they get to know *more,* they realize why in the hell, at twenty-nine years old, I'm alone; that is to say, without a significant other. "Say, love," I broke in, taking the bangs out of my dark brown hair with my index and middle fingers. I don't exactly have long hair; sort of medium length and wavy, the kind that, when you put on a baseball cap, the back of it resembles Donald Duck's rear end… very alternative rock; but, the bangs are a decent length, and I have to toss them away from my forehead from time to time. "I was just wondering, is that an

Irish accent I detect?" I said, utilizing a very amorous tone of voice and giving her my world famous *smokey-eyes*. My *smokey-eyes* move, just so that you are aware, is this squinty kind of a thing that I do with the lids of my eyes, wherein I close them approximately seventy-five percent of the way, leaving just a tiny slit visible to the onlooker, as if there were a terrible raging fire, billowing with smoke, all around me; something right out of a Prince video (you know, the Purple Rain guy)… very debauchee of me, I must say.

"Yes, darlin', I just come over not too long ago. Been here fer a little while now." Her dialect was simply delicious. I could've eaten her up like Irish pudding right then and there.

"I see… well, on behalf of the United States of America, I'd like to thank you for blessing us with your beauty. You are truly the jewel of Ireland." I took hold of her hand and gently kissed it. Now, listen… I know what you're thinking (especially if you're of the female variety); you're thinking, that was an absolutely cornball line, accompanied by an even cornier move. And, you know what? I will give that to you; but understand this: when you're in the right environment, in the right situational circumstance, and you're a fairly decent looking fellow with a bit of charm, that move is aces. It really is. Listen, and don't dare deny this… if a disagreeably looking guy just happens to come spilling into the bar at the same time, using the same line, to the same waitress, I would bet all my marbles that he'd get a drink thrown in his stupid mug; at the very least, the damsel would screw face him and think of a thousand and one excuses to beat it the hell away from the poor schmuck. There's no doubt in my mind that would be the case. Now, conversely, take a swell looking gentleman, such as myself, and apply the aforementioned locution, in circumstances of the same, and just watch as mademoiselle so-

and-so begins oozing all over you; again, I say this with every bit of confidence in the entire stupid world. One other thing that I've learned, in addition to all of that junk I just lobbed your way, what I've come to understand, is that if you give a girl the floor, give her the stage, put her on a pedestal and make *it* about *her*, you're sure to score. Honest to God. Between those two tidbits of advice, you should have no problem getting the proverbial touchdown… and, if you *don't* strike gold, then you did something terribly wrong.

"Oh, we have a charmer in our midst, do we?" She said, her cheeks now blushing.

"For sure, love, Irish ships must be searching the Atlantic, looking for their lost treasure, I'm certain." I continued to lay it on thick with my award winning smile, showing just enough teeth to captivate, but not too much to display my gums… that's just a turn off. No one wants to see anyone's confounded gums, trust me. "By the way, what's your name, gorgeous?"

"Oh, my, you must get all the *garls* with yer flirtatious ways! Me name is Reha, darlin'." She said, taking it all in - hook, line, and sinker. "And yers, love?"

"I'd give them up all for you, my little pot of gold. Mine is Jasper." I replied, biting my bottom lip. I do this thing, sort of unconsciously, when I'm *smooth operating*, wherein I bite my bottom lip. Don't ask me about that one; I have absolutely no idea, whatsoever, why in the world I do that. It's just a thing. Sometimes people do things without knowing why, and have no rational explanation for it. Perhaps, forsooth, it's some sort of innate, preprogrammed, sexual thing I was born with. Who knows? maybe my Maker knew I'd enjoy sweeping the fairer sex off of their feet and threw that extra feature into my genetic make-up. What I *do* know, what I'm undoubtedly certain of, is that it works, and that's the most important thing.

"Mr. Don Juan over here! Ok, Mr. Jasper, let me go get yer next round before I get me arse fired!" She said, giggling, now heading back, almost floating on air, to the bar to get our booze.

I have to say, as she glided away, her ass swaying back and forth like a pendulum of a grandfather clock, I'd love to have sampled *her* Shepherd's Pie. The whole time I was making waves with the waitress, the douchebag - my drinking companion – was disturbingly silent, staring in amazement at what he just had the fortuity to behold. "Dude, I can't believe it, that was insane! You could totally smash that!" He commented, with a childish, most repulsive connotation. I wanted to throw what little of my drink remained in my glass into his fatuous face, but that would, most certainly, have been alcohol abuse; therefore, I refrained my impulses.

"Listen," I said, ignoring his offensively libertine remark. "after this drink, I really need to head out. I have this thing, somewhere I need to be." I hadn't the wherewithal to come up with a legitimate excuse for abandoning his putrefactive company and, to be brutally honest, I didn't care.

"Yeah, totally. I gotta head home, myself, soon. I'll tell ya, I'm super glad we got together, we really ought to do it again soon. Hey, do you think you could hook it up with that waitress you were kicking it to? I mean, that is, if *you* didn't have any plans to get with her." He said, with an air of pathetic desperation. I wanted to take hold of the back of his head and bring it down upon the table using all of the force I could muster. I imagined doing so with unadulterated pleasure, wishing to God Almighty that committing such an act of atrocity was a socially acceptable form of ridding one's self of impertinent human beings, such as he; but, alas, in an established Platonic Republic, that is to say, a civilized society, this sort of a thing is frowned upon, and so I withheld the impulse, saying nothing in response to his inquiry.

The waitress returned with that stunningly gorgeous smile of hers, larger than life, with our next round of libations and, with the look of a child who was promised a toy from his parent, the gargoyle glared at me awaiting a *plug*, as it were, for the introduction between the two. Out of sheer obligation to give to the less fortunate, as was always instructed me by my elders (*which* elders God only knows… probably from the television shows I watched growing up), I made the introduction. "Reha, my love, this here is an acquaintance of mine, Harold. He was just saying how much he'd like to meet you." I said, half wanting to vomit from my inanition in creating this nexus.

Reha, with a countenance of extreme and utter apathy, shot him a quick and exceedingly disinterested smile. "Halo, Harold."

"H-hey, t-there. You're a really fine… you're a pretty hot… you're a little hottie, aren't you?" Harold sputtered in the most cringe worthy display of his nebulous existence. He was utterly gauche. I wished to never have met him, wanting very much to be far, far, away from his despicable presence.

"Oh… uh… tank yah, Harold…. Uh… can I get you boys

anythin' else?" She replied, utterly repulsed, with a look on her countenance similar to that of one whose pants unexpectedly dropped to the floor, in the middle of a crowded room.

After a few seconds of awkward silence – Reha's eyes bouncing back and forth between Harold and I, in conjunction with Harold's inability to follow through with the introduction, staring at her the entire time with a look of ineptitude plastered across his reprehensible mug - I finally interjected, "Uh… no, Reha, this will do, love. Thank you."

We got the check shortly thereafter, Harold the Magnificent footing the bill and me leaving a cash tip. You should always leave the tip if the person you're out drinking or eating with pays the bill, even if he happens to be a moron… it's just a matter of good manners, quite honestly, and you should definitely do it; otherwise, you'll end up with your integrity, as well as your upbringing, in question. Anyway, he and I parted ways and I couldn't have been more relieved to finally be rid of him. One minute more in his presence and I'd have slit my goddamn wrists all over the place. I mean it, one more minute, I swear on all that is Holy and pure.

Afterwards, I found myself just sort of walking, aimlessly, for blocks on end, down Second Avenue, from 79th Street, peering at people sitting down to dinner and drinks at the cafés and restaurants that were now all lit up with very pretty deck lights and centerpiece candles, as it was now evening. The air was pleasant; not too hot, maybe about seventy degrees, which is right up my alley. I hate it when it's either too hot or too cold; I enjoy it right there in the middle… that's what tickles my fancy. I noticed how happy the people seemed; everyone laughing, having a good time… couples leaning in close to each other, seemingly engaged in romantic locution. It was nice. It gave me this sort of warm feeling inside… the kind of feeling that makes you feel somewhat impregnable, as if nothing or no one could crush my will, like I could accomplish anything in this forlorn world of ours; that is, until I remembered how miserable and lonely I was.

I'm horrible with relationships, by the way. I've been part of a great many of them and, let me tell you, I am, without a doubt, the absolute worst at it. I won't give you a song and dance, either, about how it wasn't all my fault that these romantic liaisons perished, or how any of the girls had a hand in the demise of it all; that'd be a facile, way too craven, and dismissive way to blow off the issue. No, I'm fully prepared to take sole responsibility for the destruction of all of my vexatious love affairs. The thing is, if you asked me why I am this way – and I absolutely had to give you an answer… like, I couldn't blow you off and change the topic because you just so happened to be brandishing and pointing a pistol to my head, insisting that I answer your question - I'd say it has to do, a lot, with my expectations. I'm not just exclusively talking about my expectations of women, either; I'm talking about what I demand from every living, breathing human being on this crummy planet. I once had a friend, a really good friend that became my lover at one point (Samantha was her name), that really gave it to me straight – when our tryst was approaching its climax – by telling me exactly what my problem was. "Jasp," she began, "you know what your problem is? Your problem is that – although you're a really beautiful person; very giving, very loving, and all of that good stuff, you expect it all back… tenfold. You want to be freakin' compensated for all of your good doings and if you don't, if you don't get fully compensated, all hell breaks loose and you become this dejected, sort of downcast person, catechizing everyone as to why they're not as perfect as you. And honestly, dear, this kind of a thing is a complete turnoff; there isn't a girl alive that wants to deal with that kind of thing… including me." And with that, she took her belongings and beat it the hell out of my apartment.

I will go on record by telling you all right now, she really hit the ol' nail on the head. I mean, you can't get any closer to the truth than that; and, to be completely and utterly honest, I don't see one goddamn problem with it… with the way that I feel. Why on Earth would anybody, with a fully functioning brain in their ridiculous head, voluntarily give all of themselves if they're not going to get, at the very extreme least, an equal return on their investment? I'll tell you right now, if anyone tries to claim different, it's a farce; they're lying right to your face. Any billionaire, any millionaire, any weekend warrior who bought one lousy share of any goddamn stock of a company or one billionth of a crypto coin, will concur by telling you that if you put your hard earned money into anything, you'll want that money back… tenfold. Listen, I'm not spewing out anything that a million other people haven't thought for themselves; the only difference is, there aren't a lot of folks out there that would admit it, what with having to cower to the conformities of society and all that crap. Not me. I'll tell you a thing or two and not have any reservations about it whatsoever… not a one. The only thing, the only downfall – in case you're thinking of incorporating my brilliant ideology into your miserable life – is that you may find yourself strolling along Second Avenue, from 79th Street, 'peering at people sitting down to dinner and drinks at the cafés and restaurants that were all lit up now with very pretty deck lights and centerpiece candles, &c'… alone. Hey, you have to take the good with the bad; I never said it was a flawless plan. I never said that at all.

About seven hours or so later, I found myself still wandering, like a lost soul, up, down, and all around the gritty city blocks of Manhattan, until I ended up at that same bar as before… the one with the Irish waitress, Reha. I spent a few minutes outside, kind of wondering if I wanted to enter. I wasn't exactly in the mood to socialize, being that I'm somewhat of a reclusive basket case. The thing of it is, if I'm going to be altogether transpicuous with you – which, you have to agree, I have been up to this point – I am, un-clinically, diagnosed with the cyclothymia. I really am. I looked it up, ad nauseam, in the DSM V – as well as its predecessor, the DSM IV (back in two thousand and twelve) - and I can assure you that the assessment is spot on. In addition to my own self-diagnosis, many of my former belles of yore have expressed this very identical analysis just before making their untimely exeunt from my life; so, there really is no disputing the fact of the matter. One minute, I'm this super happy-go-lucky, *I've got my shit together and I look good doing it*, kind of guy; the next, I'm somewhere down in the depths of the nether regions, feeling as though only sweet death has the ability to grant me mercy from my bitter desolation and mortification. When I'm in my 'low,' nothing and no one has the ability to rescue me from this morbidly dismal mental state, in which I spend most of the time feeling utterly lachrymose, curled up in my bed, covers completely concealing me from sight, with the shades drawn. The antithesis of a lovely sight, I assure you. I say all this to say - if you were wondering where in the hell that soliloquy was going - that I wasn't sure if I wanted to go back into the bar. That was the point.

I, incidentally, finally decided to go in; at the very least I figured I'd have a drink or two. When I walked through the door, I had the ol' eyes peeled for Reah, but she was nowhere to be found, which was just fine with me. What I mean is, after Harold's debacle, coupled with my current cynical mental state, I had no real desire to see her. I took a seat at one of the booths, looking around, scanning the joint, to kind of make sure that there weren't any human beings present in which I had acquaintance; again, not being in any kind of mood to deal with mankind. It was a really spiffy place, I have to say. Very cozy. Very intimate. The bar was made up of mostly old, but polished, wood and was tastefully designed with framed pictures of the plush, leafy green hills of Ireland, as well as a bunch of its old-time watering holes from the past to the present time. A live band, comprised of two guys and a gal, were doing a swell job of covering some of the alternative hits from the 1990s; at present, '*Shimmer,*' by Fuel, undulated out of the speakers that hung atop the corners of the bar. Lost in trance from the music, I hadn't realized that a waitress was standing before me, awaiting a response to her request in retrieving for me a libation. In a trice, she captured all of my attention. Now imbedded in a kind of tunnel vision, no other sounds, or sights, or smells, or any other thing that requires the use of the five senses, could be discerned; only her bewitchingly dark brown eyes, the color reminiscent of warm hazelnut; jet black hair that shone like a stone of onyx, so wavy that it resembled the waters of a rapid, cascading down to her shoulders, as if descending from a waterfall; the sexiest little birthmark below her left eye (sort of like Marilyn Monroe's except a bit higher and more towards the left side of her nose); and enchanting smile registered in my cranium. She was honestly a rare jewel; something right out of the riches of Abbe Faria's treasure boxes, discovered by Edmond Dantes at the Isla Monte Cristo. "Hey there, I'm so sorry, love; I was lost in the music… such a great band today." I said, making up for not immediately espying her.

"Oh my goodness, aren't they? They're really, really, good. They've actually come in here once or twice before and really knocked the socks off of everyone. What can I get for you, love?" She said, drawing me in deeper and deeper, with a super sexy voice that resembled the humming of angels… not to mention her perfume, which had the pleasantly inebriating effect of some sort of love potion, conjured up by an enchantress, that danced in and out of my nostrils.

"Right now, you can give me the name of that intoxicating scent that you're wearing, as well as the name of the gorgeous woman that it's emanating from." I said, using that undeniable charm I told you about before.

"Wow, you are good! My perfume is called Macaron Rose and *my* name is Greta." She replied, with the most captivating smile, which, *en passant*, displayed a perfect row of pearly white teeth.

"Hello, Greta! It is with great pleasure that I make your acquaintance. My name is Jasper, and, if it's not too much trouble at all, I'd love a beer and your number." I said, *smokey eyes* and all.

"The beer is coming right up." She said, subsequently smiling, throwing in a slight, coquettish smile, "The number… hmm, I'll think about it." As she walked away to get the libation, she turned her head back toward my direction, furnishing me with a somewhat amorous glance on her countenance before cutting the corner and disappearing out of sight.

I continued listening to the music, as the band now covered *'Black Balloon,'* by the Goo Goo Dolls, which they did very skillfully, I have to admit. I dabble in the playing of the acoustic guitar myself (having recently learned about five or six chords); so, believe me, I can tell you a thing or two about the topic, more than the average layman, that much is for sure. When Greta returned, she placed the drink onto a coaster that lay atop the table and took a seat in front of me, reconnoitering the bar with her neck stretched out like a madman, on the lookout for anyone possessing the authority to end her employment with the establishment. "I can only sit for just a second, my manager will kill me if he catches me sitting and chatting." She opined, finally looking straight into my eyes with the smile of an absolute seraph sent from heaven. "So, you want my number, huh? Why is that?" She continued, teasingly.

"Well, I don't know." I teased back. "Maybe I'd like to get to know the sexiest girl I've ever laid eyes upon a little better."

"Oh yeah, wow, ok. I'm the sexiest girl you've ever laid eyes upon, huh? And I don't suppose you say that to every single living, breathing, female you've ever come across?" She chided in a playful manner, screwing her full, sumptuous lips to the side, squinting her eyes as though she were giving me a scolding, all the while, somehow, maintaining a charmingly inviting look on her mien.

"Listen, I think you know very well how gorgeous you are. I think you absolutely do." I avoided the question, there being no appropriate answer. I mean, think about it… let's just say I go on ahead and sell her a *wolf ticket* by telling her that I've never, in my life, said those words to another girl; well, we all know that would be complete and total bullshit – and no one wants to deal with anybody's bullshit; and, quite honestly, that's a bad way to start off a relationship… coming off like a complete liar. It's just bad business. On the other hand, if I tell her that I *have* said those words before – not just once, but about a thousand and thirty-three times - where in the hell is that going to land me? Not in bed with her, that's for damn sure. Trust me, it was better for me to mosey on passed that question.

"Hmm, sounds like you're avoiding the topic… smart man." Greta said, giggling, taking another precautionary gander around the bar.

"So, is there a 'Mr.' in the picture? I pried.

"There was; but, he's history now. He was a very jealous person and didn't take too kindly to me working here, or going to school for that matter… what with about a million and one guys asking me for my number, and telling me that I'm the sexiest girl they've ever seen and all." She said, with a laser beam stare shooting directly into my pupils to emphasize her point, before letting go the cutest little giggle.

I chucked along with her and replied, "Yes, I'm sure that can be quite a cumbersome problem to deal with." She responded with just a shrug of the shoulders and another snicker before I continued, "But, what can one do but tell it like it is? I call 'em as I see 'em, you know?"

"Yes, I see that. I do see that... So, how about you, Jasper? Is there a 'Misses' in *your* picture?" She inquired, whilst seemingly bracing for the impact of an affirmative.

"Me? Nah, no one in my life." My answer was short because the topic is somewhat of a downer for me, if you really want to know the truth. The thing of it is, as I already explained to you, my relationships all end in chaotic ruin… every single one of them. I'm not kidding. I haven't had one successful breakup in my entire crazy life. Not one. They all come to this tragic sort of conclusion that could easily become a movie of the week on television, with all of the fireworks, pomp, and circumstance included in the best silver screen dramas and action flicks. A complete shit show, if you will.

She sensed the curt reply and took out the proverbial shovel, ready to commence her digging for more intelligence. "That sounds like it comes complete with a nice long story! Rough breakup? Is it still fresh?" What she really wanted to know was if there was some girl minutes away from storming into the bar, with a switchblade in hand, looking to carve me up for some wrongdoing that I may have committed.

I half chuckled at the implication. "No, no, nothing like that. It's just… well, to be brutally honest, I'm not extremely successful in that department… in the female department, I mean. The thing of it is -"

She cut me off and grabbed the arm of another waitress who happened to be passing by. "Hey, Dorothy, have you seen Curtis? Is he around?"

"No, hun, Curtis went out for a few. Said he'd be back in an hour or so." Dorothy, the other waitress, said.

"Awesome… hey, can you get my tables for like five minutes? I'll get you back for it when I finish here. Is that cool?"

"Sure, hun, I got ya." Dorothy replied, flashing a smile and a wink at the both of us, before rushing off to tend to the tables... *Greta's* tables.

Greta, then, turned back to me. "Sorry, didn't mean to cut you off. Curtis is the boss and I wanted to make sure he wasn't slithering around. Didn't want him to catch me sitting here with you... he sort of frowns upon that kind of thing, you know? Even though you think he'd realize that it leads to better tips – *not* that I'm sitting here with *you* for a better tip!" She said, placing her hand over her mouth, with a countenance that expressed sheer embarrassment. "Oh my goodness, don't think I meant -"

I smiled and gently placed my hand over hers, which was resting atop the table, as a gesture of reassurance. "No way, I don't think that at all!"

"Oh, good, thank goodness!" She said, relieved, now delicately returning the grasp and gazing into my eyes, seemingly enamored with me. "So you were saying? You're not good in the female department?"

"Well, yeah, that was the gist of it. I just wouldn't go writing a book about relationships is what I'm driving at, I guess. Unless, of course, the book was about what *not* to do." I chortled.

"Darn, I'm sorry to hear that. Well, I'm sure you'd make tons of money writing that book, the one about what *not* to do in a relationship! I mean, seeing as how you claim to be so horrible at it, with such a vast amount of experience and all... I'm sure that's gotta have some value to it, don't you think? I'd much rather read a book about someone's failures than their successes. I mean, if you think about it, their shortcomings are the result of having actually tried something… gave something a shot; and, even though they've fallen short, it's still a sort of experience that they have learned from … something that they can teach others about. Wouldn't you agree? I think that'd be a great thing to write about." She concluded with the most endearing smile, the kind that just makes you want to stare at it all day long. The problem with that is, if you *do* end up staring at it too long, the person may think you're some kind of nut job. What I mean is, it's probably best to admire that sort of thing inconspicuously; get a good enough look at it - a mental snapshot - to ponder all about the thing once you get home or some crap like that. Don't go staring at people's mouths is what I'm saying.

"Yeah, I suppose it is! That's actually a pretty damn good idea." I returned, smiling. It really was a smashing concept. People, in general, get kind of sick and tired of reading, or hearing, about the success of others; but, give them a nice, juicy story about some poor fella's miserable trials and tribulations… that's what really floats people's ol' boats.

"See? You just gotta always look on the bright side of things. Be positive about it. Say, I have a bang up idea… you could write the book and I could be your muse! A regular Erato… I could stand there with my lyre and love arrows, being your afflatus… the sexiest one you've ever seen… while you sit and type the masterpiece of the century!" She puckered her lips and feigned shooting arrows all over the place, mimicking the Greek muse. It was actually pretty adorable… she really was turning out to be a pretty swell girl, and I found myself becoming more and more intrigued by the second.

"I must tell you," I continued, "that sounds like a brilliant plan; but, you know what'd have to happen before all of that, don't you? Before I write the *great American novel* with you as my sexy muse?"

"What's that, hun?" She asked with one of her palms now resting on her chin, with that doting countenance of hers.

"You have to give me your number." I answered with a victorious smile, bringing the conversation full circle.

"Bravo!" She sat back onto the chair and clapped. "Well, done, sir! A very sound, Socratic argument; the great philosopher would be proud as heck of you." She leaned forward again, while reaching into her shirt pocket to pull out a pen, which she used to write her number onto my very vascular, very toned, forearm… I'm extremely fit, in case you were wondering. Not obnoxiously muscular, just very fit. What I lack in height (five foot nine, if your brain cells are going nuts pondering upon it), I more than make up for with my body. I've got magnificent definition in my chest, arms, shoulders, and legs, along with these killer abs – all eight of them are prominently represented upon taking my shirt off, whenever that particular occasion arrises. Seriously. This is not just something I'm saying to hype myself up in some kind of braggadocio manner; the thing has been reaffirmed by many different people who had absolutely no reason, whatsoever, to butter me up. Like this one time when the janitor of the college I went to, Iona College, told me that I had 'such a beautiful body' on me. That guy had absolutely no grounds for paying me such a complement at all. He did it because, sometimes, you just have to tell it like it is, and he just said what was truth. It's *that* simple. No mind scrambling scientific formula required. But, I digress… back to the tale at hand. "There." Greta continued, as she completed placing the tattoo of her phone number upon my arm. "Now, I really should get back to work. These bills pay for my college tuition and I can't afford to get canned."

"Oh, sure, I completely understand. Say, what college to you go to? What are you studying?" I asked, not wanting the conversation to come to an end. I was really into her; I actually could've sat there talking for the rest of my miserable life, staring into those magnetizing eyes of hers.

"Me? I go to LIU… Long Island University. I'm majoring in social work. I love to work with people and I think it's such a rewarding field… but my real passion is acting. Like, I'd love to be on the big screen, you know? The next Philip Seymour Hoffman… only, the *girl* version of him… you get what I mean!" She explained, offering that adorable giggle again.

"That is phenomenal! I really mean that! An actor, wow, that's really something! Say, I have a bang-up idea! I could write that book and we could turn the whole thing into a movie… with you as the leading actor! It'd be a smash hit! I could see it now… Jasper Loring's 'WHAT NOT TO DO IN A RELATIONSHIP,' starring Greta!" I said, holding my hands up above my head, as if the title were lit up on a billboard.

She smiled, stood up, and tapped the spot where her number bled into my epidermis. "Don't be a stranger… call me." She said, looking deeply into my eyes before kissing me lightly on my cheek; subsequently, whisking off to tend to her tables.

I left the bar after paying the tab and waved goodbye to Greta; she threw me a wink and shot me the cutest smile I've ever seen in response. The thought of her smile followed me all the way home, taking the extra long way just to enjoy the high that I was on, breathing in the fresh night air and just sort of checking out the sights of the city streets. The lights emanating from the stores were a little brighter that night and the people's faces that passed by seemed friendlier. Everything was just right and it gave me this feeling in my chest, kind of like I could take on the world; nothing was a match for me at that point in time. If life were like this all of the time, I could conquer all. I really could. It's just really strange how such an exuberant sensation – such an apparently indestructible energy - can, in the snap of the finger, transform into perfect morbidity… slipping away like one's final breath.

I opened to the door to my apartment and flicked on the lights to the hallway, subsequently heading into the kitchen to get some water and an aspirin because I had this killer headache from the alcohol. That usually happens to me when I drink and don't eat. You should always snack on something when you're pounding a few down your throat, it'll make a world of difference, trust me. Taking my water, I headed on over to the living room where I plopped onto the sofa, turned on the television, and channel surfed for awhile with no real interest in anything that was on. Scrolling through my phone, I noticed a few missed calls and some text messages, all wishing me a happy birthday. Funny thing was, after I left the apartment to meet up with stupid Harold, I had completely forgotten that it was my birthday. It just sort of slipped my mind, I guess. To be honest, I'm not too thrilled about being twenty-nine years old… it's not something that I'm jumping through hoops about, so it was pretty damn easy for me to forget. I mean, truthfully, who in the hell wants to be twenty-nine? It is truly the end of the age of innocence. Up until now, failure could be chalked up to the ignorance of youth. Everyone in the world expects a snot-nosed child of twenty-something to incessantly ebb and err; however, it is an entirely different thing when you hit the ripe old age of thirty; at that point, people sort of expect you to know what in the hell you're doing, and the entire world holds you mercilessly accountable… and now I was at the precipice of it all. Disconcerting, to say the least.

There was some shouting and screaming coming from the street outside, three floors below my apartment window, so I got up to see what all of the commotion was about, just because there was absolutely nothing better to do. It turned out to be a husband and wife that lived in the building; and, it seemed, from what bantering could be heard, that neither of them could find the key to open the lobby door… each was blaming the other. Boredom set in quickly with the pantomime down below and, since the television wasn't much better, I decided, at that point, to turn everything off and head to bed. Upon entering my bedroom, I was hit by a chill from the window that I accidentally left open earlier on. As I walked over to shut it closed, I spotted – atop the metallic, floral patterned table resembling roses with thorns – the suicide note that I had written in my memoir and, on the twin sized bed, in between the rumpled sheets, rested the black 9mm pistol. Now sitting on the edge of the bed, I picked it up, and stared at the weapon, whilst simultaneously thinking of Greta and that captivating smile of hers; which, in turn, sort of contagiously caused a huge smile to extend across my face, I must admit to you. I could even smell the inebriating perfume she was wearing, probably emanating from the spot that she planted her velvety lips. I looked down at the phone number – along with a little heart - that she scribbled onto my arm, tossed the firearm back onto the bed, and immediately sprang over to the table to transpose the number onto the notepad before the ink faded away.

End

ABOUT THE AUTHOR

JL Caban was born in the year of Elton John's 'Rocket Man' (1972) to Joe and Lisa in a Mount Sinai hospital room in New York City and grew up in the boro of the Bronx. True to the iconic song, he has always found himself reaching for the stars. Having a keen interest in the literary arts, he found himself reading the works of classic novelists such as Hemingway, Wharton, Bronte and the like and dreamed of one day writing his own page turner. He attended Lehman College where he received a Bachelor of Arts in psychology, with a minor in English Literature, and a Master of Science in Education.

A very special thank you to my team, Michael Baes, Dar Dowling, Tom Colleran